THE MOST PECULIAR TALES

CHARLES A CORNELL

The Most Peculiar Press

A Division of

Charles Cornell Creative Partners LLC

FORT MYERS, FLORIDA

Charles Cornell Creative Partners LLC
12870 Trade Way Four
Suite 107 #697
Bonita Springs, FL 34135
www.CharlesACornell.com

Book Cover Design by Charles A Cornell
Book Cover Graphics licensed from Shutterstock.com, iStockPhoto.com or obtained from public domain sources.

The Most Peculiar Tales -- 1st ed.
ISBN 978-0-9990889-3-7

These stories are dedicated to
those who love imagination
and cherish the freedom to express it
in whatever form their hearts desire.

—Charles A Cornell

PECULIAR TALES

ACKNOWLEDGEMENTS

I'm very fortunate to have as friends and colleagues a tremendous circle of talented, award-winning authors to draw inspiration from. Imagination is infinite. They prove that every day they write.

It is with great appreciation I acknowledge their assistance in critiquing *The Most Peculiar Tales*, providing their precious time and expert literary insight in order to make the telling of these stories more enjoyable for my readers.

To my editors—Ken Pelham, Bria Burton, Lara Lazenby, John Hope, Emily Wenstrom, and Susan Lounds, thank you!

— Charles

EUROPA · 1872

DEAR READERS

Come with me my friends, back to a time that never was, to places familiar in many ways but so peculiar in others. To a land of hope and despair, whisked by the beat of the Great Mechanization. To the cobbles of a city pumped with steam and brazen with intrigue. To villages lost in time, imperiled by spectres from another dimension.

Danger lurks, in both the known and the unknown. Bring your fear, for overcoming it will strengthen you. Bring your heart, for its passion will comfort you. But most of all, bring your wits. Your journey will be well guided, by those whose curiosity probes the foundation of our psyche and whose skills are the craft of the bizarre.

Join Professor Atticus Carr, and his assistant Jeremiah Boone, as they travel the darkest alleys, and the even darker aether, to bring you *The Most Peculiar Tales*.

Should your travels produce an inclination to tell others of your escapades, by all means write your own account of this journey, in whatever tabloid you feel is worthy of your opinion. Dear reader, your reflections will warm my soul and by doing so, encourage further undertakings of pen for your future enjoyment.

Regards,

Charles

PROF. ATTICUS
CARR

BY WAY OF INTRODUCTION

A Eulogy to the Life of Professor Atticus Carr

It is without doubt I owe Professor Atticus Carr a great debt that can never be repaid. He rescued me from the grimy streets of Londinium, orphaned, a waif of twelve, destitute and begging for scraps. The good professor has now passed into the great unknown and is but a memory. The eternal debt I bear weighs heavily on me. It is my responsibility to continue his work as best as I can, and by doing so, honor his legacy.

Professor Carr was a man of varied dimensions. To the public, an *artiste* of illusion whose displays of magic and visual deception enthralled many and disappointed none. It was through this facet of his numerous vocations that I first came into his employ when I joined his theatrical company as an errand boy.

His Theatre Macabre in the West End attracted all manner of society, indulging the imaginations and wonder of those of both meager and substantial means. The less well-to-do worshiped him as an artist who could transport them from their tiresome lives into a world of dreams, if just for a brief evening. The landed gentry, with their top hats and furs, patronized his research and with their funds helped build the Institute for the Investigation of Peculiarities, a building whose grand Gothic facade stands perched on the Embankment south of Conly's Gardens, the Institute being the dear professor's eternal memorial.

It was not just his spectacular public expositions of magic, showcasing the peculiar, that defined the man I grew to know and admire so deeply. Professor Atticus Carr was infinitely more complex than his projections on stage and acts of flamboyant illumination. Notwithstanding his well-earned celebrity, those performances were simply the essence of his outer *persona vitae*, a fame that helped pay the rent and put coppers into the pockets of those who worked for him. No, the true *artiste* lay within—in his talents for invention and discovery, and in his investigations into the vagaries of the metaphysical, unseen phenomena deeply rooted in the mysteries of our time.

His title of Professor of Peculiarities was hard won; a battle honor waged first through psychic confrontations akin to physical combat and then granted *cum laude* after the fact by an academia reluctant in their beliefs. Undoubtedly, he was a consummate technician, an inventor of the most profound instruments of the science of the peculiar. As his stature and renown grew, he died as a *philosopher célèbre*; as a philanthropist to the arts and sciences; as a man of deep conviction that the peculiar would manifest itself as much in the minds of men as in the substance of events. It is with this legacy that I live the rest of my life burdened with responsibility. The preservation of his Institute has now fallen into my humble hands, an endeavour I feel so much less qualified to command than its founder. As his one-time apprentice, I will do my best.

These are *The Most Peculiar Tales*—the most famous of Professor Atticus Carr's many cases, remembered as faithfully as I can recall, given the passage of so much time.

Yours sincerely,

Jeremiah Boone

Jeremiah Boone, Esquire

JEREMIAH
BOONE

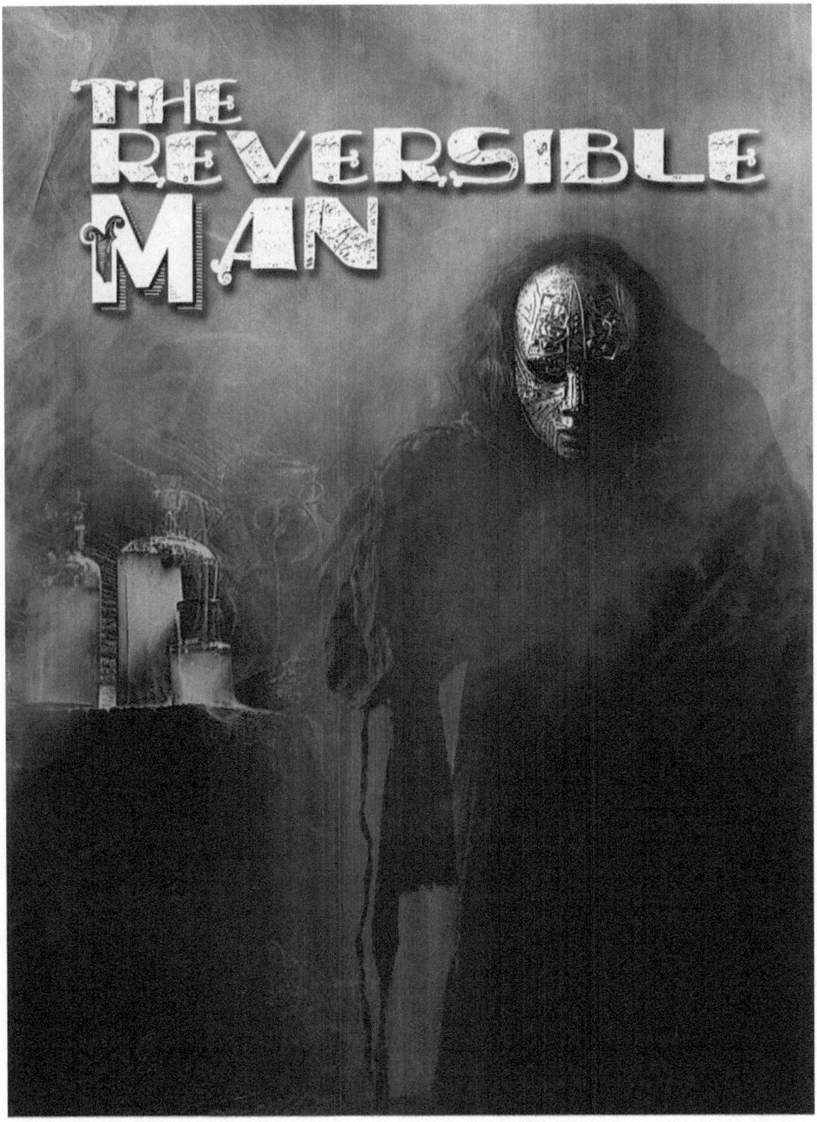
THE REVERSIBLE MAN

THE REVERSIBLE MAN

PART I

The corridors of the old Watchester gaol stank of slop and urine, washed from the cells by a lazy assemblage of prison staff who'd greeted me with indifference and whose own state of grubbiness smelt of negligence of duty. What an incredibly dire coffin of a building to be imprisoned in, I thought, as a jailor led me to Professor Carr's cell.

I found the professor leaning with his back against a cracked, whitewashed wall, his knees hunched up to his chest, resting on a bare slat bunk, a mattress nowhere to be seen. His chin hung down to a loose-fitting prison under-vest, a garment once white but now grey. I thought he might be asleep. The dour man stirred, opened bloodshot eyes, and flicked a scrap of bread off his baggy black pantaloons. His mustache and vee-shaped goatee, normally well-waxed, were straggles of limp hair, soaked in sweat. The hot, dank cell trapped the midsummer vapors as if they too had been charged with an awful crime.

"What news, Jeremiah?" he asked. His voice had lost its snap, its surety.

"Arraignment is in four days, professor. Can you cope until then?"

"What choice do I have?" he sighed, resigned.

"Quite. Well, your solicitor requested the delay. He arrives tomorrow by the early morning mail-ship having done what preliminaries he can accomplish by telegraphy from Londinium. He suggests we need more time to gather evidence of your innocence and prepare the best case we can. Apparently Judge Harringay Charlesworth leans heavily towards assuming any guilt the prosecution asperses even before the trial has commenced. He is by nature a hanging judge and recalcitrant to the blindness Lady Justice requires, especially in high capital crimes."

"And that is your good news, my dear fellow?" Professor Carr's sardonic smirk was bereft of humor. "I think I shall pass on listening to your worst."

"Forgive me. The jailor says we have scant time for this interview." I could hear the brute prowling outside the bars. "I request you hasten your instructions to me, for the little information you have given so far has provided me no compass."

"Yes, and rightly so. It seems impossible to me that I could have murdered someone I'd never met, in a place I'd never been before or traveled since, at a time when I lay on my sick bed at my country cottage."

"The prosecution asserts that your illness was but a ruse. And given the lack of a doctor or servant to attest to your whereabouts, those days you claim you were stricken alone with fever were the ideal opportunity for you to slip away into the night and execute your grave misconduct. And then there is the issue of witnesses to the crime itself, and their damning affidavits that describe you to the last buckle on your shoes, the exact cut and cloth of your famous jacket, and the features of your face. Several of them attended your most recent performance from the Theatre Macabre in Tallybridge Junction, the town where the murder took place. They have identified you from your *artiste photogravures* and other promotional literature."

"I was not there. I swear to you," the professor said.

"Please, Professor Carr, your proclamation amounts to nothing when confronted with such overwhelming evidence. Even the guiltiest villain will protest innocence right up to when the hangman fits his noose. We must have more than just your indignation. We must have *proof*. Ideally, we must identify the true perpetrator, for that arrest will be unequivocal."

"Then we must analyze the possibilities. As I have been doing in my quiet confinement."

"Please begin."

"I have reached beyond this atmosphere into the realm of the peculiar. And asked for guidance from any spirit that might pity me. And such guidance was forthcoming from the most unusual source."

"Who?"

"The victim herself."

"Baroness Purdue?"

"The same. Of course, my mystery is hers as well. She visited me last night. I felt the fingers of her aether stroke my face. Her spirit concluded that yes, it was indeed the face she last saw on this earth as the knife plunged into her heart. But she consoled me. Warmed me with the thought that beneath her true attacker's outward appearance lay a soul quite the opposite of mine, rich with malevolent intent. And from that aethereal inspection, she had concluded that I was not her murderer."

"Oh, dear Lord. If she could only testify to that fact, our triumph would be won. You do not need to convince me of the validity of spiritual messages. But sadly they are laughed out of Her Majesty's Courts."

"Still, her laments keep pouring over me like a waterfall. She is so sorry. But so helpless."

"Where does that leave us? Can we conclude that a doppelgänger exists? Surely if we told the authorities to put word out that a person masquerading as Professor Atticus Carr wanders the country, he would be easily apprehended given your nationwide celebrity. Such a man could not hide from your followers for long."

"I sense I know this man. And I fear he doesn't need to shelter his face. I fear that—his grisly work accomplished, in this first of possibly many such crimes to come—he will simply melt into the crowds, unrecognizable, anonymous, obscure. And from that ambiguity, he will strike again."

"Professor, you're making no sense."

"Yes, Jeremiah. Often the peculiar makes no sense at all."

PART II

What options were available to us? I left perplexed by the further details the professor had revealed to me and returned to the inn where I was staying, supping my lunch ale alone and disheartened, disconsolate that I could no longer rely on my master's guidance to investigate this grievous matter.

Professor Carr had concluded who the murderer of Baroness Matilda Purdue was—a man almost assuredly known to him and still free abroad to exact his agenda with impunity. Finding him and convincing the authorities of his guilt was a task even Hercules might fail, given the most peculiar means by which this high crime had been committed. And there were potentially no limits to the fiendish lawlessness that may ensue in the future if he was not apprehended. Murder, indeed. But fraud, larceny, corruption, and extortion were but a few of the many misdeeds that a man with such extraordinary powers could wield upon the innocent.

Astonishingly, as Professor Carr relayed to me, he was not an unwitting victim in the crime to which he was accused. In retrospect, he'd been an active if not enthusiastic participant. His ignorance at the time, of the consequences of his actions, had turned professional curiosity into the jaws of a bear-trap. Regardless, he was neither a true accomplice nor a heinous criminal in this misadventure, despite the guilt he felt, and something had to be done. But what?

My first inclination was to approach the High Sheriff and plead the professor's case. But that would require an understanding of a branch of the peculiar sciences as yet unpublished and unverified, even if such an officer of the law had faith that these sciences were indeed legitimate, as many did not. It appeared foolhardy to engage those whose mission was to bury Professor Carr, not to praise him.

My fare arrived at my table, but I was no longer hungry in that sense. My watch proclaimed noon. I asked the inn's hostess to direct me to the nearest telegraphy office.

"At the rail-plane terminal," she replied.

Brilliant, I thought. I can send the professor's staff at the Institute instructions on my desired course of action and then board the next rail-plane express to Londinium. The last airship had departed for the capital from Tallybridge at eleven. The next airship left tomorrow morning. Far too late. How fortuitous Tallybridge Junction was on a newly commissioned rail-plane line, giving my plan a head start.

I tipped generously, as is my wont, and hailed a balloon-cab to the station. As we rose quickly above the rooftops of Watchester, I understood why Professor Carr had chosen to acquire a country cottage here. Watchester, a quiet market town, bordered the most pastoral wolds in Britannia, gentle rolling hills of meadows and forests where serenity could be found in abundance. The squalor of the professor's confinement in its byzantine gaol no doubt had erased all such effects of tranquility. Would my efforts prevail in time? His arraignment loomed.

The rail-plane's propellers whisked me past the sheep pastures of Riffolk, the mill towns of Pottinghamshire and the industrial hamlets of the Courtolds. The two-hundred-mile journey to Londinium allowed time to reflect on what we knew and what we didn't know. Professor Carr's account had been mesmerizing. I had taken copious notes and my memory of the conversation was nearly sonographic.

It had been a chilly spring night when they'd first met. After concluding the evening performance at the Theatre Macabre, Professor Carr had been visited in his dressing room by a man who introduced himself as Dr. Miles Bennett. Dr. Bennett claimed to be both a traditional medical doctor and a practitioner of what he referred to as 'trans-psychic reconstitution'. Bennett gushed over the professor's stage display of illusion and magic. This by itself is not extraordinary; the intelligentsia never failed to be impressed by the peculiar. And Professor Carr was never left unimpressed by their generous donations to his Institute. But Bennett had not sought out the professor to be another patron of the Institute. He had sought to become his partner.

Bennett began his overture by appealing to Professor Carr's affiliation with the illusory, especially of disguise and the means by which an illusionist could distract audiences by replacing the familiar with the new. The professor recounted Bennett's discussion of theatrical makeup and its transformative properties.

"What if an exact replica of someone's face could be painted across another's?" Bennett asked. "The world of theater of course would be intrigued. Such technique would be highly profitable. But what if we could turn that opportunity into something more charitable and worthwhile? What if one could restore the features of someone horribly disfigured by industrial accident? Or take an affliction of birth that repulsed the eye and transform it into a thing of beauty?"

The professor had to admit that in retrospect, these possibilities had been the hook that had drawn him into accepting Bennett's invitation to a private exposition of the technology. Potential avenues of charity had blinded him to the possibility of infamy. Until it was too late.

Bennett's laboratory was housed in a wing of his surgery in the working class district of Pritchard's Green, an unlikely name for one of Londinium's poorest neighborhoods where the only green came from mold. The borough was uniformly depressing, a slum of terraced houses with crumbling mortar and lanes of soot-laden cobbles. Bennett said the Green was where he'd grown up and his affinity to the place had drawn him back to serve the people. This had appealed to the professor's good nature and kind heart, further ensnaring him. Having grown up in similar circumstances, I adopted a more cynical stance on the issue, as discussed with the professor in the gaol. In reflection, I said, it was more likely that Miles Bennett could find in a place like Pritchard's Green an endless supply of woeful subjects for his experiments, whether he paid the poor sods or not.

While at Bennett's surgery, the man explained to Carr that theatrical masques failed as medical prosthetics because of two things: the copious labor required and the imperfect, stony look that was created. Even wax replicas in Londinium's popular Arcade of Celebrity were, no matter how skillful the sculptor and makeup artist, still lacking in that 'special something' to make the mind suspend disbelief and become convinced that the resultant image was indeed real. This, he claimed, is where his technology had achieved a breakthrough. He called his new science: trans-psychic facial mapping.

Professor Carr was introduced to Dr. Bennett's wife and medical assistant. She was a petite lady, he recalled, dwarfed by her husband. Her facial features were innocuous, even bland; the kind of face that would blend into the crowds at a market, indistinguishable from many. I was very familiar with such anonymous-looking people, both male and female. They bred in Londinium's slums like rats. Such anonymity made them great pickpockets. It was a profession I too had been taught as a youngster, as a necessary means of survival in the harsh economy of the street.

What distinguished Mrs. Bennett was the one side of her face she'd carefully kept from the professor's initial view. She was grotesquely disfigured; her cheeks gnarled into ribbons of twisted red and purple flesh; her left eyelid melted down across her eyeball as if was stitched in place. She had worked in a tannery, Bennett had said. She'd been splashed with a solution of caustic soda, used during the liming process to swell the hides. His wife would soon be, he said, an experiment in reconstruction.

After visiting Bennett's surgery over several occasions, Professor Carr described to me Dr. and Mrs. Bennett's demeanors, quite different from each other. His wife was timid and nervous, the result, Miles Bennett had concluded, of her being shunned from society because of her deformity.

As the rail-plane sped closer to my destination, another thought came to mind. Professor Carr described Dr. Bennett as a well-dressed man who'd spent lavishly on his attire. He was athletic in build, fair-haired and handsome, the kind of attractive, educated man that the debutantes of Londinium society would swoon over. His fault was that he talked incessantly about himself and his accomplishments, although later Professor Carr could find no one among his medical acquaintances who recalled him. In conversation after conversation with the professor, Bennett persisted in his grandiosity. Why would such a dire narcissist marry such a poor and deformed waif? An epiphany came to me in the rail-plane's carriage. He would not. She was *not* his wife. She must have been a subject of an earlier—likely failed—experiment, now coerced by shame or by coin, or by both, to be Bennett's co-conspirator.

Had his hypnotic persona ensnared her, as it had done my unfortunate master? Was it possible that Bennett's tests had initially gone horribly wrong and instead of curing his assistant's maladies he had actually produced them? And wasn't his magnetic personality as much a part of the danger of Dr. Miles Bennett as the device he called the Trans-Aura Topographical Machine, the instrument to which my own Professor Carr had been a willing volunteer?

The rail-plane slowed to the terminus at Londinium's Carrington Cross Station. These questions had produced a myriad of investigative tunnels to venture down. I set about with great resolve to engage the staff at the Institute to drop whatever they were doing and devote their whole energies into the exoneration of Professor Carr and the apprehension of the criminal that we soon named The Reversible Man.

PART III

I immediately acted upon every suspicion whether substantive or not.

Professor Carr had described in great detail the apparatus Bennett was using to abscond with another person's face. A device he called a 'trans-psychic facial masque' was its main technical element, a helmet of considerable scale mounted on an articulating arm. Attached on a bench beside it was a collection device, ostensibly designed to transfer an imprint of a desired new visage onto the patient's face although both Professor Carr and I had concluded this could also surreptitiously collect such an imprint from the 'patient' and store it for future use. This was the means by which the theft of Professor Carr's likeness had been achieved and the means through which a host of subsequent crimes could be committed.

That Dr. Miles Bennett had left Londinium was not in doubt. The murder of Baroness Purdue in Tallybridge Junction, two hundred miles away, was proof of his mobility. His assemblage of instruments would require a charabanc of considerable size to transport them, along with heaven knows how many collection jars of other people's faces he'd managed to obtain from his nefarious activities. Together, his apparatus and specimen jars would need a conveyance of some magnitude and stealth. I surmised this conveyance served as a mobile laboratory so the equipment, once housed portably and accessible in a yard of his choosing, limited the risk of exposing his illegal activities through constant unloading and reloading.

So we were looking for three things. First, the recent procurement of a specialized mode of transport. And secondly, evidence that others had been duped to 'donate' their countenances to Bennett's evil cause, just as Professor Carr had done. I sent investigators down both tracks. My focus would be on the third, motive. And for that undertaking, my first inquiry surrounded the connection between Dr. Bennett and Baroness Matilda Purdue.

Was she a victim who had refused to participate in his experiments? Or was there another relationship between them? A lovers' quarrel perhaps? Could the motive behind her murder be revenge for ending an extramarital affair? Baroness Matilda Purdue was a married woman. She was also a mainstay within high society circles and that social milieu would be my next port of call. I would immerse myself in that line of inquiry while others at the Institute pursued physical evidence.

Precious time for our undertakings was slipping through the hour-glass.

The Institute's Director of Research briefed me on the dossier I'd commissioned by telegram. Baroness Purdue was an heiress to a sizable industrial fortune. Her late father had been a mill owner in Tallybridge Junction where she'd grown up on a country estate of considerable magnificence, the same estate outside Tallybridge Junction where she'd be murdered while taking her summer holiday. Her main residence was Primrose House, a mansion in a fashionable district of central Londinium: St. Stephen's Gate near the Imperial Palace. Her title had not come from her father, a gruff commoner by aristocratic standards, but by marriage to Baron Montague Purdue, First Lord of the Southern Air Army, one of Queen Ellinora's most senior military aides.

My interview with the baron required a delicate diplomacy, given my suspicions of his wife's possible infidelities, underscored by numerous inquiries to the tabloids whose readership devoured such gossip like tourists munch whelks at the seaside, and whose already published stories were corroborated by the Institute's independent contacts. Matilda Purdue was thirty years the baron's junior, a radiant beauty whose apparent appetite for lustful men had been seemingly insatiable. The baron on the other hand had tolerated such adultery because he was a gambling man and the funds from the industries she owned in the north never seemed to dry up despite his best attempts to drain her accounts. Their marriage, the tabloids had concluded, was a marriage of convenience between debauchery and tomfoolery that was oh-so-typical of the bacchanalian nature of the Imperial Court.

I sat in the Grand Reception Room of Primrose House, looked upon by glassy-eyed stares from the heads of mounted beasts—tigers, lions, bears, and gazelles. The baron had taken every advantage of his command to hunt wherever his aerial gunship had patrolled, above the savannahs, jungles, and forests of the Empire. After spending twenty minutes alone in the room, it was as if an inquisition of dead fauna were presiding over my trial of patience and their silent deliberations would at any moment proclaim my freedom or incarceration. I felt like Professor Carr must be feeling in the Watchester gaol—only my wait had the benefit of Pajastani tea and Celtish oat biscuits. Finally, the baron deigned me worthy of seeing him and arrived with great pomposity in full medal-laden uniform, feather plumes and all.

"I have an investiture to attend in Westbury cathedral, my good man. Be quick," he trumpeted as he waved his servants away with a white-gloved hand.

"Dr. Miles Bennett," I said.

"What about him?"

"You *know* the gentleman?"

"Of course I do. He was my personal flight surgeon for five years. Left the service three years ago and went into private practice. He was treating my wife before she died."

"Treating her? For what ailment?"

The baron pulled nervously at his collar. "Damn all the rumors, man. The Bennett I knew was an honorable fellow. She had a recurrent case of malaria. I shouldn't have brought her with me that time. I should have known her delicate constitution might be susceptible to the rigors of a tropical clime."

"Which is why she made *frequent* visits to him?"

"Malaria," he said, scowling.

"Her murder," I replied. "That is what I'm investigating."

"They've caught the bastard," he snapped. "He will get his comeuppance in due course."

It was a waste of time to advocate for Professor Carr's innocence. "Did she ever mention a treatment that required her to don a helmet?"

"How else would you treat malaria? It goes to the brain."

Shocked by that revelation, I asked, "Is that what Dr. Bennett said?"

"Yes, of course. He's a doctor." He looked me up and down. "I wager a fellow of your limited means cannot afford the latest exotic treatments. His methods were expensive. However, combined with the pills he gave her, she recovered fully. Do you have malaria? Is that why you're here?"

"How many other patients undertook Dr. Bennett's 'cure'? Do you know?"

"Damn it, man. Why hide such a cure, regardless of cost? Of course, I recommended him to others. Those who could afford it."

I was stunned. "Who?"

"Why is this relevant?"

"There's a possibility that Dr. Bennett's patients are in great danger because of these treatments. He's also connected with your wife's murder. Evidence of his 'treatments for malaria' needs to be presented to the High Sheriff."

"All right then. If you put it that way. Let me think." He paused, hand on chin. "There were senior officers in the foreign service of the Imperial Land and Air Armies. And diplomats returning from the tropics. Several members of parliament and many aristocrats…lords, ladies, that sort of thing…who'd traveled extensively. And my friends, owners of the Empire's largest trading companies and import-export ventures. I might have missed a few. My private secretary can provide you with the names."

"All wealthy. Of high standing in society."

"The elite of the Empire. Only the best for the best, I always say."

"Quite." I stood to leave. "Your testimony has been most illuminating, Baron Purdue. Indeed, the most valuable yet obtained, I'm sure."

He bowed. "As always, dear sir, I am of service to Her Imperial Majesty in all respects."

"Oh, one last thing. Were Bennett's patients directed to his surgery in Pritchard's Green?"

"Pritchard's Green! Who in God's name do you think these people are? Only charlatans and thieves live in Pritchard's Green. My associates wouldn't be caught dead there."

"Yes, indeed. Then where did they go for treatment?"

"Dr. Bennett came to them."

"To *them*? With his helmet apparatus?"

"He came by airship, his personal barque. An ingenious solution. He purchased a retired air ambulance from the Army and had it converted to suit his purposes. I told you, Dr. Bennett's services were expensive and exclusive. Very exclusive."

"Thank you for your most valuable assistance in this matter, baron. Exclusive indeed. And now I fully appreciate why."

PART IV

A single day passed and although my urgency had not waned, hope triumphed over despair.

The research staff at the Institute had identified the location of Dr. Bennett's surgery in Pritchard's Green. After my visit to Purdue House, our efforts could now be focused with greater precision.

One of Professor Carr's patrons was the Grand Marshal of Londinium. I solicited his support in organizing a clandestine raid by Her Majesty's Imperial Police. We found in Pritchard's Green a laboratory bereft of its main accoutrements. All that remained were square footprints on the floor where Bennett's equipment once stood and the shadows of departed cabinets on the walls, formed where dust had not collected. Bolt holes in the wall indicated where the articulating arm must have been mounted. Circular shapes appeared in the grime on shelves where collection jars had once been stored.

"This is not evidence of murder," the Grand Marshal said, inspecting the empty laboratory. "It's simply what one would normally expect of an establishment that has vacated the premises."

I rummaged through a box that one of the marshal's men had found in the debris of the abandoned surgery. It contained but a few old test tubes. Disconsolate, my eyes searched for anything, any crumb, that could lead us beyond Pritchard's Green. To one side of the laboratory was a small ante-room that contained a tattered bed. I found a dress draped over a chair, a garb like that of a scullery maid's. I searched the pockets and found a crumpled piece of paper. It had a woman's scrawl, like that of a grocery list.

"Mrs. Bennett's, I presume," I said handing it to the marshal. "The date at the top of this script indicates it was written two years after Dr. Miles Bennett left the service of the Imperial Air Army. It contains a list of women's names. Beside each name, a sum of money. Professor

Carr surmises that Dr. Bennett used his wife in disguise to lure his first victims. This list might point to fraudulent medical practices, even the extortion of funds from them. Bennett needed sizable monies to purchase his airship. Once that important acquisition was in hand, his ambitions could increase exponentially, beyond the lower caste to the moneyed elite." I tapped the list. "I think these were his first experimental victims."

The Grand Marshal examined the document. "The total is more than sufficient to cover the expense of the air ambulance as stated in the Air Army's bill of sale. I will send my officers to interrogate these alleged victims. If we can substantiate your assertions that crimes have been committed, I will grant you as much official support as I legitimately can."

"It's Mrs. Bennett I want. I suspect he may have abandoned her, as he has done with this laboratory. Her testimony might lead us to him."

"We are still far from proving Professor Carr's innocence. We have only conjecture and theory, no more. This equipment you claim exists, *where* is it? Its purpose, *what* is it? Your assertions are fantastic and most peculiar. Curing malaria is not a crime regardless of how over-priced his services were. However, evidence of extortion of his patients would warrant his indictment on those charges. But it still leaves Professor Carr facing the hangman."

"Mrs. Bennett is the key to this, I'm sure of it. As peculiar as it sounds, it's as if Professor Carr and Baroness Matilda Purdue are willing me in this direction. When we find her, we find our solution."

"I hope, for his sake, you're right." The Grand Marshal turned to the inspector in charge of the raid. "Send out a warrant for the arrest of Mrs. Bennett."

PART V

Esther Bunkle, aka Mrs. Bennett, sat in the interrogation room of No. 14 Police Squad Barracks, a bundle of nerves.

Miss Bunkle was known simply by her street name, Patsy—a fitting tribute given her history of duping others and being duped herself. Patsy had believed Dr. Bennett loved her—right up until he abandoned her in a back alley, shot in the chest, but unfortunately for him, not dead. Her arrest had been serendipitous. She languished in a holding cell awaiting trial when our warrant went out, charged over the theft of a jar of malaria pills from an apothecary in Pritchard's Green, from a man who'd previously been extorted by her and Bennett, and who'd recognized her voice and petite stature despite the absence of her facial disguise.

Her 'deformity', the industrial accident, had been a lie; her 'face' being a carefully applied theatrical prosthetic designed to reap sympathy as a part of Dr. Bennett's money-making schemes. Esther Bunkle had been a nurse in the tropics and had contracted malaria there. She'd suffered a severe remission of the disease after being released from the hospital after Bennett's attack. Penniless, she hurried to Pritchard's Green and robbed the apothecary at knifepoint. How ironic. The malady the pair had used to gain entry into the world of high society would itself finally bring her to justice.

The police grilled her unmercifully for hours until overwhelming evidence and the pain of Bennett's betrayal produced a complete confession to the crimes of fraud and extortion. The police granted me time with Patsy alone. But it was not extortion I was interested in. It was Professor Carr's freedom that was of paramount concern and the use of the peculiar by The Reversible Man to commit future crimes. Despite her admitted guilt, there remained a critical issue to be resolved—proving Miles Bennett's connection to Baroness Purdue's murder. Patsy had been left to die weeks before that sorry event and swore she knew nothing of any plan to assault the baroness or of Bennett's whereabouts. Even a tough beadle's threatening persuasion wouldn't change her story. The investigating officer finally decided her statements must be true. But Professor Carr's innocence was still in question in the eyes of the law.

"Patsy, you face life at hard labor in an Imperial prison," I began. "I have no powers to mitigate that fate. However, Professor Atticus Carr enjoys broad and endearing support from the most influential of people including the Grand Marshal. There must be something you haven't revealed to the police—perhaps in fear, or simply because you don't feel it relevant—that may unravel this web of deceit in Professor Carr's favor and by doing so improve your situation."

"Like what? I've told them about the faces we captured in the machine. Gave them all the names I remember. At least those patients I was a party to attending when they came in for treatment."

"And the authorities are alerting them to the potential dangers and deception."

"Wait—" she said, her eyes alight with inspiration. "Dr. Bennett had a storage shed. In the grounds of a house he once owned. His house had been repossessed. Perhaps there's something there that can help you find him."

"A house repossessed?"

"It had a lien on it. To repay debts. Gambling debts."

"Did he ever gamble with Baron Purdue?"

"He told me when he was in the Air Army with the baron, they used to gamble in all the exotic ports of call. But this debt was recent and domestic. And huge as I recall. Dr. Bennett could not afford the repayments and at the same time, to purchase the equipment for his research laboratory. He forfeited the property; a painful choice that left him with a vicious and vindictive demeanour. He mentioned a shed—a structure in a remote part of the estate, somewhere no one would think of looking—as a means of hiding from the police if we needed it. He intimated there was something stored there. But he was not forthcoming with an answer as to what and became angry when I pressed."

"I've seen a tumbledown shed in my mind's eye. Planted there perhaps by one whose spirit provides guidance in my pursuit. A confirmation of sorts of what you describe."

"If that leads you to what you seek, please credit my witness. Put in a good word with the judge for me?"

"I shall."

***

Bennett's former estate lay in the countryside near a rail-plane stop, an hour northwest of the city core. I withdrew all available resources at the Institute from their prior tasks and hastened to engage the local authorities. At Carrington Cross, the Grand Marshal handed me the required Imperial search warrant and held up the departure of the Londinium-to-Fordbridge Express until the Institute's forces could assemble from all points to join me.

The Institute owned one of only a few portable telegraphs in the country, a Hertzian Wave Machine, affectionately dubbed by Professor Carr a 'wireless' for obvious reasons. Carr used it during his performances at the Theatre Macabre in a segment in which he appeared to be talking to the ghost of Anne Boleyn. With this instrument I was able to keep in touch with investigators back at the Institute while in transit.

As the rail-plane sped along, they telegraphed details of an astonishing discovery. Bennett's mortgage indebtedness had been to Baroness Matilda Purdue. Upon repossession, title to Bennett's home passed to her, a scant two days prior to her murder. But even after the change of ownership, Miles Bennett held a residual indenture of some complexity on his former property. In short, in the event of the baroness's death, title would be restored to him automatically, bypassing the usual steps of probating her will. Such an arrangement could only have been agreed between lovers.

Motive in her murder had been established beyond doubt!

A police airship met us in Fordbridge and we took off, following a map to Bennett's estate I constructed from telegraphed descriptions obtained through the Registrar of Deeds. We located the hundred-acre estate and mansion house at the confluence of two rivers, and circled overhead.

A local constable scanned the ground with a *binocularis optica*. From his perch on the airship's forward observation deck, he shouted, "Down there!" The suspect shed had been found. The airship descended to the nearest flat field and myself, my team from the Institute, Sheriff Boxworthy of the Fordbridge Constabulary and a squad of his beadles waded through waves of golden hay until we met thick brambles that had grown around what may have previously been a small gamekeeper's cottage.

"Oy, what have we here?" Sheriff Boxworthy said as the brambles were hacked back and the withered door was smashed open.

The cottage was essentially a one room shanty with no differentiation between kitchen and drawing room, bedroom and office. In the center of the room was a jumble of equipment on brass tripods, and to the sides—on the floor, on tables, shelves and desks—a mess of dust-crusted jars, empty crates, old ledgers, and crumpled paper with scribbled numbers.

I found a poker beside the cold fireplace and swept away the cobwebs dangling across the instruments. "This must have been Bennett's first laboratory. And I would venture this instrument was his first prototype."

"What did Professor Carr call it?" the sheriff asked.

"A Trans-Aura Topographical Machine." I pulled on the articulating arm, its springs twanging with disuse. "This positions the trans-psychic facial masque over the subject. And yes, here on this bench—" I picked up some objects that resembled masques from a

Venetian fancy dress party. Tubing protruded from the masques and inside the tubes, the caked stains of fluid that had once circulated through them. One of the masques was still connected by tubes to a large carboy mounted on an electrical instrument that resembled a charging transformer. The crystal faces of the transformer's dull enamel dials were cracked. Evidence of an electrical fire was everywhere. I pulled a sheaf of burnt wires from the back of the charred cabinet.

"I need to get this equipment back to the Institute for examination. I believe this will prove facial imitation beyond the theatrical, evidence of the nefarious experimentation Bennett used to illegally abscond with identities."

"Mr. Boone," a constable shouted. "Over here! In this jar. My God, it's still alive!"

We rushed to the constable's side. The globular jar—about four and twenty inches high, bell-shaped at the top; fluted glass extensions sealed with stopcocks—was mounted on a circular stand of brass. The policeman had wiped the surface of its grime and through a polished section of glass, we could see a light inside, throbbing. It was a substance of pinkish hue, and as we peered through the glass, we saw a flesh-like web of red strands pulsing as if drawing blood from invisible veins.

"Dear Lord, what fiendish aberration exists inside that jar?" Sheriff Boxworthy exclaimed. "Have you seen anything like it before, Boone?"

"Never."

"It's a thing of evil, sheriff," the constable said. "Shall we raise a fire and burn it?"

"No!" I replied. "We can do no such thing. If life is what we see, it must be preserved and studied, however peculiar it may be."

"Looks like the Devil's beef drippings," the constable grunted.

"Get a grip, man," Sheriff Boxworthy barked. "And do your duty."

The sheriff swept his arms about the room. "Strip this place! Box everything, spare nothing. With haste!"

"Thank you, sir," I said. "Evil is afoot in Britannia. And we must bring all energy to bear until it is defeated."

PART VI

"I hope you're not about to waste my time with acts of legal trickery," Judge Harringay Charlesworth said, addressing defense counsel. "The prosecution has presented an overwhelming case against your client."

"He must have his day in court, m'lord."

"Undeniably. Just don't waste the court's time doing it."

Professor Atticus Carr slumped in the prisoner's dock, his head bowed towards his feet. The only witness that could be called in his defense was himself. I arrived at his trial in Tallybridge Junction but an hour before, when the last of the eyewitnesses had recounted their stories. Baroness Matilda Purdue had left a swanky *maison de cuisine* with a flamboyant man, garish in both manner and dress, sporting a curly mustache and a pointy goatee. "That man," they said, one after the other, pointing to the prisoner in the dock. "That man," another said, describing the same man who'd left the park where the murder had taken place, blood doused across his lacy cravat and splashed over his jacket.

The professor's barrister looked over at me with eyes near panic, shuffling papers as if a deck of cards, in order to stall for time. I checked my pocket chronometer. *What was taking them so long?*

A great pounding of the thick courtroom door boomed through the muted hush, startling the judge and all present. The doors flung open. The Grand Marshal of Londinium, resplendent in medaled blue uniform of state, shiny black boots and flowing cape, strode towards the judge's bench brandishing a large roll of paper tied with purple ribbon.

Judge Charlesworth stood up, his face red, his eyes blazing. "What is the meaning of this outrage!"

"By order of Her Imperial Majesty Queen Ellinora of Britannia, Empress Commander of all Her Dominions, these proceedings are forthwith suspended!" The Grand Marshal presented the scroll to the judge. "The prisoner is to be released on Her Majesty's bond and accompany me back to Londinium immediately. The charges against him are to be held in abeyance until such future date as the pleasure of Her Majesty sees fit."

The judge fell back into his chair, his opened mouth moving like a goldfish gulping for air.

Professor Atticus Carr had been set free.

For now.

PART VII

The Institute for the Investigation of Peculiarities sits between Sutherland House and St. Francis Cathedral; its facade of hamstone blocks and its roof of terra cotta tiles overlooking the dark waters of the Etham River, a course of commerce that bisects Londinium like a crawling snake.

We stood in the Institute's root cellar where the prototype apparatus of The Reversible Man had been brought, the only room large enough and empty enough to facilitate its restoration, the first order of business Professor Carr had prescribed once his freedom had been guaranteed by royal decree.

The first rays of dawn streamed through small windows high in the cellar's ceiling, windows at street level, the point where the northern boulevard of the Embankment met the Institute. The sunbeams cast an eerie spotlight on our night's work.

The articulating arm with its trans-psychic facial masque had been given a good cleaning; the stained tubes running into the helmet replaced with new ones. The electrical cabinet's wires had been repaired. The cabinet's voltmeters and transformers, its enamel dials and potentiometers, the glass carboy and all the other aspects of the machine's attachments and instrumentation had been replaced during a frenzied night of work by the professor's team of technologists. The source of ignition that had destroyed the prototype—a faultily designed set of crude circuitry—had been reconfigured by the professor's chief electrification engineer and the Trans-Aura Topographical Machine's function was certified as operable to the best of his knowledge, whatever the beast did.

Professor Carr's liberty had been secured by a most fortuitous event. One of the Crown Jewels of State, the Mabur-Noor Ruby had been stolen. Late one night, the Steward of the Imperial Armory had been seen entering the vault where the crown jewels were kept, and the following day, the tiara with the precious ruby was discovered missing. While I had been attending the raid on Bennett's estate, the Grand Marshal had been summoned to the Imperial Palace. Accusations against the Queen's Steward had been made. Eyewitness accounts verified the man's identity beyond reasonable doubt. The problem—as the Grand Marshal told the professor and I in the strictest of confidence, under pain of treason—was that the Steward of the Imperial Armory had actually been with Queen Ellinora in her bedchamber at the time of the robbery.

The Reversible Man was no longer a wild theory concocted by a frightened prisoner to countermand his unquestionable guilt. The fiend was now an imminent threat to all those whose countenances he had stolen, and to the preservation of the social order of the Britannic Empire.

In the court of public opinion, it was one thing to condemn a blaggard from Pritchard's Green to transportation for petty crimes against the underclasses, it was an entirely different thing to turn the aristocracy into high felons. The Queen was having none of it. What could be done to apprehend this villain? The wax on her decree— suspending the charges against Professor Carr—was still warm when the papers arrived in Judge Charlesworth's courtroom in Tallybridge Junction.

And that was the question before the good professor. Yes, what could be done?

Dr. Miles Bennett, The Reversible Man, had become wise to the inquiries of the Imperial Police. The day following the theft of the Mabur-Noor Ruby, a small airship had been seen off the coast of Riffolk, ablaze in the sky. It crashed in the tempestuous Northern Sea far from land. Floating remnants were salvaged by a fishing boat. The police confirmed their origins as coming from the same air ambulance Dr. Miles Bennett had procured from the Army. The Reversible Man was now afoot, a welcome development to be sure. But what of his laboratory? Had he found a permanent home for it? Or had his spree ended with the theft of the crown jewel? Was he about to escape Britannia for foreign shores? Security at Britannia's aerodromes, ports, and rail-plane terminals had been elevated to the highest level to interrogate all those planning to leave the country.

Entombed in its jar of mysterious vapors, the specimen of pulsing flesh from Bennett's laboratory sat on a table beside his restored prototype machine. Professor Carr approached the jar, as he had done innumerable times in the past three hours, the expression on his face a sign he was still contemplating the thing's purpose.

"There is more to this machine than brass and copper," he said. "Much more to its operation than inducing electrical current. There is life most peculiar in this jar. I fear we cannot replicate its production without the special fluids that once filled the carboy."

"Then why have we spent so much time restoring the machine?" I asked, tired and exasperated.

"Because a replication can be taken from a subject and kept living in this jar," he said. "But the other function of the machine I surmise is that this same object of replication can be transferred to another person by reversing the instrument's polarity."

"You mean taking this—this *aberration*—and applying it to someone's face?"

"Precisely. That is the *modus operandi* of The Reversible Man."

"What are you proposing, professor? We don't know whose replicated face this represents. We have no expertise in the machine's operation. And who would volunteer for such an experiment even if we did?"

Professor Carr felt around the edges of his face with his hand. He had the look of intrigue, beyond curious.

I was stunned. "You can't possibly be serious? You're not thinking that *you* should undertake such an endeavor?"

"Are *you* volunteering to do it, Mr. Boone?"

"Well, no, but—"

"So should I coerce one of my staff to do it? Under what mandate? Under what code of moral authority should I condone such assault on another? No, Jeremiah. I am the only one that can possibly be considered for this course of action. My own freedom means nothing if such a monstrous mind is allowed to roam free, and my liberty may yet be taken away in a court of law if he is not apprehended. If we are to break new ground in the science of the peculiar, this is the exact manner of exploration required."

I didn't know what to say. That the professor lacked fear in matters such as these, there was no doubt. But there had never been such incredible danger. "What if that which we think is reversible is actually not?"

"Then I forever become another doppelgänger of someone whose identity this blob of pulsing flesh represents. Who knows what crimes I might commit?" he chuckled.

"This is not a laughing matter, Professor Carr."

"Indeed not. We must proceed with all seriousness."

PART VIII

The hum from the machine vibrated the marrow of my bones and sent sharp tingles down the roots of my teeth. The cellar had come alive with something beyond electricity. A pale blue haze enveloped the brass end of the articulating arm that held the trans-psychic facial masque. Professor Carr, wearing a white surgical gown, reclined in a tilting chair below the opened helmet, a device that separated into two pieces—one that remained with the machine to support the back of the head, and the other, the frontal masque that lay face down on a table on a linen cloth. The professor was in position, his arms, legs and chest held tight to the chair by thick leather straps.

"The field of aura has reached the peak of its intensity," Carr said. He wiggled a palm to his engineer. "Hold it there." He looked over at me. "Jeremiah...I'm ready."

Professor Carr's private doctor attended him, as did a nurse. The only other witness was the Grand Marshal. If facial transplantation was to be the outcome, we had to be sure the authorities understood its ramifications. If the experiment proved successful, someone other than staff from the Institute needed to vouch for the professor should he adopt a new and quite irreversible identity.

The collection jar that held the aberration captive had a bottom seal around its base. Brass toggle clamps secured it. Professor Carr had deduced that the vapors inside comprised some kind of preservative gas. It was imperative we did not lose any of it in case it was needed again. The fluted stopcocks on the jar's side had been designed, he said, to siphon this gas off. Once this was done, the seal could be broken, the jar lifted from its base, and the 'thing' removed. The size and quantity of tubing attached to the specimen matched receptacles on the interior of the frontal masque. The procedure would involve placing the aberration into the masque, attaching its own tubes to the masque's receptacles, and then enclosing Professor Carr's head when the two halves of the helmet were reassembled. His face would thus be squashed into the replicated flesh of another's.

I siphoned off the gas into a glass container. The specimen appeared to stiffen as atmosphere was lost. The doctor, the nurse, the engineer, the Grand Marshal and myself held a collective breath. We were about to step beyond the known. The Institute's cellar had become the maternity ward for the macabre.

The doctor and I wore protective goggles and rubber gloves. Sweat ran down my cheeks. I unclamped the collection jar, held the bell dome with both hands, and nodded to the doctor that I was about to raise the jar from its base. As soon as I did, the doctor whisked the specimen away and placed it on a silvered dish. With delicate fingers skilled in surgery, he thumbed through the pink flesh, freeing the ends of the tubes attached to it. He turned the matte of living tissue in his hands several times while glancing at the front side of the brass masque laying next to it.

"I think this is the correct orientation," he said. He scooped the fleshy flap—the size of a man's face—into the masque as if a sous chef was delivering a handful of slippery gelatin to a jelly mold. His fingers danced in-between the masque and the 'thing', both being the peculiar products of a diabolical mind.

"The connections have been made," the doctor announced.

"With haste, doctor," Carr said.

The professor's head had been placed into the backside of the helmet. In his white surgical gown, my master looked like a Knight Templar with only half his armour. The doctor brought the front part of the masque under Professor Carr's chin, the jellied aberration it contained moving like a plate of worms.

"Do it," Carr ordered.

The doctor raised the front of the masque in a single sweeping motion until the tabs on its perimeter interlocked with matching ones on the backside of the helmet. Eight small toggle clamps locked the device shut.

Immediately upon the final contact, the sounds emanating from the Trans-Aura Topographical Machine changed in pitch and tone. The engineer attending the instrument cabinet was taken aback, nearly falling off his stool. "A circuit must have been completed," he said.

The machine's dials raced in a crazy procession. Circular windings advanced numerous counters; needles peaked and fell. The trans-psychic facial masque glowed, emitting a plasma that surrounded Carr's helmeted head several feet on every side; deep blue at first, then progressing through the spectrum—green, yellow, orange—until it blazed a bright fiery red.

Professor Carr's body shook. His arms and legs, held fast with straps, tensed and jerked. The helmet rattled as if the professor were attempting to extricate himself from its grip.

"How will we know when it's done?" the Grand Marshal asked, his voice panic stricken.

"The professor said he would know," I replied, without any ounce of confidence.

The professor's body suddenly relaxed. His chest, once tight as if holding his breath, sank. The red haze around the helmet evaporated into nothingness, leaving behind a thin layer of black soot on the coppery brass surface of the masque. Several loud clicks ka-thunked inside the machine. The humming stopped abruptly. Needles fell back to zero. Dials unwound until counters came back to null. All without anyone touching any instrumentation.

"Circuit breakers," the engineer said. "Blimey, I've never seen anything like this."

"And I doubt you ever will again," I replied with a sigh of relief.

The doctor and nurse hurried to the professor's side. They undid the straps that held his limbs down and loosened the belt across his chest. The doctor checked the professor's heart with a stethoscope. He nodded to us, indicating Carr was still alive. The doctor reached over to undo a toggle on the helmet. He recoiled as grey smoke rose from his gloved fingertips. There was a smell of burning rubber.

"The mask is hot," he said. "I hope it hasn't burned his face."

"Let me." I swapped my rubber gloves for those of stout leather, gloves like a foundryman's, and gingerly unclamped each toggle. I placed a hand under the front masque for support. As the last toggle was freed, I tugged gently. The helmet separated into two.

I stepped back.

Silky white vapors drifted off Professor Carr's face. When they cleared, everyone in the room gasped.

His face had been perfectly transformed. He had a new identity.

Professor Atticus Carr of the Institute for the Investigation of Peculiarities was now the spitting image of Baron Montague Purdue, First Lord of the Southern Air Army.

PART IX

When fog descends on Londinium, it fills every boulevard and avenue like the creeping vapors of a nocturnal acid whose purpose is to strip both man and beast of courage. On such a night we waited and watched. Light was at a premium, the street's gas lamps imprisoned in rolling clouds of grey gloom.

We heard the steam charabanc before we could see it, its engine sputtering in the darkness. Two golden orbs of fuzzy light appeared suddenly from the fog and turned into the arched portico that fronted Primrose House. The mansion's door opened. A bright clean light emerged from inside. The silhouette of a man in a long greatcoat and top hat, carrying a walking stick, greeted the cab's driver who'd stepped down to open the passenger door. The man produced a note, hushed words were exchanged, and then the man in the top hat climbed aboard. With a huff and a chug, the charabanc set off into the night.

A posse of prop-cycles quickly exited a nearby alley and followed, the noise from their smaller engines drowned by the charabanc's steamy exhaust.

"Set off!" the Grand Marshal ordered from the back seat of our police cruiser.

Our driver pulled away from the curb. The shadowlike outlines of policemen on prop-cycles were all we could see as our headlights penetrated the foggy dark.

The trap had been sprung.

The Imperial State Police had used its network of spies in the criminal underworld to spread word that Baron Montague Purdue would be acting as the Queen's emissary to repatriate the Mabur-Noor Ruby from the thief in exchange for a handsome sum. This secrecy ensured the public would know nothing of the theft in the first instance, a major embarrassment that exposed serious deficiencies in the security of the Imperial Treasury.

Soon, the Imperial State Police intercepted a letter to Baron Purdue, an envelope without Imperial stamps or postmarks, slipped under the door of the baron's office at the headquarters of the Southern Air Army. Tonight, the letter said, a meeting could be arranged with The Reversible Man. The note contained detailed instructions as to the procedures to be followed to exchange the ruby for a saddlebag of gold. The real baron knew nothing of this intrigue or his role in it. Secrecy was paramount. Instead, a different letter was sent, this time by Imperial agents, to draw the baron's unwitting participation—a gaming invitation, timed for the very same night.

A police detective sat beside our driver, speaking into a radiophone to keep in touch with the leader of the cycle squad ahead of us. The charabanc turned onto the Imperial Mall, the widest highway in Londinium. The chase increased from stroll to canter as the midnight parade filled the empty boulevard. As the charabanc finally slowed to navigate the archway of Marble Cross, the officer with the radiophone lifted the ear of his headset and said, "They're intercepting it now."

The procession ground to a halt and we bolted from the cruiser. Beadles surrounded the charabanc. The cab driver, an Imperial agent, had dismounted and the cab's passenger extracted against his will.

"What's the meaning of this?" Baron Purdue bellowed.

"That's Her Majesty's business," the Grand Marshal grumped.

"But I'm just going to a club. It's all very legal and—"

A man exited our cruiser, carrying a saddlebag, approached the baron without a word, swiped the hat from his astonished head and the walking stick from his hand, and vaulted up the cab's steps to take the baron's seat. Baron Purdue was hustled into the paddy wagon that had trundled behind us, his apparent night of gaming rudely cancelled.

"Drive on, man" the Grand Marshal barked at the agent. "The abandoned Brunell Sewage Works." The driver nodded and climbed back aboard.

"Ingenious. The perfect place," I said, as our cruiser and a posse of policemen embarked towards the rendezvous contained in The Reversible Man's note. "Somewhere no one would suspect him to hide."

PART X

"Some call it intuition," Professor Carr said, tapping the silver knob of the baron's walking stick to his nose. "But it's far more peculiar than that. It's not a question of being guided by a sight or by a sound. No signs lead the way in the traditional sense. But do not fear, a hand of the softest aether will pull me in the right direction at any sign of danger."

With those less than calming words, the professor left me in the shadows of the crumbling vestibule inside the old workmen's entrance to the derelict Brunell Sewage Works.

The ironstone building wore a mantle of damp moss, its broken windows open to the winds and swallows, and to wisps of dank fog that crept inside. I fondled a whistle in my hands. But it was not the only weapon which could come to the professor's aid. I had brought my trusted hunter's petronel, each of its compressed steam cartridges filled with enough shot to puncture the side of an elephant. The Imperial State Police of the Grand Marshal's Special Pursuit Squad had taken up positions around the building's perimeter, instructed by the professor to enter only upon either his whistle or mine. My eyes would be the only other ones to take account of the professor's daring rendezvous.

The note not only gave the location for the exchange but included a set of cryptic instructions. Once inside the workmen's entrance, it called for the baron to take fifty paces straight ahead into the belly of the old edifice, a ruin bereft of meaningful light. In the darkness, he would reach the intersection of a tangle of overhead pipes. From that locus, a marker would dangle down from the pipeworks, a basket containing a candle and matches. The baron was to light a candle, follow the pipe the basket had been attached to, and bang on the metal with his walking stick every ten paces to announce his arrival. It seemed an awkward introduction but the methods of The Reversible Man were ingenious. Arranging a simple meeting at the entrance to the Sewage Works invited entrapment by any who accompanied the baron. The fiend had ensured he controlled time, place, and opportunity. The note did not say when the baron should stop rapping on the pipe. Presumably it would become obvious once the unknown destination within the Sewage Works had been reached.

I followed Professor Carr, a safe distance behind, until he reached the first marker. The professor found the basket, removed the candle, and lit it. The candle cast a yellow pall into the industrial void. Squeaking rats scurried from the light; the scratching of claws on floorboards and pipes creating a grim aria of sound.

A rap gonged on the pipe, and the glow of candlelight drifted left. I slunk forward, petronel in hand, whistle in my mouth. The shadow of our faux baron kept a steady pace, his top hat moving with a solemn grace like that of an undertaker, the rapping of pipes akin to the metronome of a funeral march. The old Sewage Works hung with cobwebs and stank of decay, its high ceiling of iron buttresses dripping with condensation from the fog that leaked through cracks in its roof. Bats fluttered overhead, nearly invisible in the dim candlelight.

The rapping ceased.

I crept into the doorway of an old foreman's office, out of sight, and watched. Professor Carr set the candle on a work bench and I could see why this part of his journey had abruptly stopped. The pipe he'd been rapping on had come to an end, fractured by rust and age, a twisted arm of jagged metal tumbling down to a cobblestone floor.

We were in the hall where great turbines once powered the flow of dirty water through a maze of settling ponds, still black waters reflecting like volcanic glass in the light of a single candle. The processing hall was at the center of the Brunell Sewage Works, its tall atrium roof of cracked glass panels rising in a pyramid shape above our heads. Three massive hulks stood under it, now frozen. Naked pillars of arched steel marked where the turbines' framework and gears had once been active. The most valuable parts had been stripped away in the push to build a newer works for the ever-expanding needs of Londinium. Under one such gazebo of abandoned mechanics, a dark mass sat in silence—a rectangular shape from which the limb of an articulating arm protruded, hanging over the silhouette of a chair.

A minute passed like an hour, a sickly stillness sinking into the pit of one's stomach like the sour bite of a spoiled apple. The sound of a switch echoed through the steel arches, followed by a low throbbing hum. Lights appeared on the shadowy dark mass, bringing life to the cabinet of a machine like the one we'd restored. Vacuum tubes and diodes shone brightly, illuminating a helmet hanging from the machine's arm as if an executioner held a severed head. A man with dark straggly hair, wearing a bronze masque to hide his features, walked in front of the instrumentation. He wore a ragged black cape around his shoulders, a cloak that covered his whole body, down to his boots. He inspected a large glass carboy connected by tubes to both the cabinet and the helmet, a demijohn filled with a liquid that glowed with an eerie turquoise fluorescence. This fluid was the ingredient that had been missing from the prototype machine; the means, I surmised, by which an original fleshy replication of a subject's face could be created in the first instance.

The Reversible Man turned towards the professor. His words made me grip the petronel tightly. "Why are you here, Baron Purdue?"

Professor Carr—a master illusionist—could imitate a wide range of accents, both foreign and domestic. His theatrical ability to mimic someone's voice was uncanny. He knew Baron Purdue. The man had frequented the Theatre Macabre on several occasions, each time visiting the professor backstage after the revue. When the professor spoke, his voice was indistinguishable from the real one. "You sent for me. You know the Queen wishes the Mabur-Noor Ruby to be returned, don't you? A princely sum is on offer." The professor removed the saddlebag from his shoulder and lifted it up. He jostled it. The chinking of coins echoed in the hall.

"You have every ability to return the jewel," The Reversible Man replied with grit, his tone menacing.

Every ability to return the jewel? What did we *not* know?

The professor hesitated, as unsure in his reply as I was mystified.

The Reversible Man pulled a weapon from under his cloak, a long-barreled pistol with a tube of fluorescent blue liquid as its magazine. "Because you paid me to steal it for you. The ruby is in your possession. So I ask again, *why* are you here? What traitorous plot have you hatched?"

The baron paid him to steal the ruby?

The Reversible Man pulled the trigger. A projectile struck the professor, knocking him back. He slumped to his knees then steadied himself, one hand on the cobbles. His other hand grabbed the dart that had penetrated his jacket, its feathered end sticking out of his shoulder. In the dim light, I could see the professor's neck veins glowing, a glow with the fluorescence of the blue liquid. The serum advanced through Carr's blood vessels into his head. He pulled hard and grunted, but the dart must have been wedged tightly into his collarbone. He tried again and this time succeeded, letting out a scream that scattered a colony of bats in all directions.

I sprang from my hideout, my whistle bleating its shrill alarm.

Startled, The Reversible Man spun the dart-gun toward me. I had the advantage of surprise. The blast from my petronel struck him in the chest, slamming the fiend back into his machine. The buckshot from my gun sprayed the instrument cabinet and liquid-filled carboy. The glass demijohn shattered, spilling fluorescent fluid in a gush that swamped The Reversible Man's feet. Sparks flashed from the punctured machine's control cabinet, setting the liquid alight. Flames traveled up his soaked boots and caught the bottom of his cloak, rising to his waist.

The Reversible Man dropped his weapon and grabbed at his neck to release the clasp on his flaming cape. The cloak fell in a fiery pile as he stepped away. Underneath his cape, he wore a breastplate of armor. My round of shot had merely pockmarked its surface. But I had inflicted a wound on an unprotected arm. Blood spilled from it. Wincing, he wrested a dagger from a scabbard on his belt, perhaps the weapon that had murdered Baroness Purdue, and charged. I cocked the petronel's lever to chamber another cartridge, and took aim. The Reversible Man ducked behind a girder just as I pressed the trigger. Buckshot clanged like church bells off the steel.

A bright blue light—like the flash from a photographic bulb—burst from Professor Carr's head. The mystic flare stunned me, taking my gaze from my target. The bright glare subsided. I could see the professor on the floor, shaking. His body went still. I fumbled to reload, expecting a dagger to be thrust into my throat. I turned back in the direction where I last saw The Reversible Man. The villain was gone.

Footsteps and lanterns appeared in every corner of the ruined hall. The Imperial Police had heard my whistle. I ran to the professor's side fearing the worst. I cradled his limp body in my arms. Vapors shrouded his head, much like the vapors we saw after the prototype machine had meshed the baron's replicate-face onto his. When the wisps of fluorescent haze cleared, Professor Carr's true countenance had returned.

I slapped his clammy cheeks in a desperate search for life.

He coughed. His eyes opened and squinted, searching for focus as the lights from policemen's lamps darted around us. The Reversible Man had vanished into the dark aether of the Sewer Works.

"Are you all right, professor?"

"Oh, my word, Jeremiah," he moaned. "What a most peculiar feeling."

EPILOGUE

We may never know what happened to The Reversible Man, although the Grand Marshal and the Queen's Imperial Police have other designs which may in the future lead to his apprehension. What face he'd adopted that night, hidden by his bronze masque, will also never be known, although every person who attended his treatments is on high alert should a crime be committed with their stolen identity.

That Dr. Miles Bennett had escaped with considerable wealth was not in doubt. Baron Purdue had paid handsomely for the Mabur-Noor Ruby and now paid again with something infinitely more precious— his receipt: an order of Imperial execution, pinned to his chest as he dangled in the crook of a hangman's noose.

What the baron planned to do with the ruby was still under investigation. The current theory was that it was to be sold at a high profit to an enemy of the Empire. Imperial spies were trying to determine which monarch or sultan that might be.

The chemical composition of the fluorescent turquoise liquid would remain as mysterious as the evil process The Reversible Man had invented. Flames consumed every drop from the damaged carboy and the villain had retrieved his weapon with its serum darts before making his escape. There could be no guarantee that another Trans-Aura Topographical Machine would not be built again, but its components had now been placed on the Registry of Technology and could not be procured in Britannia or any of the Queen's dominions without a traceable license.

Professor Atticus Carr suffers no lasting ill effects.

With one exception.

The left side of his face twitches whenever The Reversible Man is mentioned.

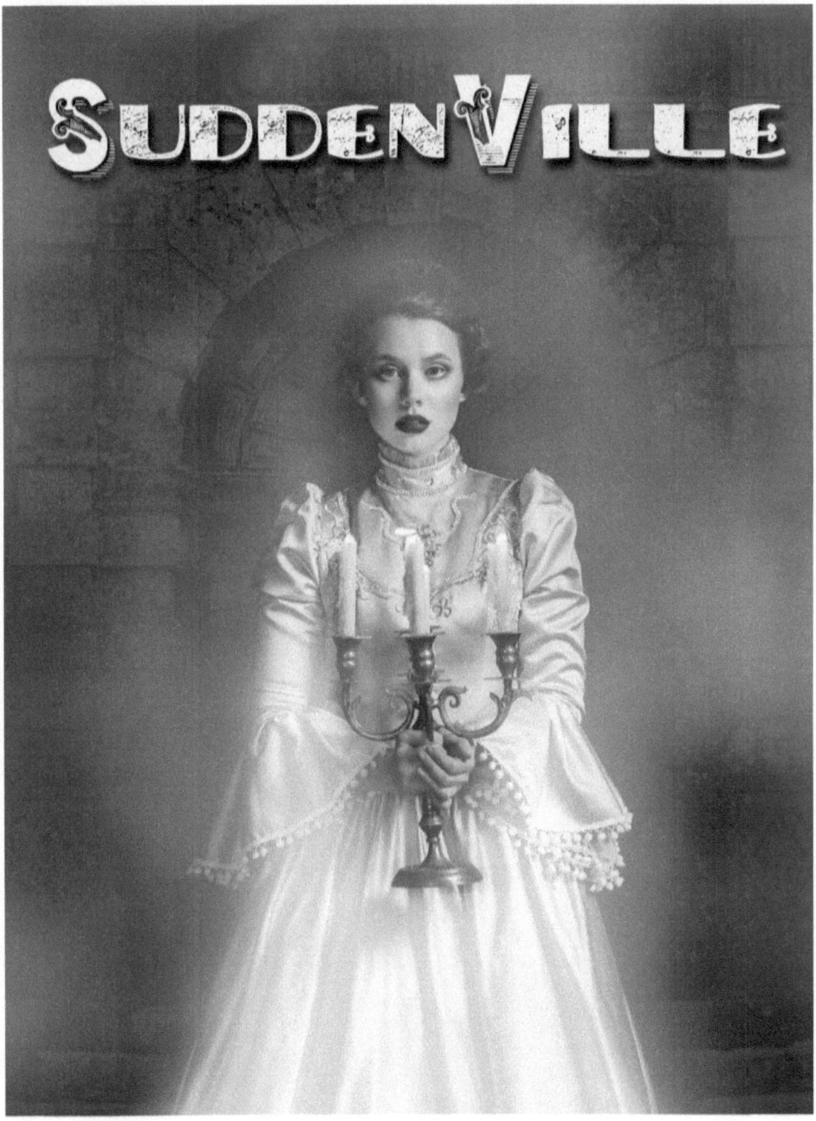
SUDDENVILLE

SUDDENVILLE

PART I

The town of Suddenville was a frightened being, deformed by a malevolence of both natural and supernatural character. Norms of daily life had been sucked into the cracks of its winding limestone walls and timber-framed houses, its five hundred souls bound inside their homes like prisoners in a gaol.

Professor Carr and I had been in Suddenville just one night prior, an evening of introduction barely sufficient to fully reconnoiter the situation to which we were now solemnly and inextricably engaged. A dense fog had engulfed Suddenville for several months, isolating the small hamlet on the northwest coast of Aquitaine from its neighboring villages. On a bright clear day, the townsfolk declared, the white cliffs of Britannia could be seen across the Channel. But brightness and sunshine had become a rare event ever since *they* arrived. Once night descended, the residents of Suddenville bolted their doors shut with an astonishing array of heavy locks and chains, and huddled inside.

The cobbles of the town had been engraved over centuries by the march of rural peasants and their horse-drawn carts, farmers whose traditions of commerce had changed little since Roman times. It was in these meandering alleyways that the disappearances had occurred.

Midnight. A quiet discomfort crept around us.

The gloomy air squeezed the very breath from our lungs.

We walked through the fog with only our wits as shields. Stiff poles appeared in the mist: gas lamps that flickered in the alleys with silent sighs as if they would expire from this Earth at any moment. Deserted streets wandered aimlessly outward from a small central square. As we trudged forward, the alley we had taken turned sharply. In front of us, at a dead end, a tall wrought iron gate sat between two stone pillars. Behind the gate, a dwelling of significance cut through the night's damp to proclaim its stubborn disobedience to the pall that engulfed the rest of the town. The mansion was large and old, two-storied, with a deep courtyard; an estate no doubt occupied by someone of wealth and prestige.

I moved the phonautograph's detector in a sweeping motion. The instrument, hanging by a strap to my shoulders, recorded the sound of vibrations. The device was Professor Carr's first choice in circumstances like the one we presently explored. The 'naught' position of the phonautograph had been calibrated using our heartbeats. Vibrations beyond that level would excite the gauge.

Professor Carr's hand stretched back to warn me. "Stop here."

"There's nothing registering on the meter," I whispered.

"But can you feel it, Jeremiah?"

"Professor, I fear I cannot."

"An echo moved through the aether." Professor Carr's mind could tune into frequencies few other mortals could detect. "A distortion dwelling in the dead air."

The professor had been tutoring me in the arts of the extra-sensory with the hope that I possessed a kernel of psychic insight, something that might develop into a talent as profound as his own. After many disappointing sessions of meditation and concentration, I had made no progress. Only by touching his hand as the professor entered trance could anything beyond mortal sight fill my mind with the slightest intuition. Notwithstanding my lack of natural ability, Professor Carr had been very kind, repeatedly consoling me, saying I should not be discouraged, that I should be patient, for patience was the key to opening the many doors that lay beyond the purely visual.

"I sense a prowler," the professor said. "This creature walks with soft footsteps, drifting shadowless in the aether."

I pointed the phonautograph's detector ahead of us, moving it slowly from left to right. The professor pushed on the gate. It swung open. Following him, I scanned the building's front entrance. The needle on the meter jumped to a peak, then rested again. Electric gears whirred as the instrument recorded this disturbance on the wax cylinder inside its case.

"The doorway," I exclaimed as we crept forward. "It's right outside the doorway."

"No longer," came his reply. "It has gone through it."

"What do we do now, professor?"

Professor Carr approached the chateau's entrance—a single oak door, ancient and tall. He placed his hand on its weathered grey wood and tilted his chin to his chest. His mind entered trance. I heard him grunt, then mumble.

He stood silent, without a twitch, time slowing to a crawl. "She will let us in," he finally said.

"Who?"

A slash of sliding metal broke the silence and cut off the need for a reply. Several more latches were released. The door swung inward. A woman appeared, holding an unlit candelabra and dressed in all-white. Her gown had a basque-bodice, its high neckline reaching up to her chin, its bell sleeves adorned with lace and the dress's fabric embroidered with pearls. Strange that she should be dressed so formally in the dead of night, especially a night such as this.

The gas light from the alleyway cast a ghostly veil across her face. Her features stood in stark contrast to the whiteness of her dress: her hair dark and tied back, a single short curl caressing each cheek; her skin a pale porcelain that set off her dark eyes; dark ruby lipstick over plush full lips. If not for her youthful unwrinkled skin, one would have thought a corpse in her funeral gown had risen to greet us.

"I've been expecting you," she said. Her hand gestured us to enter.

"Where did it go?" the professor asked. "I no longer feel its presence."

"Perhaps it's because you are no longer afraid," she replied. "Fear feeds it. Anxiety attracts it. Confidence repels it."

"But it must have gone somewhere, Miss —?"

"It's Mrs. Theodora Malon," she said, turning away. She walked into the foyer and lit the candles. "Although I fear I may have become a widow," she said as we stepped inside. "My husband is one of the disappeared."

The candelabra's flames blossomed into orbs of warm amber light as she led us into the drawing room. The room was surprisingly small for such a large mans. It had a minimum of furnishings: a chair, plush red velvet, tall with a winged back, and facing that, a chesterfield in green and gold damask with a castellated back and sturdy arms. She'd been taking tea by the room's small iron-boxed fireplace, whiffs of steam rising from a dainty china cup on a tiny side table. The coals of the fire throbbed with dying heat. She knelt by a basket and threw a handful of twigs on the embers, then a gnarled log. The fire roared back to life.

The chesterfield invited her two guests to rest. In the corner of the drawing room, I noted a small davenport desk where a writing pad lay by an inkwell, its companion feather quill dipped inside. The desk was strewn with papers—letters that had been opened, their envelopes cast aside. A candle in a brass holder had burned to a stub and was now bereft of light.

"Few strangers visit Suddenville in the best of weather. Foreign visitors are rare."

"Forgive my rudeness," my master said, introducing us. "Professor Atticus Carr and my erstwhile assistant, Jeremiah Boone. Burgher Piquette summoned us from Londinium by telegraph."

"The poor fellow is riddled with guilt. Conducting an investigation of a single disappearance was well within the purvey of the council of elders to manage, without much fuss. But with so many now being abducted, and with this awful shroud of bad weather to entomb us, Piquette realizes he should have reached out for help sooner."

"The gravity of the peculiar is hardly known in full at the outset, ma'am. We came as quickly as we could, first by airship to Spari, then by rail-plane to the coast. I fear the length of the journey was such there must have been more unfortunates lost to the nights that have since passed?"

"Every family seems to have been affected. It's as if a plague has struck. My husband was the first to disappear," she said, her voice choking. "A month and two weeks ago, when this fog first arrived. It has never left. He'd gone to the inn to conclude some business and never returned. The last anyone saw of him, he vanished into the fog as he crossed the town square."

"What business was your husband in, Madam Malon?" the professor inquired.

"Antiquities," she replied. "He had an export office in Grecia, in the village near the aeroport of Thessiki."

"I know the airship route to Grecia very well." Professor Carr had performed his *Theatre Macabre* in all the major capitals of Europa. "*The Flight of Pegasus*, the route is called in the brochures of *La Companie Aero-Oceanique*; a route popular with travelers enraptured by the history of emperors and pharaohs, but also a common conveyance of those who's business it is to rob their graves seeking the treasures of the ancients."

On the mantle over the fireplace, several small bronze statues sat on display. Professor Carr picked one up, a naked nymph, her curves aged with a verdigris patina. "Did your husband return recently with an artifact such as this to sell? Was that the business he was conducting before he disappeared?"

Professor Carr's line of questioning unnerved her. The tone of her reply was stern. "I know nothing of my husband's conquests except that of my heart, monsieur," she said.

The professor returned the bronze to its place. "An apparition passed into this house tonight. An event which would normally put one of the common folk of the village into major distress. In fact, a fit of hysteria would not be unwarranted. Yet I sense you know, in here—" He tapped his temple with his finger. "What these apparitions are, their proclivities, and their appetites. And you said at the door, you were expecting us?"

"I know what I feel. And you feel and see as I do, Professor Carr. These gifts come to few of us. But when you have them, they should be used, don't you agree?"

"We've had precious time to investigate this peculiarity and I fear precious time is left before others in the town might be subjects of further disappearance if the phenomenon is not stopped. Tell me more, madam, about what you have 'seen' and 'felt'. Tell me as much as you can. Can you describe this phantom?"

"Phantoms, professor. Plural. For they are many. They have the torso of a man, naked from the waist up; from the waist down, the hind quarters of a goat, coarse brown hair, cloven hooves. Their heads are adorned with curling horns; skin of leather and eyes of menace. Soon after this started, I walked the same alleys as you, at the same time of night, in search of my husband. One evening—it was so late it could have broached the morn—I came across a group of them as they prowled. They whispered beyond earshot then dispersed. One of them entered a home. Several minutes later I saw them regroup as if to confer, before moving down the street."

"Did you see them abduct others?"

"No. Not on that night. It was several days later that word of disappearances spread like wildfire through the village. At that point, my lone wanderings ceased, my bravery exhausted."

"But in your case, these visitations did not cease, did they? Tonight, the phantom returned."

"This particular one comes to me *every* night. And has done so ever since my husband's disappearance. It asks nothing of me and provides no answers. If I turn away from its ugly face—full of warts and green teeth—and then turn back to gaze on it again, I find nothing. It has vanished. Its nocturne concluded, without foul or harm."

"Peculiar," I said. "Quite peculiar."

"Why does this thing—I struggle for words, this *creature*—why does it torture me so? Why do they not take me, like they've taken the others? It first appeared in my bedchamber, beside my bed as I slept. That invasion repeated for several nights. Doors and locks offer no safety from it. So now I simply wait for it by the fire, all night if need be, sleeping in the chair when I can, too tired to move once it has departed, until dawn brings light to the fog and the sounds of commerce rise in the village. Only then can I return to my bedchamber and find peace."

"How can you be so sure," I asked, "that what you witnessed wasn't just a dream? Brought on perhaps by despair and anguish over the loss of your husband?"

Madam Malon rose from her chair, her dress bustling along the floor. She took several steps away from us, stood by the entrance to the drawing room, and pointed at the wooden floor. "Its hooves scratch the floorboards," she said. "The trail leads all through the house. What 'dream' leaves such marks? What madness must someone have inside them to possibly invent such a story? In truth, the creature sits where you're sitting right now during its visits."

"It sat here?" I exclaimed, jumping from my seat on the chesterfield.

"Dear young man," the professor said. "It's patently clear the being has left the house and has taken its evil with it. Sit down before you embarrass us further."

"Madam Malon, if as you say, you 'know' what I 'know'," Professor Carr continued, "Then by admission, you have confirmed these creatures are beyond being just malicious spirits but truly are daemons—apparitions metaphysical in nature, where no dimension can be protected from their presence, whether aethereal or otherwise. They are malevolence incarnate of the worst possible kind. The townsfolk of Suddenville have a right to be afraid. But not you? That you have accepted this presence—one that visits you regularly and accepts you without harm—is, might I say, most peculiar."

Madam Malon picked up the candelabra. "I'm tired and wish to seek my bed."

"Of course. Your hospitality has been much appreciated."

She led us back to the front door. "What can be done?" she asked. "Will I ever see my husband again?"

"That is the prerogative of Fate I'm afraid," the professor replied as he tipped his hat. "Good night, ma'am."

PART II

The Burgher of Suddenville, Jean-Francois Piquette cradled a snifter of calvados, the local apple brandy, in his shaking hand. It was morning, although the fog remained. He met us over coffee at the Auberge Renard, an old coaching inn on one side of the market square at the crossroads of two main avenues. Auberge Renard was the very establishment from which André Malon had last conducted business and had last been seen alive.

"Do you know if any of the villagers disappeared last night?" Professor Carr asked.

"No, thank God," the burgher grunted. His pudgy cheeks expanded as he slurped his brandy.

Piquette's hair was short and grey. Wispy eyebrows, thin lips. His odd squinting eyes made his face appear as if it had not grown since childhood, the rest of his head fattened by decades of rich cuisine.

"But several villagers heard them," he grumped, wiggling his empty snifter at the innkeeper. "Did you witness their evil patrol?"

"Our instruments registered a presence, a being that entered Chateau Malon," I answered. "But soon after its entry, it disappeared."

The burgher shifted uncomfortably in his chair, his weight making the old oak groan. "What is to be done, messieurs? The elders wish to call upon the resources of the central police authorities in Spari. I am against this. For now. I told them, how could we explain what is happening with any measure of intelligence? The investigator-general of the *Gendarmerie Publique* will think we have all gone mad and have us committed to an asylum."

"Our most pressing concern," Professor Carr advised, "is to find the door through which these daemons enter and depart our world. That, I suspect, has been the means by which they have perpetrated these abductions. Once we know where it exists, we can see if it can be closed. But, Monsieur Piquette, I must warn you. Once such a portal closes, those who have been taken to the other side can no longer return."

"Then why do it?"

"I fear it is the only way. We must devise a trap and lure the daemons into bringing your villagers back before we shut the door."

"A trap?" The burgher harrumphed, his belly jiggling. "You cannot be serious! Have you done this kind of thing before?"

Professor Carr pulled out a small leather-bound notebook from his jacket. He put on his reading glasses and flipped through the notebook's yellowed pages. "We've brought the equipment we need to find the door. Yes," he said, "that aspect is well in hand. As regards to a trap—well, let me just say that exploration of the peculiar must always make first landfall somewhere. In my experience, luring a daemon to a subject of interest has never been a problem. By their nature, they seek out the corrupt and the corruptible, the weak and the vulnerable. Finding and closing the portal will be the challenge. But if we don't try, we can't succeed."

"A subject of interest?" the burgher asked. His nervous hand shook his refilled snifter. Brandy spilled over its edges. Piquette mopped up the dribble around the glass with his tongue then backed the rest of the amber liquor down. "Who?"

"Madam Malon. I hope she will cooperate with us. It appears the manifestations have left her alone for some reason. They've had many opportunities to abscond with her and reunite her with her husband, but have not taken advantage."

"Madam Malon?" the burgher hissed. "*Madame Malon*? Of all people to save us!" Piquette held a determined finger in the air as if to stop such a suggestion dead in its tracks. "*Mais non!*"

"Why do you act with such venom, sir?" I asked.

The burgher's cheeks puffed in and out as he spoke. "Ever since she arrived in Suddenville, monstrosity has followed her every footstep. The villagers shun her. They *hate* her. It would not be unwelcome for Madam Malon to be exchanged for those we hold more dear."

"That is a cruel indictment, sir," I added. "No one has suffered in these circumstances more than she has. She is visited by a daemon on a nightly basis. How can the villagers feel such animosity towards her? What has she done to deserve such a lack of sympathy?"

Piquette beckoned the innkeeper to bring the whole bottle of calvados to the table. Once his glass had been refilled again, the burgher leaned forward. His eyes darted around the inn to see who might pick up our conversation. He said, voice hushed, "After she arrived, sheep were found dead in the fields. Whole flocks. Ewes birthed stillborn lambs."

"Evidence of disease, perhaps?" I whispered back in reply. "A virus carried from field to field?"

"Apples rotted on their branches." Piquette held up his snifter. "This calvados was made from last year's harvest and may well be our last. When the fog arrived, the groves have seen no sun to ripen the fruit. What has grown soon shrivels and falls."

"A phenomenon of weather and in both cases, of natural disease?" I responded. "Two unrelated phenomena?"

As his apprentice of under three years, I had seen and done but a fraction of the professor's incalculable experience, and breathed in but a wisp of knowledge compared to his accumulated wisdom. Professor Carr encouraged my inquisitiveness as a tool of learning, applauded my studious attempts at psychic meditation, but called me out when I was nonsensical.

Carr had said nothing during this discourse. His eyes had studied every flinch from the burgher's face. Streams of sweat cascaded down Piquette's pudgy cheeks. Clearly, my rebuttal had unnerved the fellow.

"What my erstwhile assistant is saying," the professor remarked, "is that all possible natural causes must first be examined and eliminated before jumping to conclusions, especially where the peculiar is involved."

"Coincidences? Unrelated phenomena?" Piquette harrumphed. "What say you about this, gentlemen? Several women in the village have had miscarriages. Others claim to have become infertile, even though they come from family stock whose women are renowned for their prolificacy. All of this—this 'coincidental phenomena', as you call it—has occurred since Madam Malon arrived in Suddenville from abroad."

"From abroad?" the professor inquired. "Madam Malon is not from Aquitaine?"

"No," the porky man replied. "She is from Grecia. André met her there on one of his archeological expeditions. Suddenville is the seat of his family, the Malon dynasty. It was natural for him to bring his new bride back to his ancestral home. We all wish she would leave, now that her husband is gone. Perhaps that is the answer. Many have talked over the possibilities."

"What possibilities?"

"Extradition, professor. By force if necessary."

"An extreme course of action, my dear Monsieur Piquette. And highly illegal. She is his wife. Perhaps his widow."

"There are archaic laws on the books regarding witchcraft that have not been repealed. A solicitor in Spari is looking into any legal recourse that might apply."

"Try her for witchcraft? And what proof could you provide a court even if such foolishness were pursued? What proof could you provide that would link her to these daemons?"

"*You* can provide that proof for us, professor. If such a trap can be laid, with her as bait, the whole village can see if she is consumed by this evil or is in fact, its orchestrator."

"The science of the peculiar should not be used to reinforce the superstitions of the ignorant." Professor Carr wagged his finger at the burgher. "Your remit to me was to investigate this peculiarity and remediate its effects. My task is not to lay judgment on the heads of its victims. And I will not participate in punishing them."

"You are not in Britannia. You are in Aquitaine, sir," the burgher said, straightening in his chair, his voice raised. "It is not for you to say how we should judge those whose transgressions undermine our civil harmony. Yes, by all means necessary and with posthaste, lay your trap. Engage Madam Malon if that is your intended course of action. But leave the consequences of your success to those whose monies have funded it, the same paupers who will lose everything dear if you fail. How much time will you need to prepare? When will this event occur?"

Professor Carr didn't reply to the burgher's question, asking instead, "You have not told us everything, have you?"

Piquette jolted in his seat. "Sir! What is this unfounded accusation?"

"The business you conducted with André Malon the night he disappeared."

The burgher's eyes shifted back and forth. His chubby cheeks grew red. "How dare you—"

"I dare because I seek the truth. And I know what I seek. In *here*." Professor Carr tapped his temple with his finger. "There is far too much that is peculiar about this village, about these events, not to believe what comes into my mind from the other side. In this case, from André Malon himself. He is trapped. Imprisoned. And he cries out to me. He says, ask the burgher for the truth. So that is what I have just done."

Piquette's chin slumped. He had been caught hiding a secret from the very agents who needed as much information as possible in order to save both his skin and the hides of his fellow villagers.

"Gentlemen, come with me," he finally said, after a moment of tense introspection combined with a further deep gulp of apple brandy. "Whatever truth you seek is yours. I have no will to prevent you restoring to Suddenville what has been lost, by whatever means is necessary."

PART III

A gray-timbered building sat forlorn at the opposite side of the market square from the inn. Its old beams sagged, its walls askew as if a strong breeze might bring it down. The lettering on its sign was faint. As the foggy mist of the village passed over the sign, condensate from the coastal sea air dripped down like tears onto our oiled raincoats.

The sign hanging from the building read, Le Shoppe des Curiosités, Propriétaire: Jean-Francois Piquette.

A carousel horse sat in the window, its child-like smile an ironic twist. Piquette unlocked the shop door. As we entered, a collection of small bells tinkled and the old door rattled and shook as if one more slam would disintegrate the wood from its hinges. Above our heads, hanging high in the ceiling, were rows of old oil lamps, their shades turned an opaque yellow by dust. Angled glass cases and tall shelved cabinets held objects ranging from tiny silver boxes to rusty agricultural tools. A hand-blown flagon of green Flemish glass caught the professor's momentary interest but the grimy layers of dust that blanketed every artifact indicated few people had bought antiques from Monsieur Piquette in a long time.

The burgher rounded the shop's main counter, its register coated with cobwebs, and disappeared through a door into a back room.

I wiped the dust from a glass case with my kerchief. I'd spotted a weird shape through the grime. I thought it was a small coconut, hairy and round. "Good gracious," I said, stepping back into a mannequin dressed in the uniform of cavalry from the Revolutionary period. I steadied the dummy before it had a chance to fall.

"What is it, Jeremiah?"

"Is this what I think it is, professor?"

Carr peered down at the object in the case. "If what you think this is, is a shrunken head, then yes, it is just that. These trophies are produced by tribes on islands in the Pan-Asium Ocean to celebrate victory in battle over another tribe."

"Wouldn't a commemorative coin suit that purpose just as equally?"

"Perhaps," the professor laughed. "But you can't eat the brains of a coin, can you?"

The shuffling of feet and the huffing of breath announced Jean-Francois Piquette's return to the shop proper. He held a wooden box with silver hinges and plopped it on the counter.

"I'll be back again. The final piece is very heavy. Please, examine what is inside while I'm away."

Professor Carr opened the box. It contained a scroll tied with a leather ribbon and a strange device that consisted of small wooden tubes of decreasing length held together in a row with knotted wicker.

Piquette returned with a dark-colored urn, between two and three feet tall, and as wide as a cask of brandy. He fumbled as he held it, the urn slipping from his grasp through sweaty fingers.

"Here, let me help," I said. I took the urn from him and placed it carefully on the counter. "Oh my, it is indeed heavy. Its body is not ceramic but solid rock."

"Basalt," the professor noted as his hand swept the surface. He turned the urn slowly. "Etched with Grecian patterns. Figures of men and women prancing in some kind of dance. Around the circumference, motifs of grapes and vines."

"An urn for wine?" I asked.

The professor felt the urn's weight. "Too heavy and hard to lift. More likely for ceremonial oils, Jeremiah. The opening at the top is wide and the urn has no pouring spout. It would sit on an altar. A priest would dip his hands in the oil to anoint a worshipper who had come into his temple, much like the taking of bread and wine at a Christian mass."

He tilted the urn to peer inside. "Ah," the professor said. "What have we here?"

Carr reached into the broad mouth of the vessel until his arm disappeared almost to his elbow. His face grimaced as he tugged on something. "It's a lid, firmly shut. I feel a lock, metallic, bronze perhaps. It won't release. Something is holding what feels like a small box firmly to the bottom of the urn."

"A locked container? Deep inside a jar?"

"Curious," the professor replied. "And by its location, I surmise this hidden chamber contains something of substance, something important."

"What?" I asked.

"One hundred francs I paid for the whole lot," the burgher said, before an answer could be given. "The contents of the box and the urn together. Generous to a fault, I am. Five hundred francs, André Malon said they might fetch in Spari, if I found the right buyer."

"Four hundred francs profit? That would be quite a tidy sum." Professor Carr stroked his goatee. "Why didn't Malon sell them himself, given these artifacts may be worth so much more than what you'd offered him?"

"Malon said he needed the coin. For urgent repairs to the chateau. Anyway, I doubted they were worth as much as he claimed. Malon bragged about the profits he made in the antiques trade but he was always scrounging for money. He owed substantial debts, to the village blacksmith and a stone mason, and to the inn. Nonetheless, I was sure I could find profit in these objects, so I was glad to buy them. Malon had done some business with me before. What I had bought previously always attracted buyers, as he said his discoveries would. I had taken his finds to the city. As you can see, this shop is but a storehouse. Collectors in Spari trusted the integrity of my wares once they were provided with Malon's certificate of provenance."

"And on that night? The night he disappeared?"

"He delivered these artifacts to me—a collection he said had come from the same location in Grecia, the scroll tells where—then left my shop with a bag of francs. He crossed over the square, passed by the inn, and then—my last sight of him—he disappeared into the fog. In the morning, the bag of coins were found in the alley beside the chateau's courtyard. His beret lay there also. But André Malon was never seen again. From that day forward, villagers disappeared in a similar manner."

"And the money? The bag of coins?"

"Given to Madam Malon. Of course. What else?"

Professor Carr had a look of doubt on his face over the shifty Piquette's last claim. Nevertheless, he offered, "I will credit you two hundred francs from the account of my services to Suddenville in exchange for these artifacts."

The burgher didn't hesitate to accept the professor's generosity. "Done! They're yours. And good riddance to them, cursed as they may be."

We left Piquette's Shoppe des Curiosités to return to our rooms at the inn. There, Professor Carr gave me a list, my instructions. "Begin our preparations, Jeremiah. Have the wagon with our instruments delivered from the inn to Chateau Malon. We will base our operation there. I am confident Madam Malon will cooperate. Her urgency to see her husband again will trump any inconvenience this may cause her."

PART IV

Whatever sun had shone through the swirling mist had deserted the village and its surrounding pastures and orchards hours ago. Woodland animals had surely crept into their burrows. The last peasant, lantern in hand, hustled his horses into a barn, the man's dog whimpering by his side. The Auberge Renard was shuttered and locked tight. Within minutes of nightfall, the muddy streets of a darkened Suddenville had emptied of life and a grim silence painted the town with dread.

I secured Professor Carr's instruments onto a two-wheeled hand-gurney, a conveyance modeled after similar ones from the Orient, a cart finely balanced and sprung to the professor's design by Londinium's most capable master coach-builder.

The phonautograph took its place on a large brass platen, ready to detect aethereal vibrations. Beside it sat a lumino-oscilloscope, the professor's most treasured device. It contained exotic isotopes that reacted when the current from a trans-dimensional portal entered its cylindrical collection chamber, a cannon-like barrel that made the oscilloscope resemble a blunderbuss. A separate mechanism, fixed parallel to the barrel's length, fired two darts—probes attached to wires that uncoiled in flight. The objective of such firing was not to incapacitate a target but to use the oscilloscope to confirm the presence of a portal and its size. As the dart entered, an exchange of energy would occur, the signal returned along the wires, registering the portal's shape on the oscilloscope's luminescent screen.

Detection of a psychic disturbance was a fundamental aspect of the science of the peculiar. Reaction to the consequences of such success was entirely another matter. What unearthly forces are unleashed when such a conflagration stands before us? Even the professor was unsure.

"The instruments are fully charged, professor."

"Then our trap has been laid. We will draw the creatures to us. Steel yourself, Jeremiah, not simply with brawn, but with brain. This is an adventure that will test the strength of both body and will."

The trap was twofold.

The human element was Madam Theodora Malon. Her plush velvet chair had been removed from the drawing room and placed in the courtyard in front of the chateau's door. She would sit facing the daemon or daemons, should a cluster congregate. By doing so, whatever magnetism had drawn one of their kind to visit her, might compel others to do the same.

The second element was bizarre—the Grecian urn procured from Monsieur Piquette, the one once owned by André Malon, an antiquity that had traveled far from its origins and whose mysterious purpose the good professor seemed to have interpreted. He had said nothing to me about it, just that the urn was essential to completing the Triad of Peculiarity—bringing humanity together with the physical and the metaphysical; united in common purpose, a means of energizing all dimensions at once.

"How will we release the abducted?" I pondered.

"Ah, that is the conundrum," the professor said, angling the instrument cart so it pointed towards the mansion's iron gate. "For that, I have few answers, my good fellow. My hope is to channel psychic energy into the portal, to provide the abducted with a beacon which they can locate in the dark aether, a signal to guide them back into our dimension. We will engage someone else with a similar talent. I have asked Madam Malon to assist me in this endeavor. She has a keen desire to beckon her husband back from the brink and will act in a similar manner as his beacon and guide. I hope many will follow André Malon's lead to escape their bondage."

The dog inside the barn howled, baying as if its cry could be heard on the other side of the world, a rolling moan of bestial anguish set to the tune of the Devil. Behind us, the mansion's door opened. Madam

Malon emerged in her white-gowned finery. Her lithe ghostly body, in its hooped bustle, floated down the short steps onto the limestone slabs of Chateau Malon's forecourt. She took her place in her wing-backed velvet seat, her countenance stoic and resolute. Her pale arms stretched out beside her on the chair's arms, her regal pose forged from hope and courage. At her feet sat the basalt urn procured from the burgher, its curved dark body silhouetted against the folds of her lacy white dress.

"I sense they're coming," the professor said.

"I sense them too," Madam Malon replied. She sat ramrod straight, eyes staring into the gloom.

I flipped a switch on the oscilloscope. The device flickered to life, humming as the voltage from its battery charge warmed its isotopes. I increased the current on the rheostat to prime the electromagnetic thruster that would fire the dart-probes. The smell of heating copper rose into my nostrils.

The dank night air was stoked with a deep, unworldly silence. Sound was gripped by the dead fingers of the dense fog; footsteps would not resound at distance through its misty vapors. The villagers of Suddenville had retreated behind armored doors, candles and gas lamps extinguished, perhaps holding their breaths in their anxious sleep.

The bulb glowing on the oscilloscope's panel turned from red to green—the isotopes inside the instrument had collected ions from a disturbance in the aether. Suddenly, the needle on the phonautograph's meter whizzed upwards until it bounced off its top limit. I gently turned the platen to redirect the detector. Once again the needle fell, then rose violently, then fell again, vibrations indicating a presence. I swept the phonautograph's beam from one edge of the courtyard's entryway to another. The meter rose and fell four more times, confirming the presence of an invisible group standing in the gap formed by the chateau's opened gate.

"Five of them, professor," I said, gulping. I felt a cold clammy sweat emerge from my pores.

"Symmetry is our friend, Jeremiah. The natural order of the universe dictates the lead-daemon will transit through the portal first, to take his position as leader in the center. When his four subordinates follow, they will stand to each side of him. Verily, I feel the strongest of their auras resting in the middle of the grouping of five you describe." He pointed to the gap in the gate. "Indeed, that must be where the portal makes its center. On my command, Jeremiah, and not an instant before, get ready to fire the darts. Aim true, for there is but one chance."

The dust in the courtyard swirled, lazy eddies at the start, progressing into stronger upward spirals. As it did, the daemons' feet and limbs were the first to appear from the aether, shaggy-topped hooves beneath iron-muscled legs. Their bodies took form as the dust rose, revealing coarse fur that ran up to their waists. A whisper of hair marked the middle of their bare chests, branching outward to well-defined pectorals. Arms like gladiators. Shoulders like roof beams. Their faces emerged, and finally their horns. That was when—my God—I gasped in terror. And prayed.

"Steady, Jeremiah. Not yet. Remember, wait for my command."

Professor Carr pulled the scroll he'd bought from Piquette out of his jacket. He had shown me the contents of the scroll but as it was scribed in a language I did not know, the scribbling meant nothing to me. As he unrolled the ancient paper, it was clear Professor Carr understood what was written. He shot a quick glance to my side. "It is a tune they want. And they shall have it."

Tension rooted me to the spot. My hands gripped the instrument gurney as if my fingers would weld with the handle. Clammy sweat had turned into rivulets, taunting the nerves of my cheeks. The professor's comment caught me completely off guard. A *tune*? Did I hear him right?

Carr's other hand went into his jacket, pulling out the final object he'd bought from Piquette, the bundle of wooden tubes tied together with reeds. "Music," he remarked, his voice unwavering. "The universal language. The song written on this scroll in ancient Grecian is *An Ode to Lynx*, the keeper of secrets and hidden truths. Lynx was a nymph who was the daughter of Pan. Her mother, his consort, Echo."

"Professor," I bleated like a frightened lamb. "Before us stand a quintet of daemons. By their nature, their intent towards us cannot be benevolent. I do not wish to be absconded from this existence to live beyond the aether, in a dominion where pain and suffering walk side by side with anguish and torment." I mustered more conviction. "We must *act*. Or we must *flee*. But in all names holy, a *song*?"

He held the scroll up with one hand and focused on its script. Professor Carr's message did not detour from whatever strange purpose he had in mind. "Anyone with a musical ear can play this tune using this primitive set of flutes. The notes have been carefully marked in an ancient code not unlike modern musical notation."

Professor Carr moved the wooden tubes to his lips. "This set of flutes is called a Pan's pipe and with these reeds, I will play to these satyrs what they long to hear, *Lynx's Ode*."

"But the oscilloscope, the darts?"

"Not yet I said. Only on my command," he ordered. He placed his mouth over the Pan's pipe and pursed air through it, sliding from one flute to another. Melancholic notes emerged from the reeds, shifting in pitch from heavy to sweet and back again.

The satyr-daemons crept forward, heads tilted in curiosity, limbs stalwart in their stride.

"Not yet," Carr reiterated, as my fingers hovered over the dart-gun's controls. "They will retrieve it first. Our bait. Their gambit has always been to take hostages, in exchange for *her*."

I looked back over my shoulder, to where Madam Malon had been sitting. Her chair was empty. "She's gone, professor!"

"Madam Malon was not what I was referring to. It is the urn they want and the secret chamber that lay within. The scroll tells us why. In addition to the music, it describes a ritual. The urn had been entombed in a sacred Grecian shrine beneath the Temple of Pan. It was unearthed by André Malon and brought here."

The tallest daemon, the leader, growled. Its deep voice set my teeth on edge.

Professor Carr took a step towards it, pointed back at the urn sitting at the foot of the empty chair, and yelled, "Take it and leave! Be gone!"

The daemon snatched the urn from the ground as if plucking a tail feather from a chicken. He cradled the heavy jar in his arms, carrying it back to the group of satyrs as if it had no weight at all.

As the daemon turned his ugly back to us, Professor Carr yelled, "Now, Jeremiah! Fire!"

I pulled the lever. A pair of darts sprang forth towards the daemon's back. They passed right through the phantom, through the gate behind, and struck a point in midair halfway between the chateau and the hovel across the alley. The darts hung there, wedged in dead space as keenly as if lodged in solid wood.

Professor Carr jumped to the back of the gurney and turned the oscilloscope up to full power, sending a surge of electro-luminosity down the wires and into the darts. The charge intensified. Ribbons of pale blue light encircled the wires. Within an instant, the instrument's current was reciprocated by a more powerful surge coming back along the wires towards us. This bolt of peculiarity ran into the oscilloscope's chamber. The instrument's crystal screen lit up. Outlines of people appeared on the face of the glass.

Professor Carr held the palms of both hands tight to his temples. His face crunched into a grimace as he stared across the courtyard. "The portal is open!" he announced.

I felt a sensation tingling across my face. It made the hairs on my head stand on end.

The professor closed his eyes, his face illuminated by the flashes and sparks running along the wires. I assumed he was channeling his psychic energy, the rescue beacon he swore to send. Professor Carr had chosen to fight, not flee.

The daemons huddled around their leader, the satyr that held the urn. Hairy clawed fingers stroked its curved sides.

"Look, professor," I said. "The screen is lighting up! More shapes are appearing."

"My signal has been received. Their determination will break through."

A rush of figures emerged into the alley from the other side of the portal, leaping as if straddling a ditch, blowing through Pan's phantoms as the daemons in turn dissolved back into the dark aether from whence they came.

One by one, the lost villagers returned from beyond—men, women and children—until the courtyard filled with their bodies and with their joy.

"Professor, I sense a loss, someone missing, someone left behind."

"A kernel of psychic insight? Bravo, Jeremiah! The first shrewd whiff of clairvoyance you've ever displayed. And what you 'feel' is indeed true."

After a scant few minutes, the blue surge of luminosity along the wires diminished. The circumference of the portal, as it appeared on the oscilloscope's screen, shrank until it condensed to a pin prick. As it did, the thick fog that shrouded Suddenville was sucked into this tiny aperture in a rush of damp air.

Above our heads, a swath of twinkling stars, set on a black heavenly carpet, illuminated the clear, cloudless night sky. The dog that had been locked in the barn barked madly and scratched at the barn door from inside. One of the abducted, a young boy, perhaps twelve, ran over. The door was unbolted. Under a bright silver moon, a happy reunion befell a father, his son, and their faithful pet.

Professor Carr slumped to his knees, his hands braced on the grit of the courtyard, his body and soul exhausted, spent. A crowd gathered around our strange equipment. Questions flew until they blended into a cacophony akin to the cackling of a flock of blackbirds.

"Go," the professor instructed, waving my attentions away as he rose to his feet. "I'll deal with the villagers. They are owed some kind of explanation, however brief. Find her. Inside Chateau Malon."

"Her husband, how tragic. I thought André Malon would be the first to escape. But for some reason, he did not appear. Has he been lost to the closing of the portal?"

The professor smiled. He panted, deep breaths, recovering his strength. "Go and find the answer inside the chateau."

I did, with great haste. I ran into the candlelit mans, calling out the name, 'Madam Malon'. I headed straight into the drawing room with its fireplace and its floor with hoof-scratched marks. A white dress—emptied of its former wearer—sat draped across the chesterfield. The letters that had lain across the davenport desk had been flung mysteriously around the room. The correspondence littered the floor. Several creased papers had landed on the discarded gown.

I picked up a few of the letters and read through them, each one a window into an infatuated soul. They were love letters from André Malon to his bride, Theodora. They expressed his desire to never be separated from her, in this life or the next; words typical of a deep romance, reciprocated by the later bonds of marriage. These notes held a solemn promise, in language that was irrefutable. Under no circumstances did André Malon consider his life worth living without her; no despair worse than her mortal demise; no joy greater than eternal companionship, in this life and beyond. Such was the message contained in one particular letter, in a poem, written, as its adoring words stated, on the eve of their wedding.

Footsteps came down the hallway. Professor Carr entered the room. I looked up from my reading, bemused. "Where is she, professor?" I asked. "Madam Malon has disappeared. No one answers my call."

"The wrong question, dear fellow. The right one is, *who* is she?"

"Why, André Malon's wife, of course. Who else?"

"Then answer this, why did André Malon not return to her—on this side of the portal—when he had every chance to do so? You have read his devotion to her, his strong determination that he would not part from her side. Once the daemons had what they wanted, their disinterest unlocked the aethereal shackles that bound their captives."

"I have no answer for a daemon's intent. Do you?"

"To find the answer you must become a student of those artifacts, as I quickly became. In order to gain such wisdom, you must know the Grecian language, as I do, and Grecian myths. They are the key to this puzzle."

"You mentioned a nymph, Lynx, daughter of Pan and Echo."

"The legend was etched in the scenes across the urn's surface and further detailed in the scroll of priestly notes. Those notes described the sacred rituals of her sect which included their ancient ceremonial music. You may ask, what was so precious inside the urn to the very existence of those daemons, that would drive them into every nook and cranny of Suddenville in search of it? The urn's very removal from the Temple of Pan placed a curse upon whomever stole it. The urn's secret lay locked at the bottom."

"You know what was inside, even though you could not break the lock?"

"Without the scroll, this peculiar episode would lay in a perpetual mystery as deep as the fog that engulfed Suddenville. What lay locked in the urn? Ashes, Jeremiah. The mortal ashes of the Grecian nymph, Lynx, daughter of the god-satyr, Pan. She took human form thousands of years ago. Lynx is their goddess and they wanted her ashes returned to the Afterworld."

"Her ashes? Yes, I suppose that explains much. I saw their eagerness to retrieve the urn and by doing so, allow us that brief opportunity to open the portal for the safe return of the villagers of Suddenville. But it still does not answer the mystery of Madam Malon. Why did Theodora Malon flee, leaving her fine gown behind? And where has she gone?"

"Ah, such are the proclivities of the strange and metaphysical. *Why*, you ask?" Professor Carr swung a cavalier hand above his head as if announcing one of his stage illusions. "*Where* has she gone? The answer is nowhere but everywhere. The mortal we knew in this world as Madam Malon is herself but a creature of the night, the aethereal embodiment of Lynx, Pan's daughter, whenever she chooses to walk among us. She was not simply visited by the leader of the satyrs. He was holding an audience with her to receive his instructions."

The professor picked up one of the love letters. "André Malon stole her ashes and she stole his heart to get them back. As it was in the times of the ancients, and for thousands of years since, Lynx often steps into our world, casting off the cloak of a phantom to manifest her being as a magnetic human beauty, a visage that has enraptured countless men."

"Like her father, Pan," Professor Carr explained, "Lynx owns a temperament of immortal mischief." He held Madam Malon's dress. "An evil playfulness lay inside the bosom that filled this ghostly white garment. Lynx, the legend tells us, is the purveyor of hidden secrets, enslaving her betrothed through their blind love for her. She then revels in their struggles, as mischievous daemons always do. Once a mortal male has tempted Fate and swears to be by her side for Eternity—as evidenced by the letters of André Malon—she lures them into the aether, to imprison their soul, fulfilling their giddy wish. It is by their own love stricken will and foolish choice, they are tricked into joining her. The assembly of her past lovers now dance alongside her daemons, while father Pan plays his flute."

"Peculiar, professor. Indeed. Most peculiar."

A MOST PECULIAR TIME

PART I

The approach to Harandon Hall was measured in pain, the most uncomfortable coach ride I'd ever experienced. It was not so much the pit-strewn highway with its rock-slide obstacles but the sheer speed and nauseating sway of the coach as Professor Atticus Carr exhorted the driver to hurry along the rough road as if time itself was about to end and we must outrace the coming apocalyptic calamity.

"Why such haste?" I asked. The contortions of my face and the grinding of my teeth must surely have been a clue to my escalating discomfort.

"Our remit, Jeremiah, is to arrive well before sunset," the professor said. "Colonel Bridges was quite adamant about that. And his promised remuneration is more than adequate to sustain such a request."

"Then why," I moaned, "wasn't it enough to charter an aero-charabanc?"

A heave formed in the pit of my stomach, an intestinal swell with potentially caustic consequences. If I'd known in advance, I wouldn't have had so much cheese with my sherry at luncheon in Port Mersey.

Gratefully, the coach slowed and the horses resumed a normal gait.

"We must save our pennies for the transport of the instruments we may need," the professor eventually replied to my question, as he stared out the coach's window at the wild barren mountains on the West Britannic border with Cymrushire. "But until the situation is reconnoitered," he continued, rubbing his goatee as if stroking the back of his favourite cat, "how will we know *what* is needed, and more to the point, *why*? First principles first, dear chap."

"How exactly do you know Colonel Henry Erasmus Bridges? It seems you've ruthlessly cleared your calendar for a total stranger. I've never heard you mention him before. I collect your correspondence and his summons was the first letter you've had from him to my knowledge."

"Well, the truth is, I don't know him. I know his wife. And you do as well. The former Arabella Witherall."

"I'm sorry, professor. That name isn't familiar."

"Because it's her *real* name. You know her only by her stage name, Tranquility Belle."

I slapped my thighs. "My goodness, no! Of course. The fairest songstress ever to grace our stage, any stage for that matter. Some said they only attended your shows to hear her sing. Such was her hypnotic celebrity. Then one day...*poof!*...as if you'd spirited her away in one of your illusions, she was gone, her rhapsodic voice never to be heard again."

"Because, dear fellow, she married Colonel Bridges. And he is a very private man, as are his circle of wealthy industrialists. The wedding was held in the south of Aquitaine and I was one of a few outside that circle to be invited, as a guest of the bride, the first and only time I met the gentleman, ten years ago. I hope she has found the same happiness off the stage as she enjoyed on it. We shall see. It was her recent letters to me, not his alone, that produced such haste. Her words sounded increasingly desperate."

"Do you still love her?"

He paused, his eyes wandering the grey landscape. "We all loved her," he sighed. "But in our hearts, we knew we couldn't have her. At the time, she belonged to the world, not any one man in particular. Such was the shock we all felt with her quick engagement and even quicker nuptials. Colonel Bridges must have provided her soul with something more nourishing than just raw infatuation."

"Ah, yes. The magnetism of wealth. She was a product of the slums, as I was, professor. You plucked us out of the grime, polished us up, and showered us with opportunity. I live satisfied and grateful for what I have. But for others, there will always be the yearning for ever more coin, a flaw instilled from birth. No doubt we shall find out what dire circumstances have befallen her and whether the golden idol she worshiped has been a false cure."

"Indeed, Jeremiah. My sentiments exactly. Curiosity is a precursor to the study of the peculiar."

The coach rounded a bend and to my surprise, a vista of astonishing proportions lay beneath the broken clouds. The road had taken us to an altitude of three thousand feet; the Cymru Mountains wrapped around us on three sides. Below us, over the precipitous cliff at the edge of the road, a hidden valley stretched from the foot of the grey rock peaks to a winding river fed from the mists that clung so tightly to them. The valley was lush, its pastures separated by hedgerows that curved gently like soft green earthworms across the land.

Smoke curled from the chimney tops of a small village. "Harandon," Professor Carr said. "And over there, that castle on a promontory by the river, that must be, I wager, Harandon Hall."

Indeed, it was. A full hour passed by as the coachman made our tricky descent into the village, a hamlet of Tudor homes whose timbers were twisted with age. Our arrival at Harandon Hall required yet another climb, this time not so calamitous, up a long private avenue through a forest of broad oaks under which sheep grazed freely. It was a fortnight past the summer solstice. Sunset was several hours hence. The weather in the valley was so much brighter than during our inbound journey; warm and pleasant, under clouds that drifted like stuffed pillows. It was as if the valley was protected from the gloom of the mountain peaks by a glass dome.

The last of the oaks that framed Harandon Hall passed by the coach. We emerged onto a wide gravel courtyard in front of the spartan castle, an edifice displaying none of the outward opulence one might expect from the abode of a gentleman with such commanding wealth. Harandon Hall was built from rusty-red blocks of the local Grinshill stone; its facade plain and unadorned, unlike the Gothic palaces being built by the industrial aristocracy of today with their forest of spires and nymph-infested fountains. The mansion's rooms were marked by rows of monastery-style windows, each with archer's slits at their sides. Its simple castellated roof line and pair of round guard towers stood unambiguous to the hall's original purpose: a medieval fortress, protecting its lord against mountain barbarians in the time of swords and shields. It wasn't ugly *per se*, just stark, appearing more like a giant—albeit grand—tombstone than a fanciful palace. And there, perhaps, was the first indication of marital disappointment.

We were greeted by Colonel Bridge's butler, Mr. Humphrey, a tall starchy man in his sixties, grey-haired, shaped like a bowling pin; and by his Head Housekeeper, Mrs. Shoelittle, again quite senior, mousy and thin, a foot shorter than the butler's six-foot height, with a reservoir of nervous energy even when she was standing still. They lead us into the hall's foyer, a cold two-storey-tall entry room with a set of stone stairs in front of us, the main reception room to the left and the colonel's library to the right. To one side of the stairway's base was a heavy, dark-stained table of Tudor origins by the look of its carvings, where a stunning porcelain vase sat, filled with a bouquet of freshly cut flowers. The pastoral motifs on the vase were set on a background of rich cobalt blue and enhanced by hand-painted gilt frames. The eye was drawn immediately upon entry to the vase and its flowers, a radiant feminine touch in what was an otherwise austere entrance where the grotesque heads of dead game encircled the high gallery above on faded plaques.

"A wedding present," the Colonel said as he strode into the room and noticed me admiring the vase. "Aquitanian. A work of art."

"One of the finest examples of decorative ceramic I have ever seen," I replied. "Beautiful."

Beautiful too was the lady who entered a few paces behind Colonel Bridges, whose delicate, flawless face brought back haunting memories from my teenage youth. I would sit in one wing of the theater, backstage behind the curtains—all my chores and preparatives for the night's performance done—to listen to her sweet birdsong voice as if her aria was conducted solely for me. Such was the nature of the infatuation Professor Carr had spoken of. So sad that her retirement from the performing arts meant others could no longer benefit from her soul-soothing rhapsodies.

"Lady Bridges," the professor said, as he bowed, took her hand, and kissed it. As Professor Carr raised his head, his eyes lingered on her face ever so slightly, a memory recaptured perhaps, then he turned away. "What an impressive home."

She huffed; a sputter, half sigh, half cough. "Well Henry certainly thinks so. But I dare say the hall has its own opinion. It certainly seems to express itself quite boldly and with increasing frequency."

"How so?"

"Put in plain English, it hates me being here. And it wants me gone."

"The house?"

"More accurately, something living in it," Colonel Bridges informed us. "Something ephemeral and malignant."

"That's a mild word for it," Lady Bridges sneered. "Let's call it what it is…*evil*."

"Ah," Carr replied. "The reason for the fear expressed cryptically in your letters to me."

"Letters, professor?" Colonel Bridges asked. "I recall only sending one."

"Is there somewhere comfortable that we can adjourn to, Colonel, to discuss this matter further?"

"Forgive Henry," Lady Bridges said. "He's a bad host at the best of times." She turned to her housekeeper. "Tea in the drawing room, Mrs. Shoelittle. We will have dinner as usual after sunset." She looked up at the clock and then outside through the still-opened entrance door. The sun was low in the sky, touching the mountain tops, peeking through the clouds that shrouded them. "And tell nanny to bring the children down for an early supper."

The drawing room of Harandon Hall featured a tall, wide fireplace, the kind that in medieval times was large enough to cook roasts inside it on a spit. The embers of a nearly dead fire glowed in the hearth. Colonel Bridges nodded to Mr. Humphrey who pulled a chain. Two young maids arrived with buckets of wood and kindling. The room was large, its ceilings high. Even though the early summer had warmed the valley to a pleasant temperature, it was cold inside the hall. Soon a roaring fire chased away the chill and a trolley of tea and cakes arrived to nourish us.

"The nature of evil," Atticus Carr said as he sipped his tea, "is a relative thing. Mankind professes to know how to define it. But as the future arrives, our current understanding is found either wholly inadequate to describe the present situation, or grossly overstated when comparing blame with the past. Put another way, one man's evil is another man's righteous inquisition. In my experience, judging the peculiar depends on the circumstances of its creation and then, the conditions of its perpetuation. So, pray tell, what have we here?"

Colonel Bridges shifted uncomfortably in his wing-backed chair as if sitting on a rock. Bridges was about fifty years old, his wife about thirty-five by my reckoning, given the year and age she was on the day she left the troupe, when I was just a youngster myself. Undoubtedly handsome even in his later years, the colonel was a broad-shouldered muscular man, his strength evidenced by the grip of his handshake, steadfast and firm, as befitting a man with a military pedigree.

Beneath the finery of his tailored grey morning coat, his silk brocade waistcoat held a pocket watch with a thick gold chain. He took the watch out, flipped open its cover and stared at the time. "Very soon, professor, you may have your answer. At least part of the equation, for in truth only the passage of more time here at Harandon Hall will be sufficient to get the full measure of this aberration."

"It's his first wife," Lady Bridges announced. "I'm sure of it." The curls of her golden hair shook as she shivered, her sudden chill juxtaposed with the glowing red blush on her cheeks produced by the enveloping warmth of the fire.

"Come, dear. We've had this discussion before and she can't possibly be the reason."

"She followed us here," Lady Bridges insisted. "I know it in my bones. A woman always knows the presence of another woman in her man's heart, whether such woman still walks the earth or not."

"Your first wife is deceased?" I asked. Professor Carr, as usual, shot me that look of his that expressed both how silly that question was, and his desire for me to let our benefactors talk.

"Yes. But before I met Arabella," the colonel answered graciously, rescuing my embarrassment. "Many, many years before. Miranda was a diplomat's daughter and I was a junior military attaché to our Queen at Court in Londinium. We were young and in love. And when Miranda's father was recalled to Aquitaine, our pending forced separation became unbearable for both of us. Did we marry at too young an age? Perhaps. I was twenty-three, she just nineteen. The folly of youth? I don't think so. We were very happy for two brief years and then—" His words choked in his throat, his chin dipped.

"It was tragic," Lady Bridges continued on his behalf. Her husband covered his watering eyes with his hand. "I will grant that. I never knew her. But I do know how my husband loves. It is a deep, all encompassing commitment, as much love as any woman would ever demand. Miranda died in an airship crash one dark wintry night, on the way to see her ailing father in Spari. Such was the love between her and Henry, I suspect her spirit has never been far from him ever since. But I fear his marriage to me has been a step too far for her."

"Your children," Professor Carr asked. "How old are they?"

"A boy, six. A girl, four. Why do you ask?"

"Has whatever you feel is watching you, ever manifested itself before their birth?"

"No, not that I recall."

"So, when did such manifestations appear?"

"In the past year," she replied.

"Ever since we moved into Harandon Hall," the Colonel added. "I purchased the estate at auction. The previous owner died in sudden circumstances, leaving many debts and a gang of squabbling heirs."

"Oh, I see," the professor remarked, his fingers stroking his beard. "Then we've peeled away one layer of this mystery already. Where we begin is not so peculiar after all."

PART II

The Bridges' children, Joshua and Charlotte, took their supper in the library across the entrance hall from the drawing room. A table, sized perfectly for them, was set with fine china and silverware to one side of the colonel's impressive mahogany desk. Their food was served by a maid from a trolley.

The library was a near-replica of the drawing room, with the exception that where paintings hung above and on either side of the fireplace in the opulently furnished reception room, the walls of the library, as expected, were completely covered by oak bookshelves, filled with leather bound volumes and an innumerable quantity of intriguing curios from Colonel Bridge's worldly travels. Apart from the desk, its companion desk chair, and two small chairs opposite for visitors, the richly carpeted library had no other soft furnishings, its breadth consumed by a cornucopia of children's toys. A globe of the world stood in one corner next to the open entranceway from the foyer. Armies of lead soldiers and a kingdom's worth of toy knights surrounded a medieval castle. At the opposite end of the room, a dollhouse, its roof higher than four-year-old Charlotte might be able to reach, towered over a palomino riding horse with a gold silk mane. Between the siblings' toys, as if in charge of playtime, stood an elephant, four feet tall to its shoulders, modeled to the exact detail after the famous Fotheringham Clockwork Elephant, the real one now lost with its inventor in the wilds of Pajastan.

Lady Arabella Bridges fidgeted, standing by the cold unlit fireplace, her eyes glued to every forkful the children ate as if waiting to pounce should one of them choke. Colonel Bridges and the professor sat facing each other, deep in conversation about the colonel's military career as an airship officer, sherry glasses in hand.

My sherry never touched my lips, held in a purely ceremonial grasp as my constitution was not yet ready to consume alcohol again.

I paced the bookshelves admiring the library's literary works, a collection that spanned the ages from the early days of the printing press to modern journals scribed by explorers, scientists, and engineers whose topics elucidated the wonders of discovery and the advancement of technology in the Ellinorean age.

"The books on that shelf," the Colonel said, noting my interest in one particular section, "were left here by the previous owners. I really don't know what they're about. The English is Tudor and quite archaic for my taste, difficult reads that try my patience."

I pulled a volume from the shelf, it's title rather unusual, '*Being a Treatise on The Spelles, Manners, and Trickerie of the Gipsy, and other Woodland Dwellers*'.

I was perusing its finely illustrated, yet fragile pages when Lady Bridges abruptly announced, "Henry, have you forgotten the time?"

She went to the library window and looked out. The afternoon's light was fading into evening, the sun behind the mountains ready to set. She checked the mantle clock on one of the library's shelves and clapped her hands. "Children, finish eating. You may have cake in your room later. Hurry now." She turned to Mrs. Shoelittle, who had supervised the serving of the children's dinner, and said, "Fetch nanny. Tell Humphrey to gather the staff."

Colonel Bridges glanced outside as well. Curious, I thought. Up until now, it seemed the house had been the focus of their concern, yet for some reason the grounds now commanded their attention.

He rose from his chair and waved his arm. "This way," he said, ushering us towards the far end of the library to a door invisibly blended by a carpenter's skill into the millwork of the bookshelves. The door opened up into a hall, rooms on the left, mullioned windows running down the right. Outside was a cloister, a covered flagstone walk parallel to the interior hall, its arched openings typical of the monastic architecture of the Middle Ages.

We exited Harandon Hall through a modern extension added at the rear to the castle's exterior. It was a delightful orangery with white-painted window frames, big enough to house ten-foot-tall tropical palms, an array of broad-leafed jungle plants, and brightly-petaled flowers of all kinds, both the familiar and domestic, as well as the exotic. Outside the orangery, a gravel path led to a large octagonal gazebo complete with wicker settees and high-backed summer loungers. It sat to one side of a large pond, the estate forest to its back.

Our host's immediate entourage assembled under the gazebo's protection—the colonel, his wife and children; the children's young nanny, Rachel; the professor and I. From our vantage point, we could look back towards the outdoor cloisters adjoining the castle proper where Mr. Humphrey and Mrs. Shoelittle had corralled the kitchen staff, footmen, and maids.

The underside of the clouds caught the reddish-orange light from the setting sun. Beams burst upwards behind the Cymru mountains. The vista was idyllic, the kind of setting one yearns for during the depths of a dreary Britannic winter.

Professor Carr stood like a hunting hound braced to pounce, his body ramrod straight, his eyes alert to any movement or sudden sound from the forest that lay barely fifty paces from the gazebo. "Do you smell it?" he asked me, turning in a circle as he searched the air with his nose, then stopping as his eyes focused on the pond.

I stepped beside him. "Yes," I replied. "It's quite strong. The odour of a spent fire, charred wood."

"Do you see a fire pit anywhere near this gazebo? No, I don't either. And we are too far from the house to catch whiff of its smoke. Besides, the breeze is such that any chimney smoke will be pushed away from us, towards the river."

"That patch of dead ground over there. Perhaps that is the source?"

The professor turned where I pointed. I followed him out of the gazebo. We walked twenty yards to a section of ground beside the pond, a nearly perfect circle of bare earth.

"Nothing will grow in it," a voice behind us said, as the Colonel caught up with us. "We've seeded it innumerable times. Laid the best manure as fertilizer. Even placed swaths of sod over top. It dies quickly. No grass will grow, no weeds either. You've seen how lush the estate's grounds are. It takes a platoon of gardeners to keep the flowerbeds in order and prevent the forest reclaiming its birthright over our manicured lawns. But not here. Not in *this* spot."

A pair of mourning doves cooed in the trees. The bleating of sheep filled the air. Professor Carr raised his head to the sky, darkness descending.

The roofs of a cluster of farm buildings peered through the trees. As we wandered back, an ebony black horse bolted from inside the woods and raced across our path, its eyes aflame as if hornets were stinging its haunches. It galloped across the green towards Harandon Hall. A footman left the cloisters to give chase.

As soon as we were back at the ladies' side, the squeals of what must have been a whole herd of pigs ripped through the air from the direction of the farm; their pitiful voices like no squealing I'd ever heard—frantic, as if the earth was about to swallow them up and they were scampering up the sides of a crevasse in a frenzied attempt to avoid falling into the abyss.

A pair of pheasants flew from the bushes, darting several feet above the gazebo, wings beating feverishly. A gunshot rang out, a crack like thunder. One of the pheasants fell from the air, tumbling end over end in the grass. I could see no one in the vicinity that could have fired that shot, no telltale smoke from the end of a barrel, hidden in the brush.

Then there was silence.

An eerie, penetrating silence.

A stillness gripped the trees; no sounds from any bird or animal, as if death had descended like a blanket and snuffed all life from the natural landscape. You could hear the beating of your heart.

It was dusk, that time between day and night, where shadows disappeared and the sun yielded slowly to the moon. Light still lingered, sufficient to make our way back to Harandon Hall along the gravel path.

I walked behind Lady Bridges, the nanny and the children; the colonel and the professor in the lead. To say the children were distraught would be an understatement. They were nearly mute with fear, mewing like kittens as they clutched their nanny's dress, having been terrified by the squealing of the pigs and jumping out of their skins at the sound of the gunshot. Lady Bridges was similarly upset, although tried hard to maintain a stoic demeanor for the children's sake. The Colonel seemed non-plussed by the whole alarming turn of events, episodes that would send any normal person into a state of distress. His face had hardened, his back had stiffened. I concluded it was his military background that had steeled his constitution to withstand all manner of battlefield gore and thus took sudden terror in its stride. For the professor and I, the strange occurrences—although quite unique among our considerable experiences—were also absorbed as matter-of-fact as possible, a necessary step towards patiently understanding our remit.

We reached the cloisters where Mr. Humphrey and Mrs. Shoelittle waited, having ushered the servants back into the house.

"Humphrey," the Colonel said. "Send a boy to search the lawn around the gazebo. A pheasant fell there. As soon as the bird has been retrieved and hung in the kitchen's cold store, advise me."

"Will do, m'lord."

Once inside, Lady Bridges parted ways with her children, kissing each of them on the cheek and reminding them that cake was waiting, a clearly pre-planned treat to sooth their anguish. The nanny took them down a hallway that led to a back staircase and the trio vanished from sight.

"Well, let's survey the damage, shall we?" Lady Bridges said.

"Damage?"

"There's always some sort of damage, professor," she replied. "The question is not *whether*...it is *where,* and *how much?*"

"This way, gentlemen," the Colonel pointed. "Through the dining room."

The dining room adjoined the kitchen towards the back of Harandon Hall. It was long and oddly shaped—not square or rectangular but oval, the room's plaster meticulously laid so no corners were present. The ceiling was coffered and painted with the most elaborate mural—vines which extended from the room's side walls to stretch into a blue sky where white doves flew among chubby cherubs, some of the winged baby angels blowing trumpets.

The dining table, a large stalwart piece of mahogany furniture, could seat ten people on either side, plus one at each end. Its legs were carved with similar vines to those in the walls' paintings, a motif that appeared on the chairs as well. The dinner service had been set for us— place settings for four; an arrangement looking entirely lost at one end, as if an afterthought.

A draft blew in from the kitchen, bringing the smells of cooking— the scents of fresh bread baking in an oven and the savoury roasting of meat. Quite suddenly those aromas were overwhelmed by a floral perfume as if the room had been filled with gardenias.

"What is this wickedness!" Lady Bridges exclaimed. "That is *my* perfume. My favourite perfume. What is the meaning of this? Why has that witch brought it in here?"

The sickly scent clung in the air, so strong it was almost pungent and nauseous.

"The *why*, is why we've engaged the professor, my dear," the Colonel said. "Explanations are as thin as morning frost." He surveyed the glasses on top of the sideboard, sniffing to see if perfume had been dropped into them. But no. Then he examined the table's silver centerpiece, an airship of considerable detail, quite possibly one of his prior commands. "No damage here, thank goodness."

We exited the room at the opposite end to where we'd entered and found ourselves on the other side of the stone stairway in the entrance foyer. We had come full circle through the ground floor of the Hall. I lingered in the dining room, hoping to find a missed clue, when a scream pierced the air. I rushed forward to the professor's side. Lady Bridges stood aghast, clutching her mouth. Her beautiful, freshly cut flowers were dead—not just wilted, but rotten and slimy as if eaten by slugs.

"My flowers!" Lady Bridges sobbed. "Every time, such a ghastly and personal attack."

"You arranged them yourself, I presume?" the professor inquired.

"I care for my blooms as if they were my children. I sow them from seed, watch them grow, cut them, and yes, arrange them. I have always loved flowers, the feel of them, their delicate nature. It is my hand that labors so, and it is my heart that suffers from this heinous misdeed. It is her will to torment me, to take whatever beauty I create and smother it in death."

"And that is why, Lady Bridges, you believe it is the colonel's unfortunate deceased wife who has come to haunt you?" Professor Carr paced in front of the flowers. "Every time, you said? You mean, this isn't the first time this has happened with a vase of flowers?"

She nodded, crying into her handkerchief.

Footsteps thumped down the stone staircase. The nanny, her face distraught, raced down the stairs. "I heard a noise in your bedroom, ma'am, when I was putting the children in their beds. Your hairbrushes have been knocked from your dresser onto the floor, as if a hand had swept from one side of the dresser's top to the other. And your favourite bottle of perfume—it was also knocked over and all the scent inside drained out. But ma'am—" The nanny burst into tears.

"What is it Rachel?"

"There's no perfume in the room. No scent. *None.* Even when you place your nose right into the wet spot on the carpet. That perfume— it's so strong, so rich in its bouquet. A single drop is enough to bring life to the gardenias whose essence it contains. But a whole bottle? Where has the scent gone?"

Before an answer could be given, the Colonel bounded out of the library's entrance. "In here!" he said from the adjoining library. "More devilment!"

We rushed in.

Books had been scattered all over the floor, knocking down six-year-old Joshua's carefully arranged parade of soldiers. Empty spots marked where the books had fallen from the very same shelf that had taken my fancy.

"You see, professor," the Colonel continued. "None of my staff could have done any of this. They were purposefully brought outside to ensure that any phenomena that might transpire inside Harandon Hall during sunset was truly the work of the aether and not manipulated by flesh and blood."

The butler, Mr. Humphrey, stood at the library's entrance and announced, "The pheasant, m'lord. It has been found and brought to the kitchen."

"Quick, Professor Carr, there's no time to waste." The Colonel grabbed my master by the arm and nearly lifted him off the floor in his hurry to retrace our steps. I followed in ever quicker strides as he and the professor ran back through the dining room.

The kitchen was indeed large; the bones of its design begun in medieval times—large central preparation table, open fireplace on one wall, and then updated to add coal-fired stoves around the perimeter. At one end was a gamekeeper's cold store, a windowless stone shed with a door to the outside where game was brought in from the hunt to hang before butchering. A single pheasant hung lamely from a wrought iron hook.

"Knife, Humphrey," the Colonel ordered. A sharp carving knife was produced from the kitchen. He turned to address us. "You heard a gunshot, yes?"

The professor and I nodded.

"And saw this bird fall prey to a hunter? So it follows, there should be an entry wound of some kind, correct? Examine it please, professor." He passed Carr his handkerchief.

Professor Carr twirled the bird on its hook, fluffing and poking its feathers back, and squeezing its limp body. "There is no wound." He looked at the handkerchief. "And no blood either."

"Very well. But we do know it's dead. And let me I assure you, if we examined the inside of this bird, you will find no buckshot, no bullet. So how, one might ask?"

"You've seen this phenomenon before."

"Like my wife said, professor, as in her case too, yes, several times. Exactly the same. But that's not all. Now please affirm that this bird is newly killed, under a half an hour ago, correct? Wild pheasant is usually hung between three to seven days before preparation, according to culinary specifications. Also correct?"

"Yes, of course. The best chefs agree."

"And the fowl is thus tenderized over time and delicious under fork. But not this bird. Handkerchiefs, gentlemen." Colonel Bridges produced another one of his own from his pocket and showed us his intent. We placed our handkerchiefs to our noses.

He slit the pheasant open with the carving knife, from its neck to its chest and down its belly.

I gagged.

The smell from the bird was rank. Its insides were putrid, in an advanced state of decomposition. White maggots crawled out between folds in the rancid flesh.

"God help us," the professor said, as we exited the cold store, coughing.

"Dispose of the fowl, Humphrey. Burn it!"

"Quite right, m'lord."

Safely back in the kitchen, well away from the noxious odors, the Colonel said, "You see gentlemen, this is the evil we are dealing with. And please take careful note of the time. Sunset. Always at sunset.

Never if it is overcast or dull. We must see the sun. See it in all its heavenly glory. Watch it slip away below the horizon and then see its light dying as if night had conjured its murder. And then—" He sputtered. "We get *this*...this *evil*."

"Truly, colonel," Professor Carr acknowledged, "a most peculiar time indeed."

PART III

The evening's meal was eaten under a cloud of tension, conversations interrupted by even the smallest sound, however innocuous and normal. Such was the fear that embraced Colonel and Lady Bridges and their staff.

The first order for Professor Atticus Carr after dinner was to inquire of the Colonel the location of the nearest telegraphy office. "On the other side of the drawing room," came the surprising reply. The library was primarily the playground for the children. Colonel Bridges' *office proper* was a two-storey affair, housed in one of the former castle's medieval guard towers; the lower floor's ancient weaponry stores now used to keep his voluminous files of commerce, the upper floor being a place where the Colonel could conduct business in absolute privacy.

The Colonel's upper-floor office had a commanding view of the estate, its round shape and many windows conforming to the tower's exterior. It benefited from the most up-to-date telegraphic equipment, providing the professor with the appropriate facility to send his instructions to the Institute for the Investigation of Peculiarities in Londinium. Upon receipt, the night porter would rouse our technicians from their apartments at the Institute so the shipment of the equipment we needed could be readied overnight to be flown in by chartered airship. Hopefully, everything would arrive before the next sunset.

The morning brought calm to Harandon Hall. Lady Bridges and the nanny left early with the children so they could ride their ponies at the stables. Their departure from the Hall avoided exposing the helter-skelter disarray of the playroom to the children's impressionable eyes. The shambolic disorder from the previous night had been left undisturbed per Professor Carr's instructions.

"To the library," the professor said as soon as the last mouthful of our breakfast had been swallowed.

"What are first principles when coming upon a peculiarity such as this, Jeremiah?" he asked upon entering.

"Observe. Then catalog those observations into notes. Sketch the scene. Preserve any evidence that may deteriorate with time. Analyze."

"And from such analysis?"

"Derive meaning."

"Then that is exactly what we shall do."

In our experience of poltergeist phenomena, rarely is such mischief wanton and random. There is purpose behind every spirit's action. The barrier between the aether and our physical world is often very thin. Someone with psychic abilities can traverse its boundary with relative ease. Professor Carr is one such extraordinary individual. For the rest of us, only the physical evidence of a spirit's presence communicates meaning to the living.

"Do not disturb the pages," the professor advised. "Not yet."

I mapped in my notebook the location of the books strewn about the library floor. Professor Carr examined the empty spaces they left behind on the bookshelves. Five books had been displaced, clearly thrown around the room to create as much chaos as possible, thus drawing attention to them. Joshua's toy soldiers were scattered all over the floor. Charlotte's dollhouse had been knocked over by a particularly heavy volume that sat next to it in triumph. The rocking horses had been toppled. Each book had landed open, a fact by itself rather odd since surely some would have landed in the closed position just by chance.

"Professor," I said, kneeling on the floor. "A common element has emerged. On each book, a toy soldier has been placed on top of the opened pages as if to mark them. It prevents any drafts from turning the books to other pages. I say 'placed' because it is impossible for such an occurrence to be produced purely by happenstance."

The professor responded immediately, going from book to book, quickly scanning the open pages and taking notes. "Excellent observation, Jeremiah." He tore a paper from his notebook and ripped it into strips. "Place these as bookmarks," he said. "Then remove the soldier, close the book, and catalog its title."

I did as he instructed. One such volume was instantly familiar, *'Being a Treatise on The Spelles, Manners, and Trickerie of the Gipsy, and other Woodland Dwellers'*. It had done the most damage to the orderliness of Joshua's parade.

The others included *'The Arte of Musketrie'*, and a book written in Latin, *'Modum Executionis- Habentis Maleficia'*, the pair having knocked over the two rocking horses. *'An Accounte of the Visite of King Charles I'* lay open beside the clockwork elephant. Beyond doubt, the most surprising of all—the heavy volume that had tipped over the dollhouse— was a 1623 edition of *'Mr. William Shakespeare's Comedies, Histories, & Tragedies'*, one of the bard's most famous publications, a collection of thirty-six of his plays, referred to by collectors as his *'First Folio'*.

"Professor, may I ask, have you connected with the spirit that has done this?"

By professional habit, Professor Carr never revealed the nature of his metaphysical contacts until such time as it produced a positive clue in our inquiries, although that was usually quite soon after an initial encounter such as the one we experienced upon our arrival. His reticence to say anything, either at dinner last night or at breakfast this morning, puzzled me.

"No, not exactly 'connected'," he replied, as he finally opened a window into his psychic wanderings. "What we have here is an *imbroglio* of metastatic proportions. Harandon Hall is a battlefield. We're not dealing with just one spirit, but *three*. It's possible there could be more, but the animosity and emotional entanglement between these three departed souls is so vicious and spiteful that the war that rages in the aether between them is drowning out other voices."

"So it's definitely *not* the colonel's first wife?"

"Most assuredly not, Jeremiah. My soul screams out with an overwhelming feeling—it's hard to describe the instinct; it's gnawing, subliminal—that this battle has been going on for centuries, not just a few short years, although to the departed, events are occurring as if they happened yesterday. These books provide first evidence of a theory. I suspect they were known by the deceased, contemporary to their lives, and will likely point us to the circumstances of their deaths. They most certainly speak directly to the diabolical discord that boils around them. This display is not haphazard but a message I'm sure we are meant to decipher."

Mr. Humphrey appeared at the entrance to the library with an envelope on a silver tray. "A telegram, Professor."

"Ah! Progress is at hand."

Indeed, it was a reply from the Institute. An airship was en route, having left after first light. It's anticipated arrival was around the three o'clock hour, depending on the winds.

"Let us retire to the drawing room and examine these texts, Jeremiah. We are done with our deliberations in the library." He turned to Mr. Humphrey. "Have the maids restore the playroom to its prior order. When the children return, they must not be distressed."

"Of course."

"And Humphrey...could you and Mrs. Shoelittle join us at your convenience? I have a few questions."

"About?"

"Harandon Hall. What else?"

***

The arrival of the aero-barge *The Royal Connaught* was a welcome sight for the children, Joshua and Charlotte, a distraction from things their young minds weren't fully capable of understanding. Of late, their lives had only known disruption and trepidation. A ground mooring anchored the airship in a tethered position above the expansive lawns of Harandon Hall. The children went up to the ship's mizzen deck to view the countryside from the air, a sight that brought a smile to their little faces.

A steam crane unloaded several valuable pallets of instruments. Professor Carr hadn't left anything to chance. Equipment for every metaphysical eventuality had been requisitioned. This spectrum of technology required a skilled technician to accompany it. That assignment had fallen to one of the most talented engineers at the Institute, Alexei Patroznik, an emigre from Dizel Russka.

Alexei was a former protégé of the infamous Doktor Mechanika, Russka's Armaments Minister. Alexei had run afoul of Russka's autocratic rulers who accused him of spying for their sworn enemies, the czarist Empire of Korolya. He escaped with his life but his arrival in Londinium was met with suspicion. Neither Russka nor Korolya were friends of Britannia. Professor Carr had innumerable connections within the corridors of power at the Imperial Court. Before Alexei could seek sanctuary elsewhere, the professor gave his personal assurance to the Queen's Secretary of Internal Security to allow Alexei to stay. A royal warrant of residence was granted to Patroznik as a 'scientist of exceptional potential and value to Her Majesty's Empire'.

Alexei had been a boy genius in Russka, graduating *summa cum laude* from the University of Mockba at the age of fourteen in electro-mechanical physics. His expertise was in the unusual properties of light and sound. One day, while experimenting with a machine that was a prototype weapon to generate lightning, a stray charge nearly electrocuted him. He lost all his hair; eyebrows and eyelashes included. They never grew back and his skin adopted a funereal tone. As most brilliant scientists often are, Alexei was a quirky chap, shy and reserved. His studiousness and odd demeanor had been mistaken for treachery and factions within the Russkan hierarchy trumped up charges against him. At the tender age of nineteen, he fled with just the shirt on his back, another waif rescued by Professor Carr.

Once the cargo was safely on the ground and Alexei and I had descended down the paternoster lift, the airship withdrew its moorings and set sail back to the capital. The hour was approaching five o'clock. If we hurried, the equipment could be set up and calibrated before the next sunset. The day had been another bright one, and as Colonel Bridges had stated about the phenomenon, we were most assuredly due for more bedevilment at the hands of an inglorious full sunset.

Farm carts delivered the instruments from the grounds to the Hall. There was no time to waste. Professor Carr instructed their placement, focusing on the drawing room and library but also on the dining room and kitchen. His psychic intuitions were to be respected.

His interrogation of Mr. Humphrey and Mrs. Shoelittle had been only slightly illuminating. As he'd suspected, by their dialects and age, they were of local stock and had been in service in their current positions at Harandon Hall during the previous owner's tenure. They recounted that nothing overtly different had happened during that era, just the same kinds of poltergeist behaviour as we had already seen. Freshly picked apples rotted upon the arrival of sunset. Clocks would chime even though the time wasn't an hour or half hour. A random gunshot rang out. Dead fowl were found prematurely decomposed.

After the previous owner's death, when the Hall had been put up for sale, the supernatural manifestations continued during viewings by prospective buyers. Rumors about spirit possession deterred reasonable offers. The squabbling of the heirs had been precipitated by the consequences of that mischief. None of them wished to live there. The Hall had to be sold at any price. Eventually it was decided to put the Hall up for auction in the hope that some unwitting overseas buyer might pounce on the opportunity of a low reserve. It didn't require that. A domestic bidder prevailed, a man who couldn't resist a bargain, Colonel Henry Erasmus Bridges. The frequency and severity of peculiar occurrences escalated substantially once the Bridges took up residence.

Unpacking and setting up the instruments consumed many hours. The commotion brought the attentions of our hosts, their children, and their curious household staff.

"Done, professor," Alexei said, a pair of skiascopic goggles perched on his forehead. "The luxautographs are ready. The aether-optometric chronometers have been calibrated."

"What are those strange glasses?" Joshua asked. "What do they do? Can I see them?"

"They detect minute changes in the light density of shadows." Alexei took off the goggles and handed them to the inquisitive boy. "See? The glass prisms in the lenses. They refract very dim light."

"What does that mean?"

"He's five, Alexei," I reminded my colleague.

Beads of sweat glistened on Alexei's bald head. "Whatever disturbs a shadow becomes visible to the human eye."

"Can I try them?" Joshua asked.

"You won't be able to see any—"

"They're broken," Joshua whined as he put the goggles on and stumbled about. "I don't see anything."

The goggles were not able to 'see' spirits but to detect the presence of their passage, an effect known as a 'skiascopic transit' where the spiritual disturbance of the aether affected physical light. The professor and I had our own sets of skiascopic goggles, accessories essential for the operation of a luxautograph, another of Alexei's inventions, truly a scientific breakthrough, an instrument so new it had only been used in the laboratory, never before during an actual investigation of the peculiar. Professor Carr had placed a bold wager on his faith in Alexei and in the progress of the young man's science.

"Let's take a look at one of my luxautographs, shall we?" Alexei retrieved the goggles and led the boy to a large tripod-mounted device quite similar in size to a photographic studio's box camera.

"What do they do?" little Charlotte asked, pointing to its insulated copper cables, vacuum tubes, glass-encased ion collection cone, and ferrous armatures.

"It creates its own electro-magnetic field so it can capture the reflected ionization of the air as aether concentrates around a spectral presence."

"A speck *what*?" the girl replied.

"Um, when the path of ionization—"

"Alexei," I scolded with a wag of my finger.

"It photographs the invisible."

"My mommy says we have ghosts," Joshua said.

"Did you know we have ghosts? They're invisible," Charlotte added.

"Are you taking pictures of ghosts?" Joshua asked.

"Oh, for goodness sake," Professor Carr grumped. The professor had been measuring the luxautograph's angle of view with a protractor when the boy nearly tripped him up as he wandered in and out, under his feet. Atticus Carr encouraged young minds who visited the Institute to wonder at our technology and ask questions. But after a while—the past hour to be exact—the children's repetition of the phrases, *What does this do? And what does that do?* had became even too much for the otherwise patient professor. His huffing drew the attention of the supervising adult, their nanny Rachel.

"Come, Joshua, Charlotte," she said. "Playtime is over. Let the professor and his assistants get on with their work. We'll take supper in the orangery tonight. Won't that be nice?"

The little ones were escorted out of the drawing room. The time was half past seven o'clock. We could expect the arrival of dusk in a little over an hour.

Seven luxautographs had been positioned strategically around Harandon Hall. Our task was to stand watch within reach of one or more of the luxautographs and when a skiascopic transit was detected through our goggles, trigger the operation of the nearest 'spirit camera'. It would, hopefully, capture the ion particles reflected by the spectre. The luxautograph did not produce just a single photographic image but many. Once triggered, a roll of film ratcheted across a drum inside the main cabinet. The spectral ionization exposed it. The film strip, when spliced into its separate images, could be flipped together to view the motion of the aether, similar to the amusing zeotropes holiday makers watched at seaside arcades.

Soon, everything was in order and in its place—Colonel and Lady Bridges ensconced in their plush chairs in the drawing room, ourselves in position around our designated luxautographs. The evening's peculiar performance was about to begin. Another bright day meant the sun would fall behind the Cymru Mountains as magnificently as it had done the night before. The haunting would soon commence...using our trembling hosts as lightning rods.

PART IV

As the last beam of the sun's rays was extinguished, the sound of breaking glass erased an eerie silence.

"Don't move," Professor Carr barked at Colonel and Lady Bridges. The professor stood in the entrance foyer, the drawing room on one side, the library on the other. "Jeremiah, it came from your direction, did you capture it?"

"Yes, I did," I yelled, my finger on the cable that triggered the dining room's luxautograph. Its gears whirred as the film drum cycled. "But professor, you should come and see this."

I had been standing in the back hallway that separated the kitchen from the dining room. My goggles first detected aethereal movement but it was my eyes that were astonished by what happening next. I quickly triggered the instrument in the kitchen then followed the apparition into the dining room and proceeded to activate the luxautograph in there too.

"The glass that shattered was not one of these," I said as the professor stood at one end of the dining room table, I at the other. Fine crystal wine glasses were suspended in the air, clustered in two groups, one on one side of the table, another group on the other. They hovered like fishing floats bobbing on a pond.

"What was broken is on the floor, there by your feet—a bottle that had been carried from the kitchen, straight across my path and then flung at the wall. It was at that moment that the wine glasses lifted from the sideboard, one at a time, as if plucked, then gathered as you see now on opposite sides of the room."

"Careful, Jeremiah. Do not move!"

We stared transfixed for at least a minute at this act of peculiarity. Then a sudden, very loud rapping came from the front door of Harandon Hall. At the same instant, several of the glasses whipped across the dining table to the other side of the room, shattering on the wall. A retaliatory volley of glasses went in the other direction.

"They're fighting," the professor said. "Hold your ground."

"Be assured, I'm not going anywhere."

Professor Carr inched backwards, his eyes still fixed on events in the dining room. "Alexei," he said. "Start the device in the library, then use the hidden door to make your way outside. Run to the front and set the outside luxautograph in motion as soon as you get to it. Look quick now."

"Yes, professor."

"I'm going to open the door, Jeremiah. If your luxautograph runs out of film, reload it with great haste and keep recording."

Professor Carr stepped back until he reached the front door. He placed a hand on the large wrought iron ring that held the latch closed, his eyes gazing back past the stone staircase into the dining room that lay behind. The professor had dispensed with his goggles, relying I presumed only on his psychic mind-sight to direct his affairs.

A chill wind came from behind me as soon as I heard the professor turn the ring to unlatch the front door. The remaining suspended glasses dropped to the dining room floor, straight down. The front door flung open under its own power, knocking Professor Carr over. I hurriedly finished changing the film cartridge in my luxautograph, activated the device again and rushed to the professor's side. The weight of the door had dazed him.

"Outside!" the professor exhorted, recovering his senses. "Outside!"

A gunshot rang out, like the one we heard near the gazebo. A mourning dove fell onto the front steps that led up to the entrance. Carr raced past the dead bird, into the gravel courtyard, stopping in its center. Alexei and I gathered there with him to view the next manifestation. Above us loomed a single, ominously dark cloud, alone in the starry night sky, its body twirling in a circle, sparks of electricity flashing in its folds. The cloud hung over the gazebo's pond, the water's surface glistening in the early moonlight.

Colonel and Lady Bridges ran out the front door to join us. I wondered if it was fright or curiosity that compelled them? Likely, I concluded, abject terror at the thought of being left alone in the Hall.

The earth shook as a massive lightning bolt descended from the cloud and struck the ground near the gazebo. Its incandescent bright flash blinded us, its peel of thunder violently passing right through us, the sound shaking us to our bones. Lady Bridges fainted into her husband's arms.

The dark cloud dissipated into nothing. The sky turned completely clear. Stars twinkled as if nothing at all had happened.

The opened door behind us slammed shut, leaving us in the dark.

"How much more of this can we take?" Colonel Bridges said, tapping his wife's cheeks as Arabella gently moaned, cradled in his arms. "Has the Devil himself invaded Harandon Hall?"

"Thankfully not, Colonel," the professor replied. "Our three souls are imprisoned in Purgatory by their history of misfortune and misery, a tempestuous fate that Eternity has dictated they must remain trapped. Unless, we can do something about it."

"Can you?" the colonel pleaded. "Can you do something...*anything*...to stop this madness?"

"Now that we have a record of tonight's events, we can certainly try."

"I'll double your compensation! No...*triple* it!"

"That won't quite be necessary, Colonel. But additional donations to the Institute are always gratefully received. Come, Alexei, Jeremiah. Our work has only just begun."

***

The images from the luxautographs were developed, spliced and deposited into viewers. The result was remarkable.

"The apparitions' movements, as you can see, yield clues to their intent," the professor explained to Colonel and Lady Bridges. "But simply taken on their own, the lux-prints are open to interpretation and debate. To someone with psychic insights like myself, the *three* spectres involved displayed distinctive auras as they moved, a feature of the aether we do not yet have the technology to capture. You will have to trust me on this and let me guide you to my conclusions. During this most recent manifestation, I focused my mental energy on these auras, to help me find deeper meaning behind the spectres' actions."

Professor Carr picked up one of the viewers. "This set defines our most important subject. You can tell from the lux-prints that we have a female. The outline in the movement indicates she is wearing a wide bustled dress. She is central to the maelstrom that has engulfed Harandon Hall. She is the spectre who smashed the bottle, as you can see in this series of views, a compilation of prints taken first in the kitchen, then through into the dining room."

"Who is she? Do you know?" Arabella asked.

"Yes." On one of the tables, the professor had arranged the books that had been strewn about the library. He picked up the volume titled, *'An Accounte of the Visite of King Charles I'*.

"This is the most important of all of the books that had been opened," he continued. "It is her story she wishes to impart to the living. It is her torment that is central to these peculiar circumstances. Her name is Lady Samantha Stansberry."

The candles that lit the room flickered.

"She is never far from us. In fact she is here now, standing in the corner." Professor Carr pointed in the direction of the drawing room's exit to the guard tower. "Welcome, Lady Stansberry. We do not fear you," he said on behalf of us, despite our misgivings. "We embrace your sorrow. Let it be our sorrow as well, until such time as we can vanquish your sorrow from the aether."

A draft came down the chimney. The fire's embers flared.

"She agrees," he said.

Professor Carr opened the book, *'An Accounte of the Visite of King Charles I'*, at the page I'd previously marked with a strip of paper. "Here is the record of the tragic events that consume her soul. I will read the entry…by the Royal Warrant of King Charles I, the execution of the gipsy Cosmo St. Angelo will occur—" Carr paused for effect. "At *sunset*…in accordance with the accepted doctrine of the *Modum Executionis, Habentis Maleficia,* for his crimes of sorcery and devil worship."

"The Method of Execution for Witchcraft," I said.

"Well done, Jeremiah. Your study of Latin has brought results." The professor picked up the book of that title. "The *Modum* is a doctrine to guide the judiciary during the reign of Charles I. In September of 1642, from the *Accounte*, King Charles I passed through this region in the early years of a civil war when this country was known as England. He personally presided over the trial, here, at Harandon Hall."

"A witchcraft trial?" Lady Bridges gasped. "Here?"

"In this very room." Embers flared again. "We shall see in the morning what the tempest of tonight has brought us," the professor continued. "For lightning has surely marked the very place of that execution, a spot well documented in the *Accounte*, a spot I have concluded, Colonel Bridges, where no grass will ever grow. The *Accounte* is specific in its detail of the execution of Cosmo St. Angelo. He was hung, then drawn and quartered. I wager that if we dredge the pond, we will find the charred remains of the gallows that were used—burnt after use and then cast into the nearest waters, according to the specifications of the *Modum* doctrine. His body parts were burned with the timbers and the ashes cast into the pond, ridding the earth of a warlock's soul. The smell of smoke and burned wood still lingers around the pond and gazebo. But the fellow was innocent of all charges."

"How do you know?" she asked.

"His aura revealed a purity of soul impossible to achieve in one of daemonic intent."

"So this madness now has two names," the colonel inquired. "You said there were three spectres. What of the third?"

"Lady Samantha Stansberry has left us clues in the only way she knows how…the books." Professor Carr picked up the heaviest volume, Shakespeare's *First Folio*. "This was opened to the first page of *Romeo and Juliet*. For it was her lover, Cosmo St. Angelo that pounded so violently on the door tonight. He wishes to rejoin Lady Stansberry in eternal bliss but is prevented from doing so by the aethereal powers of the mastermind of this tragedy, her husband, our third spectre…Sir Montague Stansberry, Baronet of the Borders, Sheriff of Harandon."

A thunderclap shook the Hall. I leapt to the window. Storm clouds had appeared over the Cymru Mountains, their dark shapes outlined by flashes of lightning that lit the night sky.

"The three auras revealed much to me. Baron's cruelty towards his wife during their short marriage drove her into the arms of Cosmo St. Angelo, a wealthy merchant of gypsy heritage. *The Accounte* describes how the Baron had the man arrested on charges of high treason, on suspicion of siding with the King's enemies, Oliver Cromwell's Parliamentarians. The accusations of witchcraft came later, at trial, when evidence could not be provided of any alleged political treachery, so other indictments were needed to seal the poor man's fate."

"And once a trial of witchcraft proceeded," I commented from my studies of the peculiar, "it rarely ever ended in acquittal."

"Very true. Those were fearful, superstitious times. There were reasons aplenty for every disagreement, many of them imaginary in nature, reality distorted to suit the accuser."

"You say the baron prevents her gypsy lover from leaving this plane?" Lady Bridges asked. "Why is that? Did he not get what he wanted with the man's execution?"

"It is not the gypsy's soul he holds, but his wife's. One evil crime was followed by another. Baron Stansberry sealed his damnation in the manner of his wife's murder," the professor announced.

"No wonder she haunts us!" Lady Bridges exclaimed.

"After the trial, while she still grieved for her lover, he shot his estranged wife with his hunting musket." He picked up the fourth book, *The Arte of Musketrie'*, and opened it to the illustration of the gun it displayed, another of Lady Stansberry's pleas. "If we study the scenes of spectral movement in their totality, the story of her death emerges. The lady fights with her husband—the shattered bottle and wine glasses. She is chased around the house. His hunting musket stands by the front door. She grabs it to defend herself. They struggle. The baron prevails. They argue again and a single shot rings out. Then Lady Stansberry lay dead by the door."

Suddenly, several candles flared brightly, fading to a dull red before being fully extinguished.

"A curse was cast on the baron's soul by St. Angelo's gypsy clan," Professor Carr said, opening the final book to its marked page. The professor read from *The Spelles, Manners, and Trickerie of the Gipsy'*, "He who has taken the life of a gypsy by foul means shall attend for Eternity at the Gate to Hell, one foot in the grasp of Lucifer, the other on the ground of his crime, to live a desecrated existence as a corpse, with maggots as his companions." Carr closed the book. "Despite the curse, his evil is strong. Baron Stansberry has Samantha's innocent soul in his grasp and refuses to allow her to ascend and seek redemption. His maleficent strength also repels her lover's desperate attempts to free her."

"Dear God," Colonel Bridges remarked.

"The single gunshot we keep hearing but with no hunter in sight? The baron's nefarious deed," the professor added. "The dead birds, rotten to the core? The gypsy curse. The wilted flowers? His spiteful attempt to repudiate his wife's love of life and her natural beauty. We have a twisted, bitter hatred for a delicate young woman with a heart of gold, now trapped with her lover in Purgatory. This *imbroglio* is entirely of Baron Stansberry's making. And will be forever more if this eternal drama is allowed to repeat."

"How can we end all of this professor? Can we end it?" the colonel asked.

"Keep your money in your pocket, Colonel Bridges. Everything I think we need has already been dispatched and resides within. How we utilize such instruments is the crux of our next task. It will be difficult, no doubt. For if I'm right in my theory, we must separate the spectres from each other; encourage portals to open; and without prejudice, let the spirits be drawn into the one best suited to their misdemeanors."

"Portals? Heaven and Hell, professor? Does science have such power?" Alexei asked. "Indeed, does any man? Surely, if the science of the peculiar interferes with the workings of the Divine, it will be at our grave peril."

"Quite right. We must all embrace our faith. There will be risks to be sure," Professor Carr replied. "But our actions in matters of the peculiar, as always, will be merely a catalyst for justice, wherever no earthly court presides. The only spirits we need to separate are Lady Stansberry and her husband. For it is their quarrel that imprisons Cosmo St. Angelo. If she is set free, his aether will be drawn to her by the power of their eternal love. For Baron Stansberry, let Divine Judgment decide his fate."

PART V

The storm clouds in the night turned into an overcast drizzle by the next day. With the possibility of a day without a visible sunset, would Harandon Hall get a reprieve? Regardless, we worked at a quickened pace to ready Professor Carr's choice of peculiar instruments should the sky clear and our intervention at the next sunset proceed as planned.

Colonel Bridges left the hall after breakfast to rally men from the farm. His crew dredged the pond by the gazebo using grappling hooks and lances, probing the pond's waters as if they hoped to harpoon a whale. The professor desired a chunk of timber from the executioner's gallows, if such charred wood had survived. The stagnant bottom of the pond was devoid of oxygen, he said, and thus created an environment that should have naturally preserved a sample, regardless of how many centuries had passed.

Alexei and I laboured under the arches of the cloister, protected from the light rain. We readied another instrument brought in from the Institute, a lumino-oscilloscope, like the one the professor and I used at the daemonic possession of Suddenville.

"I share your concerns," I said to Alexei as we worked. "Portals to other dimensions are not theory. Suddenville proved that. From that experience, one must respect the unpredictability of such phenomena, truly beyond mortal control and certainly not in our power to initiate. Professor Carr's plan frightens me. This instrument detects a portal once it has opened on its own accord. Surely he doesn't believe he can conjure up a portal through its use alone?"

"Of course not," Alexei replied. "But he and I have been working on another device that uses the spectral energy of the aether to encourage such creation. Spirits are bound by metaphysical laws as yet not fully understood, but through observation and experimentation, we have discovered various degrees of predictable behaviour of aethereal energy."

"That device," he pointed to a crate yet to be unpacked, "may be just the apparatus to energize the mechanisms we need in this endeavor. To isolate the spectres from one another, we must use their latent metaphysical kinetics. Like earthly magnetism, it can be encouraged to attract or repel."

"But the portals themselves? Doors to Heaven and Hell? Is that not beyond any man's means to create?"

"The professor and I theorize that aethereal energy has a potential energy like voltage and the speed of a spectre's motion is like the kinetic energy of an electrical current. Isolation of that energy of motion—stopping that spectral kinetics, trapping it within what could be called an aethereal energy field—ceases the motion of a spirit relative to our earthly presence. But in doing so, it does not diminish the potential energy that is inherent in the very nature of the spectre's existence in the aether."

Alexei gestured with a flamboyant flip of his hand, as always carried away with the internal musings of his brilliant mind as it delved into the import of his theorems, barely taking a breath between sentences.

I raised a finger to note a point of clarification, for those of us of lesser academic acuity. Basically, his explanation dumb-founded me. "How does the metaphysical magnetism of spirits, as you call it, encourage the creation of portals?"

"Ah." He finally understood that simplicity would win over my heart and mind. "Think of it this way, Jeremiah. Potential 'good' will be drawn to Heaven. Potential 'evil' will be drawn to Hell. Always. An eternal truth. Once spiritual 'motion' is prevented, we will let the potential energy of the spirits—their 'voltage' if you will—open the portals relevant to their eternal destinies. It is their preordained fate that dictates the outcome, not a choice on our part."

"Our actions in matters of the peculiar will be merely a catalyst for justice."

"Precisely. As the professor explained, the baron has one foot in the doorway to Hell due to the curse the gypsies placed on him. His daemonic power has blocked the metaphysical forces that would naturally draw Lady Stansberry's spirit towards the door to Heaven. We will attempt to sever the captive force of his evil from her, so she can float freely in the spectral direction of her choice."

"A bold theory. Revolutionary. But what if it's wrong?"

"We learn from our failure, return to the Institute, do more research. Then try again, at another time, at another place."

"And doom our current benefactors to a life of perpetual misery?"

"Harandon Hall may prove to be uninhabitable by humankind. We shall see."

Alexei and I fitted the lumino-oscilloscope to a mount on its gurney, a handcart that allowed us to wheel the instrument from one place to another. The instrument detected the shape and size of trans-dimensional portals on the oscilloscope's luminescent screen. This new version had dispensed with the mechanism that fired darts, fitted instead with an ion-beam generator using the same exotic isotopes contained in Professor Carr's original design. This eliminated the need for a coil of wire attached to the darts to conduct the electro-luminosity given off by a portal. An ingenious upgrade by Alexei Patroznik, Professor Carr's ingenious new protégé.

"So, now we must focus on *that*." Alexei pointed to the unopened crate, standing eight feet tall, six feet wide and six feet deep.

The crate resembled a permanent cargo trunk, fitted with bolts to keep its sides together. As the trunk was unbolted, an apparatus— Alexei's newest invention—came into view. It was a remarkable but outwardly delicate looking device. It consisted of a set of very tall, sealed glass cylinders standing on end in a circle. Appearing behind the tubes, at the instrument's core, a sturdier looking set of circular brass rings acted as supports for five copper-coiled dynamos. At the base of the instrument lay a small panel with silver-plated prongs.

"We attach an electromagnetic field generator here," Alexei said, pointing to the prongs. "To charge up the machine. Once charged, it can run for twelve hours."

I continued my examination. Each glass cylinder was attached to the central body of the device by what I determined was a folded articulating arm. "Forgive me, Alexei, I can't imagine in a thousand days and nights how this device might work."

Alexei laughed. The opaque skin of his cheeks wrinkled into little washboards as he smiled, one of the few times I'd seen levity erupt from his usually bland face. "It's still a prototype," he said. "And a bit bulky, I admit. With development, I'm sure I can make it smaller. Technically, it's a spectral kinetic interferometer. But I call it Patroznik's Carousel." He finished his exposé with a flourish of his hand and paused, as if waiting for applause, then said, "And why not? A name that's easier for laymen to say. Let's charge it up and I'll show you how it works."

Our pending endeavour—to breach this barrier of ignorance surrounding the peculiar and replace it with knowledge—was the reason I remained entranced by the possibilities offered in my employ at the Institute and fully committed to its mission. "I can't wait to see it in operation."

Alexei cranked up a micro-steam-driven generator, like the ones that powered our luxautographs, and attached its cable to the Carousel. I was intrigued by the device's name as soon as he'd said it, an ode to the inventor without question, but it was the whimsical idea of using a fairground carousel to entrap ghosts that was beyond peculiar. Of course, the science behind his new apparatus, I came to learn, was infinitely more complex than the carnival moniker he'd coined.

The Carousel began to spin. The articulating arms extended, their attached glass cylinders moving from the vertical to the horizontal position. They swung around like a centrifuge. Electrical charges like miniature lightning ran up and down the inner body's dynamo coils. Alexei adjusted the output of the generator until both it and the Carousel hummed in unison.

He stood back to admire his invention. "The gas inside the cylinders will acquire a tremendous charge of electro-luminosity. And *that* is the key."

A slender leather case, the size one might think held a clarinet, had been included with the shipment. Alexei opened it. Inside, in its plush-velvet padded interior, hid a copper bar about three feet long, two inches in diameter, with a rubber hand-grip. The bar bristled with fine filaments, making its surface look like it was covered along its entire length with copper-coloured dandelion heads.

"Vulcan's Wand," Alexei said.

I felt its weight, musing over its purpose. "It's lighter than a cricket bat."

"The core is hollow."

Engrossed by this strange wand, part baton and part brush, I didn't hear Professor Carr approaching. He reached from behind and snatched the wand away. "Aha! I see you've made some improvements, Alexei," he said with a grin. "And the Carousel? Marvelous! Absolutely wonderful." The gas inside the slowly spinning cylinders had become cloudy and glowed with a pale blue light. "That will do just nicely."

***

When watching a sun as it sets, enriched by the daily discourse and progress of human enterprise, I usually feel peace and accomplishment, a sense that the natural order of the world and mankind's role in it has come full circle during daylight and will rest until dawn. Tonight, at a quarter of the hour before nine o'clock, the entirely opposite was true.

The sun, ever majestic in its decline, signaled the arrival of a wretched darkness. My soul was filled with apprehension and raw naked fear. I had felt this same fear on one of my previous adventures with Professor Carr, during the daemonic possession of the village of Suddenville, where we faced a terror there beyond words and precedent, with equally dire consequences should the professor's plan fail. Our triumph in that instance had aged us, physically and spiritually. We prayed we would never encounter such dark aethereal forces again, knowing full well, deep in our hearts, that the Institute— its leader and its followers—was the tip of a spear piercing realms of the peculiar that opened into unimaginable dimensions. For the professor to endure so, even thrive under such stress, was a testament to his resolve.

Patroznik's Carousel had been moved to the center of the gravel courtyard in front of Harandon Hall. Alexei attended his invention; the device to be activated by the professor's instruction. My job was to operate the lumino-oscilloscope, a skill I had mastered, and upon detection, advise Professor Carr when and where any supernatural portals opened. Professor Carr took Vulcan's Wand in hand, its purpose still a mystery to me. He stationed himself in the foyer, the locus of spectral activity, being the intersection of the conflicts between Baron and Lady Stansberry inside the Hall and the cursed grounds of the estate that lay beyond its entrance. The front door was propped open, not for the spirits' sake, as physical objects provided no barrier, but for ours, so the professor and ourselves could enter and exit the Hall at will. On the earth of Cosmo St. Angelo's execution— the ghoulish arena damned by the gypsies' spell—the remains of the gallows, soggy charred timbers resurrected from the bottom of the pond, had been arranged in the shape of a Christian cross.

The moon's light kissed the tree branches. An owl's hoot, somewhere deep in the forest, broke the silence. Darkness fell like a theatrical curtain, suddenly and with complete abandon. It was as if the spectres knew what was about to happen and had summoned additional forces to douse the sun's light as thoroughly as one would snuff a candle.

We left Colonel and Lady Bridges huddled on the drawing room's buttoned chesterfield, arms locked in a tight embrace. Mr. Humphrey and Mrs. Shoelittle stood by the fire, ready to assist if called. The top floor of Harandon Hall was a sanctuary, the mainstay of spectral activity being confined to the lower floor's rooms, the ones surrounding the Hall's entrance, the site of Lady Stansberry's murder. The Bridges' children, their nanny and the rest of the household staff had retired to their bedrooms upstairs.

The play—more peculiar and grim than any horror spectacle ever performed on the Theatre Macabre's stage—was about to begin.

And begin it did.

An object flew out of the dining room, past the stone staircase, whizzing by Professor Carr's head, inches from striking him. The silver centerpiece, the model of the Colonel's airship, shot out of the entranceway and tumbled to the gravel courtyard, coming to rest at Alexei's feet. The sounds of breaking glass filled the still night air. The *battle royale* had commenced.

A single gunshot rang out, echoing around the turrets of the guard towers. The owl—its nightly predation intercepted by Baron Stansberry's aethereal musket ball—plunged with limp wings to the foot of the front steps.

Professor Carr bounded out of Harandon Hall, yelling, "Now, Alexei. Now!"

Patroznik's Carousel had been humming at idle. With a flip of a switch the articulating arms that held its gas-filled cylinders rose and spun.

Sweat beaded on my brow and trickled over my eyebrows onto my cheeks, its salty sting touching my lips. I felt my legs tremble and a rush of sickliness rise from my stomach. I strengthened my grip on the oscilloscope's gurney, ready to aim it where necessary.

The Carousel achieved its peak luminosity, the pale blue light from the glass cylinders spreading wide around the grounds, illuminating the gazebo and the trees surrounding it. The silhouettes of tree trunks and their clawing branches appeared as if a ring of spectators had joined the proceedings, an audience of stiff witnesses to the spectral reenactment of the baron's heinous crimes.

Professor Carr approached Patroznik's Carousel, wand in hand. He held it in the air less than a foot from the spinning cylinders. A bolt of electro-luminosity jumped from the machine to the tip of Vulcan's Wand and raced down its length, curling around its brush-like filaments until the entire wand was bright with pulsing blue light.

Professor Carr, holding the wand high, backed away from the machine and marched at a brusque pace towards the cursed remains of the gallows. The bolt of electro-luminosity followed him, attached from the wand's tip to the spinning Carousel, stretching like a twisted electric laundry line. He stopped at the edge of the barren earth where the gallows' timbers lay.

Inside Harandon Hall, all of the candles were snuffed out by forces unknown, plunging the castle into darkness. I heard Lady Bridges scream. A cold chill swept past me. Looking through my skiascopic goggles, I saw the outline of a spectre race by. It wore a bustling dress. Barely a second later, another deeply chilled blast of air rushed out of the Hall in pursuit, the image in my goggles' lens of a man carrying a musket with a fluted end.

Professor Carr struck the gallows' timbers with Vulcan's Wand. His act anchored the bolt coming from Patroznik's Carousel into the center of the cross formed by the charred wood. He stepped back and a second line of electro-luminosity emerged from the timbers, attached to the wand. The bolt followed him as he walked towards the gazebo. I saw the spectre of Lady Stansberry approach the pond, her arms held out in a beckoning motion. A third apparition rose from the waters, a man by its shape, however the ghostly body was separated into parts—arms and legs dangling with gaps between the limbless torso where they'd once been joined. The third spectre, I deduced, must be Cosmo St. Angelo, hung, then drawn and quartered in 1642.

The spectre of Lady Stansberry stopped in front of the cross, the bolt of electric blue rising from it dancing in the dark. Professor Carr ran as fast as I've ever seen him run to encircle her ghostly form with his wand's line of luminosity, joining this electric charge to the first line that stretched from the Carousel. He had lassoed a spirit!

Professor Carr held Vulcan's Wand straight out in front of him like a fencer would hold a sword. Through my goggles, I saw the spirit of Baron Stansberry draw near him. It shunted backwards as if bouncing off a stone garden wall. Carr had produced the separation of spirits he'd boldly envisioned. Patroznik's Carousel worked!

"Jeremiah," he yelled over to me. "I sense a turbulence in the aether."

I pointed the oscilloscope in his direction. "Above you, professor," I screamed back.

A swirl of spectral energy appeared on the oscilloscope's screen directly over Professor Carr's head. I removed my goggles. A visible disk of bright white light hung horizontally just above the treetops, its edges billowy and blurred. It rotated like a flat tornado, the inside of its whirlwind sparkling with tiny lights. It illuminated the figure of Lady Stansberry. Her features came into clear focus; a beautiful, ivory pale face, curls of golden locks cascading to gently curving shoulders, dainty waist, her young bosom heaving with the toil of the spectral chase.

She floated upwards towards the center of the bright portal, her hands extended, beckoning in the direction of her lover. His spirit hovered over the pond, near his place of execution. As the ghost of Lady Stansberry rose higher, her features faded, consumed by the bright aether like sugar dissolving in water. A moment later, she disappeared completely. As soon as she was gone, a beam of light reached out from the portal's center and passed into the dismembered body of Cosmo St. Angelo. His arms and legs—cruelly separated by an unjust execution—merged back into the rest of his body, making his spirit whole again. St. Angelo's spectre traversed the line of the beam as if flying on gossamer wings and disappeared through the portal.

The bright portal over Professor Carr's head closed. Darkness reigned again, save the eerie glow still cast by the bolts from Patroznik's Carousel. "Nobody move," the professor shouted, waving the wand. "No matter what happens, no one approach me!"

I put my goggles back on. An apparition paced back and forth in front of the professor, an arm's length from the glowing tip of Vulcan's Wand, its electro-luminescent force keeping the evil of Baron Stansberry at bay.

A rumble shook the earth beneath my feet, its vibrations reaching the Carousel. It knocked Alexei to the ground. "Professor!" he yelled.

"Do not forsake your care of the machine on my account, Alexei! Whatever happens next is beyond anyone's control."

Suddenly, like a fencer thrusting at his opponent, Professor Carr lunged out. The tip of the wand speared the ghoul. As the professor withdrew, the electric charge the device carried stuck on the baron's chest. A dancing line of luminosity connected Baron Stansberry to the cross formed by the gallows' burnt timbers.

The earth inside the execution ground, lit by the bolts from Patroznik's Carousel extending from it, began to turn, accelerating in speed until all definition of the soil was lost. The unholy spot turned black, swirling like a pool of thick oil. The cross-shaped timbers crumbled like dry mortar, loosing their shape. The pieces flared into bright red flames amid a whooshing roar, the sound of a tempest's wind, until no flames remained. Two hands crept out of the emptiness of the swirling black pitch; hands gnarled and covered in warts; long thin fingers, with sharp curled claws like those of a hawk. It pulled on the flickering bolt of luminosity attached to the spirit of Baron Stansberry, drawing the bolt down into the portal like a sailor hauling a rope. The apparition—Sir Montague Stansberry, Baronet of the

Borders, Sheriff of Harandon—resisted, squirming and twisting. Stansberry's ghost was drawn toward the pit, a daemonic portal opened on ground bearing the curse of an innocent man's execution. His screams pierced the night, their echoes lingering with the unsettling vibration of a tuning fork, rattling my bones.

Fog emerged from the portal, a creeping mist that rose to the height of the trees and dampened the light from the Carousel's bolts. The air became saturated with a sick odour, sulfurous and rotten. A nauseous weakness engulfed my body, as if I was about to faint. I fell to my knees, hands on the instrument cart, the only things preventing my total collapse.

Loud rumbles shook the earth. Baron Stansberry drifted into the fog, pulled ever deeper into it by unseen hands, until his apparition evaporated in a final whiff of smoke.

Professor Carr stumbled away from the gazebo. "Shut it off!" he yelled.

Alexei tripped the breaker on his machine. The articulating arms with their glass cylinders retracted. The Carousel spun slower and slower. The bolts of luminosity—pursing through the grim fog into God only knew where—diminished in brightness until the force of the Carousel's dynamos faded to naught and the bolts completely disappeared.

Alexei and I rushed to the professor's aid. He'd fallen face down in the gravel, exhausted. As we lifted him to his feet, he moaned, then dusted himself off and said, "Dear God, such evil."

The rank air jumped to life. A foul wind blew from the direction of Harandon Hall to the place where the daemonic portal had opened. The three of us turned back to face the bank of fog. We watched as the swirling black pit sucked the mist away. The oily churn ceased. The pit's surface glossed over, then the ground resumed the earthen brown appearance of its origins as if nothing after sunset had ever happened. Above us, stars twinkled. The crisp fresh air of a cool summer night returned.

"What have we witnessed?" I asked, not expecting any answer, for the conclusions were beyond imagination.

"The unspeakable," Professor Carr mewed in a soft voice. "Gentlemen, remember this day well. For we have had a most peculiar time indeed."

THE DARWIN ROOM

PART I

Lord Montgomery Todd-Marling, a crusty old aristocrat of quite unbearable stuffiness, rubbed the top of his silver walking stick as if by doing so he could drill a passage under the door into the professor's office.

"I'm so sorry, m'lord," I said, bowing awkwardly as I fumbled with a set of keys. "Professor Carr is not here and we weren't expecting you." I unlocked the door. "Please, do come in. Tea?"

"My time is precious, Mr.—"

"Boone, Jeremiah Boone."

"I'll come straight to the point. Professor Carr is wanted immediately at the Palace. The Queen is quite upset. A dragon has been eating her corgis."

"Excuse me, sir. Did you say a *dragon*?"

"Are you hard of hearing?"

"Not really. It's just I've only heard dragons talked about in legends. It's quite another thing to learn one is roaming modern Britannia eating dogs."

"My dear fellow, if the Queen calls it a dragon, then that's what it is. She's seen it with her own eyes. And she's sketched it."

Lord Todd-Marling produced a folded paper from his frockcoat pocket. Indeed, the drawing was on royal stationary marked, 'Her Imperial Majesty Queen Ellinora, Rockingham Palace, Londinium'.

I looked over the sketch, not sure what to make of it. It was a quite remarkable rendering but in truth, a sketch not unlike most depictions of the many types of dragon mankind has imagined to exist in our mythological past. The Queen had probably grown up throughout her childhood bombarded with images of such a creature—in paintings and tapestries; on heraldic coats of arms; and carved in the stonework of the realm's castles, palaces and cathedrals. By now, I presumed, she could draw a dragon in her sleep.

"Well, young man. Stop gawking and get Professor Carr. This is an emergency. One more dead corgi in her garden and I'll be thrown in the Tower."

Lord Montgomery Todd-Marling was the Queen's Royal Warden of Parks, one of many titles he bore. The most important of course were his hereditary titles, followed by his appointments within government and the military. Finally, there were titles of purely ceremonial worth, usually ones that allowed the aristocracy to pick the pockets of Her Majesty's Treasury doing nothing of any significance except barking orders to civil servants who basically did all the work. Being the Royal Warden of Parks was one such position.

"I'm afraid, sir," I replied sheepishly, "Professor Carr is still in his bed. He had a rather extended performance at the Theatre Macabre last night."

"Well then rouse him. The Queen's airship is anchored outside. Do you want me to enlist her Royal Marines to haul him out in his nightshirt? Didn't I say this was an emergency?"

Dead corgis? A dragon? I muttered under my breath as I scurried down the hall.

"Hurry, man." Lord Todd-Marling yelled as he stamped the end of his walking stick on the wood floor as if its vibrations would make me run faster. "You mustn't keep the Queen waiting."

I'm hurrying, you toffee-nosed, old git.

I rounded the corner and ran square-on into Professor Carr, fully dressed in his gold-trimmed formal frockcoat. "Thank god, you're up, sir," I said, panting. I held the sketch forward. "From Her Majesty, the Queen. She bade you come to the Palace with great urgency."

"A little psychic birdie tweeted in my ear I might get a most peculiar summons this morning, and so this must be it. I was advised to get a wiggle on and get dressed for a grand occasion." As Professor Carr walked back with me down the hallway, he caught sight of Lord Todd-Marling. "Ah, a dragon of another ilk. To the Palace then. And I thought I might get a day off."

"A walk in the park, sir. Apparently."

***

Set in seventy lush acres, the Royal Gardens alternated between grand patches of pristine green grass, cut as smooth as a fine beaver top hat, to flowerbeds bursting with colour, to a woodland made of small copses and knolls as if the trees were squads of toy soldiers arranged by a giant child.

The Queen's Royal Kennels were a leisurely stroll from the back terrace of Rockingham Palace through a box garden of roses. The Royal Groundskeeper accompanied us, a Mr. Tibbetts, quite a curious man, short but wiry and lean, pointy nose, blond curly hair like a baby's, who walked with the energy of a greyhound, darting away from our path to inspect a plant and then darting back to our side as if throttled by the tug of a leash.

We approached the kennels to the sound of yapping corgis, the dogs excited no doubt about the prospect of being taken for a walk. The great oak door of the kennels dangled open on one hinge, its wood scored with raptor-like claw marks.

"I suppose a dragon might do something like this," I said, inspecting the wood.

"Or a lion. Or tiger. Perhaps a bear. Let's not jump to any conclusions," Carr advised. "Peculiar as this may appear at first glance, one can't take the Queen's witness as gospel. Not yet. There may be a more apt explanation."

"Will we meet the Queen to interview her?" I said, with excitement in my voice.

The professor chuckled. "That's hardly likely. Once a royal proclamation of fact has been uttered, one is supposed to accept it at face value. The only way a queen is interrogated is after her throne has been usurped."

Each corgi had its own pen. Mr. Tibbetts opened all of them, corralled the dogs into an unruly group and tied them to leashes. "I'll leave you to it," he said as the gaggle of squat canines pulled him out of the kennels into the garden.

We examined the scene of the crime. Several pens had been recently damaged and then repaired. Claw marks marked where the beast had scrambled over the railings to capture and then drag its prey. A trail of scratches had been left on the flagstone floor, grooves still containing tiny tufts of bloody dog fur that had not yet been scrubbed away.

We left the kennels to follow the beast's trail. There was much evidence in the grass and soil as we followed the markings around the back. The size of its claw prints, and the distance between strides, left us the impression this was indeed a large creature, easily as big as a lion. Unlike a lion, tiger or bear, it had walked with a lizard-like gait, marks in the grass indicating where a tail, thicker than a wild cat's, had swished across the ground behind it.

"Could this have been a crocodile, professor?"

"They are not known to leap about, as this one appears to have done. And crocs are quite stout and heavy. A crocodile of this size would yield considerable weight. It would have completely collapsed the railing around the pen if it had jumped onto it. This creature is quite agile and nimble under foot. And I imagine somewhat slender and muscular, like an iguana perhaps."

"Must have been a damn big iguana to abscond with a dog."

The trail, ominously marked with more signs of blood and fur, led us back into a section of the garden's woodlands. Tall grasses had been flattened, small bushes trampled. The trail ended suddenly at the base of a broad oak.

"Did it take flight, professor?"

"Wild is your imagination, Jeremiah. Look below the tree. Branches have been displaced from higher up and have fallen to the ground. There are scratch marks on the bark. The creature jumped into the tree, breaking its weaker limbs, and then ran through to the next tree."

We marched on through the garden, finding other clues that proved the 'dragon' had leapt from tree to tree. Finally, our trek ended at the high stone walls on the eastern edge of the Palace grounds, a barrier fully fifteen feet tall.

"This is how it got into the garden, and how it got out, leaping from the tree to the top of the wall," the professor concluded.

"Surely someone would have seen such a beast with a small dog in its jaws bounding through the streets?"

"The area beyond that wall houses Imperial ministries that are devoid of staff in the dead of night. Yes, perhaps there's a chance a night porter saw it. But the biggest question is: where did it go? Where is its nest?"

"*Nest?*"

"If it was hungry, it would have devoured the corgi on the spot and then snatched another until it was satisfied. Mr. Tibbetts said the creature had returned over two nights, plucking only one animal at a time. It's taking its prey back to its nest, to feed its young."

"A dragon's nest? In the center of Londinium?"

"Peculiar as it sounds, that is the only conclusion I think we can reach. Which makes our next course of action quite delicate. We can't set a trap for the beast, for that will keep its origins hidden from us. No, we must entice it back, then track its movements as it returns to its lair."

Professor Carr did something I've never seen him do before. He climbed a tree. "Be careful," I yelled as the professor navigated his way through the branches the 'dragon' had traversed. A thick sturdy limb extended over the wall, thankfully one that could carry a man's weight. Professor Carr stepped onto the top of the wall, removed a handkerchief from his pocket, and rubbed it across the bricks.

When he returned to the ground, he folded the handkerchief, and said, "I'll ask the Palace to provide a pair of hunting hounds for our use. This cloth should have acquired sufficient scent to track our creature. We'll encamp outside this wall tonight using a butcher's goose as bait. Let's hope that by offering fowl on the menu, we will tempt its palate."

PART II

In most of Londinium, the city at night still breathes life. Alehouses, inns and cafes stay open until the wee hours. The aero-trams and steam charabancs operate continuously; delivering workers to factories that run uninterrupted; conveying night staff to and from the hotels. When the darkest hours provide the greatest privacy, the sordid side of Londinium buzzes like a Brunswick propulsion engine—inside private clubs, gambling rooms and opium dens; and of course, with the street-side solicitations of prostitutes who tout for business wherever a pulse exists.

A quarter of the population of the city works under the moon and stars—if that is, you can see the heavens through the city's smoky air. There's barely a district in the city where you won't come across someone doing something at night. The lone exception is the Imperial Quarter, that stark complex of edifices that hold dominion over the Empire's bureaucracy and surround Rockingham Palace and the smaller residences of lesser royals. At night, it is as deserted as a graveyard.

The street outside the Palace's walls was quiet. A single footstep echoed like a bell. The professor and I huddled for warmth, each of us with a hip flask of brandy, sitting on folding chairs in a tented put-me-up that I took with me last year on holiday to Waignton Beach. We were encamped with a pair of the Queen's favourite hunting hounds— two placid beagles, Argos and Ben, who, we were assured, would contain their excitement for the chase until instructed. Our tent was located two gas lamps upwind from a carefully positioned carcass of a fresh goose, hung from the stanchion of a gas lamp at such a height as to prevent being snatched by a stray dog but hopefully not too high to deter a 'dragon' from its evening meal.

A single distant strike from the clock over Horseguard's Arch marked the one o'clock hour. The air hung with a clawing mist, part fog, part smoke. Across the street, the slates on the roof of the Imperial Ministry of Technology clattered with a sound like dominoes falling on a table. The beagles stirred, their gentle whimpers silenced by Professor Carr's hushed command. He carefully swept the tent's front curtain aside so we could peer down the street. The light from the gas lamps glowed like floating halos in the dense gloom, preventing us from seeing what was scampering across the roof. But we could hear it. It would scurry then stop, like a wary squirrel searching for a nut.

The silence of the deserted Imperial Quarter returned; a pause that momentarily erased our suspicions, as if we'd only imagined we'd heard the sound. I gulped a generous mouthful of brandy from my flask, my nerves as twitchy as the two beagles. The quiet was disturbed by a loud scratching that ran down the side of the building. A dark shape dropped into the middle of the deserted street near the lamp that held our bait. Our night crawler had arrived to feast.

The silhouette of the beast—for we could but see its outline—suggested a reptile. Lithe limbs with a low slung belly. A long neck reaching up to a smooth earless head. A tail that snaked across the pavement. Midway along its arched back, a pair of sharply angled wings suggested a creature as yet unknown to natural science. However, the dragon's wings were small in relation to the rest of its body, each wing as proportioned to the beast as a fan was to a lady who was fending off the heat. *A youngster?* I thought. *Still not fully developed?* This might explain its inability to fly but if the professor's theory was followed, would it be old enough to have young of its own?

The creature approached the dangling goose. It rose on its hind legs and the true size of it made me gasp. It stood at eye level to the meat; from the ground to its head, seven feet tall. It took the goose in its jaws and pulled, separating it from the rope as easily as a child plucking a petal off a flower.

The beagles strained at their leashes, catching the scent they'd been trained to detect using the professor's handkerchief. Argos, the most energetic dog, let off a yelp. The creature's head, with the goose firmly snared in its mouth, turned in our direction. It stiffened, frozen in the moment just as animals do when a predator lurks. Argos bolted out of the tent, barking, then lurched back with another yelp as he ran to the end of his leash. The 'dragon' whirled around. It leapt towards the Ministry's wall in a single rapid bound like that of a giant kangaroo. It scaled the wall, reached the pinnacle of the rooftop, and then disappeared into the darkness on the other side.

We took to the chase, following the beagles' lead, running across the street and along the side of the building. The night air was scented by a musk we couldn't smell but our hounds definitely could. Argos and Ben were more accustomed to chasing foxes in a pastoral setting, not in navigating the back passages of a city, and so we stumbled against locked gates that led into courtyards we couldn't enter, the dogs feverishly trying to scale them to no avail.

"Around here," Professor Carr yelled, tugging Argos away. "The other side!"

"Professor, how will we ever gain advantage over this thing?" I puffed. "It clearly has the speed to elude us."

"Hounds never catch up to the fox when the chase is still in process," he replied as we ran along the side of another tall government ministry. "It's only after the fox tires and thus stops, that the dogs encircle it. As long as they can still detect the smell of it— their olfactory glands known to be supreme receptors of scent even at great distances—we can track it."

After a half an hour of grueling pursuit, the creature ran out of rooftops to jump across. It was still quite far from us, given the faint sound of its claws raking the roof tiles in the Imperial Quarter. Its unmistakable shape eventually landed on the avenue that led into

Billingsworth Park, the private estate of Lord Alphonse Billingsworth, a prominent and very wealthy industrialist, and husband to the Queen's aunt, Georgina.

The 'dragon' scampered up the park's ornate iron fencing and leapt down the other side. The estate was fully fenced and heavily guarded. Lord Billingsworth had been the target of an anarchist's recent assassination attempt due to the hereditary peer's bizarre ideas. He advocated for the most extreme theories of social engineering, especially eugenics; policies the cranky old aristocrat trumpeted in Parliament every chance he got.

The entrance to the grounds was further down the street from where we'd lost sight of the 'dragon'. A guardhouse, its church spire-styled roof poking upwards into the gloom, flanked one side of a massive wrought iron gate emblazoned with the Billingsworth family crest. The shadows of security soldiers from the Queen's Household Guards, alert and vigilant, patrolled its gas lit rooms.

"I fear we've lost it, professor. Billingsworth Park borders the River Etham. If the beast gets across the river, the hounds will lose its scent."

"That may be the least of our worries." The professor placed a hand on the bars of the tall iron fence. "I sense a malevolence around us, Jeremiah. I can't quite get a bearing on its dimensions. It's coming from inside the park, but I feel its presence coming down the street as well."

Professor Carr's words had barely left his lips when a steam-Clarence—an enclosed carriage with armour plating, a model with richly-appointed specifications, a popular choice with the high aristocracy—cut through the murkiness of the night, pistons pumping, its curved engine pipes spewing coal smoke. It drew up to the gatehouse. A side window opened and a guard stepped onto a Juliette balcony to examine the identity papers produced by its passenger.

As we approached the gatehouse, the two beagles erupted in a cacophony of teeth-glistening barks. The passenger leaned out of the carriage and gestured to the guard with his walking stick, pointing our way. He wore a top hat. The rest of his features were consumed by the night. A moment later, the giant gates to Billingsworth Park opened. The steam-Clarence let off a hiss as its driver engaged the gears and the weighty vehicle chugged inside.

"Time is of the essence, Jeremiah. And fortune favours the bold. We must plead our case to the guards."

The professor's gambit—telling the truth about the beast as we knew it—was met with laughter, a soldier's blunderwaller to the ribs, and a warning. Both of us, and our two dogs, crazy as we seemed to be, would be shot on sight if the guards ever saw us lurking in the dark around Billingsworth Park again. Apparently, none of the uncultured brutes had seen Professor Carr perform at the Theatre Macabre. This was one of those rare and most unfortunate occasions where the professor's celebrity alone could not pay the price of entry. There was nothing more we could do except retrace our steps back to our lookout outside the palace walls to wait for the cab we'd instructed to pick us up at dawn.

The chase had pumped the blood and brought sweat to my brow but as we ambled back through the Imperial Quarter, my body cooled and the chill of the night nipped at my tired bones. We were a block away from the Ministry of Technology, along the main avenue leading to Rockingham Palace, when a chugging noise broke the silence.

Professor Carr wheeled around and pointed in the sound's direction. "Look sharp! Danger approaches."

The boxy shape of the steam-Clarence emerged from the gloom, its pistons fiercely driven at maximum speed. The carriage raced up the boulevard with little regard to the safety of anyone in its way.

I was the first to see the pistol poking out of the side window. I owned a similar weapon, the profile of its double-barrel unmistakable. "Down, professor!"

We dropped to the pavement as shots rang out, the projectiles whizzing over our heads, clanging harmlessly off a courtyard's gate.

The steam-Clarence careened around the corner and disappeared as quickly as it had arrived.

"A warning shot," the professor said, calming the angered beagles. "Too far above our heads to make any claim the bullets had deadly intent. Someone doesn't want us near Billingsworth Park. That's very clear."

When we finally arrived back at the spot where we'd camped out, my put-me-up tent and its folding chairs were gone. No doubt some uncouth ruffians had absconded with them. Who said the Imperial Quarter was deserted at night? It's an undeniable truth about life in the city, as our chase and its frightening result confirmed, there isn't any place in Londinium where the night doesn't belong to those with the audacity and guile to make it their own.

PART III

We met Lord Montgomery Todd-Marling in his chambers in Rockingham Palace. His office was a jumble of ephemera and memorabilia, décor typical of someone retired from active service in the military. In Lord Todd-Marling's case, his collections reflected his many tenures as a governor of several Imperial Overseas Protectorates, tiny colonies scattered in the far flung corners of the globe.

Todd-Marling, bald, bushy white sideburns, ruddy cheeks dotted with liver spots, easily eighty years old if he was a day, sat his slim, aging frame in the most oversized desk chair I'd ever seen. The chair, quite possibly a relic of some previous appointment where he sought to impress some potentate of an indigenous people with the power of the Britannic Empire by means of a piece of furniture, virtually swallowed him whole.

"As Royal Warden of Parks, surely you can grant us the authority to search the grounds of Billingsworth Park?" Professor Carr inquired.

Todd-Marling harrumphed, a sound quite particular to the aristocracy, a combination of expressing one's indignation while clearing one's throat. It was an affectation of the high gentry that was perfected over a lifetime, first being taught in boarding school, to show displeasure at someone of inferior social standing, and then fine-tuned into old age while in command of a legion of toad-like sycophants employed to do your bidding regardless of how ridiculous your demands were.

"We're talking here about a member of the Imperial Family," he blustered. "Such a request must come from Queen Ellinora herself, since it pertains to the domicile of her most beloved auntie."

"A dragon, potentially living in the grounds of her most beloved auntie's estate," Professor Carr reminded him, "has eaten several of the Queen's corgis."

Lord Todd-Marling harrumphed again, this time an octave higher. His protest signaled a conundrum. He might be forced to prostrate himself before Her Imperial Highness and ask her approval on a matter that logic and circumstance would say was entirely within his purview to decide without bothering her. Such was the mechanics of the Imperial Court. Were it a machine, it would have been abandoned a long time ago for something much more technically sophisticated. In truth, his reaction was understandable. The advancement of modern times and the people's desire for egalitarianism were the twin enemies of the nobility, the highest strata of Britannia's society. They treasured protocol at all costs. It kept the rabble at bay. The veins on Lord Todd-Marling's forehead throbbed under the strain.

"You are quite fortunate that Lord Billingsworth and Her Imperial Highness, the Duchess Georgina, are not in Londinium at the moment. He's voyaged on an expedition to the Cormorant Islands in Oceania. She's taking the waters at Mercier Spa in South Aquitaine while he's away."

"Then who comes and goes into the estate, especially late at night?" the professor asked.

"Their son, Baronet Arthur Billingsworth, the Queen's cousin. He's a surgeon. Quite busy, often called out at odd hours."

"Then we must speak to him as well. Perhaps in his nighttime excursions, he's seen the creature we pursued."

"All right then," Lord Todd-Marling conceded with a grump. He withdrew a large sheaf of parchment from his desk drawer. "Since Duchess Georgina is away, I won't trouble the Queen with this trifle. I'll draw up a Royal Warrant, under my own signature, to allow you access to the estate's grounds. But you must promise not to disturb Dr. Billingsworth and his work any longer than you have to."

He procured sticks of wax and several large stamp seals from his desk, then shooed us out of his office with a waft of his hand like we were unwanted pigeons on a window sill. His private secretary ushered us into an ante-room where we were told to wait, sitting on some very uncomfortable rattan chairs.

Lord Todd-Marling's ante-room was a gallery of sorts, containing an eclectic collection from his worldwide travels—tribal art and primitive objects; native weapons of war; knives, spears and such like. Framed prints and articles documented his accomplishments, the chief one being the appearance of His Lordship outside his various governor's mansions, each time surrounded by a retinue of servants, locals of varying degrees of poverty, and bayoneted soldiers to protect him from having his head shrunk and put on display.

To give my backside some much needed relief from its torturous perch on the bamboo seat, I wandered the room, a mixture of captivation and studious intrigue fueling my curiosity.

"Professor," I said, as I stopped in front of a set of photogravures, many of which showed two elderly gentlemen in safari shorts and pith helmets. "It seems, by the inscriptions, that Lord Todd-Marling and Lord Billingsworth have a shared interest in zoology."

"Hmm, I see," he remarked, coming to my side. "Illustrations from a book they co-authored. Published by the Imperial Society of Geographers and Explorers."

"These engravings—such odd-looking animals," I said. "They appear to be mutations."

"A most peculiar but not entirely unusual phenomenon. Accidental cross-breeding in the wild. This one," he pointed, "was a very famous case from Pajastan where a *liger*, a cross between a lion and a tiger, was discovered."

The professor and I perused the framed pictures, each with an explanation underneath.

"Well, I never," I said. "A *zonkey*? Half-zebra, half-donkey? And here, a *yakalo*? A cross between a yak and a bison?" It was quite an extraordinary exposition of rare zoological discoveries. "Professor, look at this article. From the Londinium Daily Review of last year. The headline, 'Archbishops and Lords Battle Over the Future of the Human Species'."

Professor Carr read out loud from the framed newspaper clipping, "A great debate occurred last night at Duxbridge University's Hall of Oratory, pitting on one side, the Archbishops of Tallybridge and Yorkstable, and on the other, two lords of the realm, Lord Todd-Marling and Lord Billingsworth. The latter argued their case that science should take radical steps towards furthering experimentation based on Master Charles Darwin's theories."

"Isn't Darwin the one who thinks apes gave birth to man?"

"Evolved, Jeremiah. Over a considerable period of time. Darwin's Theory of Evolution. These two archbishops have been the most vocal in condemning Darwin's theories, calling them blasphemous, borne from the mind of someone perverted by the Devil."

"That must have been quite a debate," I mused.

I wandered over to a set of photographs, again showing Lord Todd-Marling and Lord Billingsworth on an expedition of some sort. Behind them, a row of cages contained some extremely large lizards. "Professor, more images published by the Society of Explorers. Here they are again, together, on the Cormorant Islands. The cages in the background—do they not contain something resembling our dragon?"

Professor Carr retrieved a reading monocle from his jacket and peered closely at the photograph. "It's quite blurry and obscured, but the silhouettes are the same. Except these dragons have no wings. They're large monitor lizards of some sort, that's true. The islands of Oceania are reported to contain the largest lizards on the planet. Curious indeed."

The lord's private secretary, a dark-suited gentleman cut from the same snotty cloth as his master, returned to the chamber with a scroll tied with a broad red ribbon. "Excuse me, Professor Carr. Your warrant."

"I'd like to speak with Lord Todd-Marling again, if I may," Carr replied, tapping his monocle on the picture's glass. "To inquire about a matter of new interest in this case."

"I'm afraid His Lordship has just left the Palace. There's a debate in the House of Commons later this afternoon on a bill he and Lord Billingsworth are sponsoring. M'lord will be speaking in Lord Billingsworth's absence, in support of the 'Act to Establish the Institute of Genetic Verification and Improvement'."

"Ah, yes," Carr said. "I've heard of that proposal. The creation of a laboratory to study methods to eradicate genetic defects and undesirable traits in the general population. It will use, I am told, experimental means of the most dubious and unethical nature, such as promoting the mass sterilization of segments of the underclass who've been deemed unworthy of reproduction."

"The idea has quite popular support among His Lordship's peers," the courtier parroted.

"No doubt it has. But if there's any common sense left in this realm—I know, that's a particularly obscure trait amongst politicians—then His Lordship's bill will die a natural death in the House."

I tugged at Professor Carr's elbow. "We have our warrant," I whispered in his ear. "Shouldn't we make forthwith to Billingsworth Park? Before nightfall brings our beast onto the streets?"

"Yes, we should," Carr sighed. "At least in that regard, we have the power to influence the immediate." He turned to Todd-Marling's private secretary. "We will take our leave, sir. I only hope our future is protected by men of reason. Perhaps a blinding bolt of sanity will strike Parliament during His Lordship's debate."

PART IV

The boulevard outside the main gate into Billingsworth Park heaved with people carrying placards, a crowd that moved like an oil slick across water, expanding and contracting in a wave of unrestrained fluidity. This mass of humanity, cut from every walk of life, spilled into the road and blocked the traffic coming into the Imperial Quarter.

The smallest contingents within the crowd hailed from religious associations and women's rights groups. Vicars led elderly parishioners whose banners of purple and gold, adorned with biblical passages, extolled the divine origins of creation. Parallel to their march, demonstrative but quite demure women chanted and sang peacefully, wearing sashes that proclaimed, 'A Vote for Equality is a Vote for Mankind'.

The vast majority of the protesters, however, were an unruly and growing mob, arriving in soot-spewing industrial lorries festooned with the emblems of the Union of Anarchists and other fringe groups; scruffy men, muscular and angry, likely unemployed and looking for trouble. They owned tough-looking countenances, yelled obscenities and pumped fists in the air. 'Revolution Not Evolution,' read one of the anarchist's signs. 'Hang Billingsworth, Traitor to the Species,' read another.

Standing at a safe distance, among a posse of astonished journalists gathered from every news agency in the city, I said, "I fear all hell is about to break loose, professor."

Patrol ships from the Imperial State Police hovered overhead, their propellers buzzing, the airships' shadows floating across the crowd below. On the ground, the Royal Londinium Constabulary was out in full force to contain the demonstration from spreading. A line of constables armed with shields and truncheons separated the crowd from the adjoining government buildings, although the main thrust of the protest appeared to be directed towards Billingsworth Park and Lord Billingsworth in particular, given his name and several synonyms for dung were shouted together. The guards at the park's gatehouse hung out of the highest of its windows, weapons drawn in anticipation of the worst.

A scuffle broke out far from the park's entrance between a group of women and several constables. One of the women had chained herself to the park's iron fence. The woman was quite plump and I'd imagine if she stayed overnight, our renegade dragon might think she was quite a juicy morsel. I feared for her, one way or the other.

This incident—remote as it was from the center of the crowd, and if left restricted just to those few women involved—would have been inconsequential and dealt with easily by the police. However, the authorities' arrival to impose their will on the women sparked a gang of anarchists to seize an opportunity. The original altercation flared like a match to kindling as the anarchists rushed the small squad of constables and overwhelmed them. This emboldened the larger phalanx of constables with shields. They charged the crowd, making no effort to discriminate between male or female, benign worshiper or the heathen. Truncheons met brass knuckles in a fray with bloody consequences for the extremes on both sides of the political divide, but also with significant injuries to ordinary, otherwise placid citizens caught up in the mayhem.

As if this were not enough to draw Imperial patrol ships down to street level, a lone anarchist scaled the park's fence and jumped inside. He ran towards the estate's mansion, its façade semi-hidden behind a grove of oak, with what looked like a bomb. A patrol ship swooped down. Several armed marines descended on tethers, quickly corralled the man, and beat him into submission.

"I think our enquiries will have to wait," I said to Professor Carr as the chaos whipped the journalists next to us into a frenzy of scribbling.

"Mastering the obvious, Jeremiah. Definitely your most charming trait, my dear fellow. Oh well, never mind. I know a nice tea shop not far from the College of Aeronautics. Their scones are quite delectable. At least this ruckus will keep our dragon temporarily in its lair."

***

It's not often I call nightfall a friend. But in this instance, darkness—along with a convoy of paddy wagons and a flotilla of patrol ships—had cleared the streets in front of Billingsworth Park. We trudged towards the gatehouse through discarded signs, some blood-splattered, warrant firmly in hand.

This time, the magic touch of Lord Todd-Marling's scrap of Imperial bureaucracy did the trick. Professor Carr, ever the flamboyant showman, embellished his presentation of the scroll with a flourish worthy of his best stage introductions, just for good measure. The gates into Billingsworth Park swung open. The two beagles, Argos and Ben, well fed and watered, champed at the bit to get the chase started anew. Given their feverish sniffing around every oak tree, the dragon's trail must have enflamed their nostrils and with their unbridled enthusiasm, our pursuit resumed in earnest.

The royal residence inside Billingsworth Park was called Ethamside Palace, the name derived from its prominent situation on the river. A former fortress from pre-Tudor times once sat on the site. The medieval moat had long since dried up but a drawbridge with thick iron chains still spanned what was now a deep grassy ditch. The ancient inner keep had been completely torn down at the start of the nineteenth century and a manse of considerable size and luxury had replaced it, paid for, as most royal residences were, by taxes on Imperial trade. This new and very opulent palace was surrounded by ruined stone walls. Great gaps appeared at frequent intervals to mark places where the original battlements had been heavily bombarded over the ages.

Argos, the most frenetic of the two beagles, insisted on leading us to a particular spot near the grassy ditch, fifty yards down from the drawbridge. Scuffed earth on the sides of the old moat marked the trail of our dragon as it had made its way in and out of the residence's grounds which lay on the other side of the ruins.

The gloom of the previous night had lifted. The sky above was cloudless and sprinkled with stars. A full moon provided light. "Physical evidence, and a canine's keen nose, point the way," the professor remarked as we clambered down one side of the ditch and up the other, then through the gap in the wall.

Argos and Ben pulled tightly on their leashes, panting with zeal over their undertaking. Inside the wall, an expansive courtyard led up to the mansion proper. A single gaslight shone in a window, otherwise Ethamside Palace was bathed in darkness.

An odd smell percolated in the air. Londinium was full of odd smells, but this one was particularly putrid and unusually out of place even though the grounds adjoined the River Etham, a waterway that was always a polluted mess. The odour had a sharpness that bit the back of the throat, a completely distinctive trait very unlike the sulfurous pall given off by sewer gas or the rancid stench of dead fish, but just as repelling. It was hard to place exactly what kind of fume would produce this effect.

Three stories tall, made of dark red brick, Ethamside Palace loomed above us in the glow of the moonlight. A white-columned portico extended over the entrance where a circular drive allowed steam carriages to drop off their passengers under cover from the elements. In the middle of the courtyard, a fountain, shaped like a giant cake plate, sat atop a circular pond. Water dribbled lazily over its sides, the moonlight casting a silver sheen on its surface.

Suddenly, through the trees, a bright beam of light shone up the road that led from the gatehouse. The *chug-chug* of pistons sent us and the dogs hiding behind one of the large topiaries at the far end of the courtyard. A steam-Clarence, by its size and the unique style of its engine pipes the same one as the night before, trundled across the drawbridge, its heavy wheels clunking over the planks. We held the beagles' muzzles to stop them yelping. The carriage's headlamps swept across the mansion's façade as the vehicle turned into the courtyard and ground to a halt under the front portico. Its headlights went out.

The driver, a man in a waistcoat wearing a coachman's hat, dropped out of the front cab of the steam-Clarence, lit a hand lantern, and withdrew foot plates from under the passenger compartment. The vehicle's side door opened. Another man stepped down, dressed in a doctor's black frockcoat and top hat, walking stick in hand. He assisted a red-haired woman from the carriage, her florinda jacket and crinoline petticoat rather unkempt and undistinguished, a muddy brown in colour. The front of her dress was low-cut, exposing an ample bosom, her appearance not untypical of a lady-of-the-night.

The coachman opened the luggage compartment at the rear of the steam-Clarence and retrieved the double-barreled pistol that had fired on us in the street. He placed it in a holster on his belt. Next came two empty cloth sacks and a large suitcase. By the ease at which he handled it, the case must have been empty as well. A small leather bag emerged, this one quite heavy, evidenced by the strain the man bore to lift it. The bag clanged when dropped on the ground. Lastly, the coachman distributed gas masks, the kind of breathing apparatus sewer workers wear.

"If that pipe's still spewing, this may be our last time here," the coachman said as he handed the others a sack and a mask. His accent was gruff; his language twanged with the lilt of someone from the East End of Londinium. "So look sharp, Julie. And be picky with your takings."

"Don't worry," the woman replied, her tongue equally coarse. "Haven't finished in m'lady's quarters yet. By the glitter of the last lot, I'm sure we'll be well sorted."

The man in the doctor's frockcoat picked a handful of tools out of the small bag. "These'll do the business. Shouldn't take this dodger long to crack into the lock-box. Easy bread and honey, I reckon, eh? Cor, can't wait to see what's inside."

"Right then, you lot. Off we go," the coachman replied, wagging the gun in the air. "Me trusty Bess here will keep the monster at bay. I'll have a butcher's in the dining room and scoff the silver. Get back here lickety-split and the job's done." The coachman picked up the empty suitcase and led the way into the mansion, its front entrance clearly unlocked.

"A crime's afoot," the professor said as we rose from hiding behind the bushes. "Some clever Dick has impersonated Lord Billingsworth's son, and with his accomplices, has grand larceny on his mind."

"But where's the real Baronet Billingsworth? And why the masks?"

"We're about to find out. But not through the front. That invites an egregious conflict. We must pursue entry from the back of the building."

I had brought my petronel, a micro-steam-driven weapon with a kick like a mule, ostensibly to defend ourselves against the 'dragon' but ready to be put in service against rogues should the need arise. We had also brought with us two flare guns of regulation calibre, the kind used to hail a patrol ship in an emergency. "Should we alert the Imperial Police?" I asked.

"In due course. This mystery needs keen observation first. The main gate would not stop a rampaging armoured steam carriage from busting through. We must know more of who they are, in the event of their escape."

Lights had been lit inside the palace, partly illuminating the courtyard. We slunk through the topiaries, mindful of being seen, following a walkway through an arbor into the back gardens. We skirted servants' quarters and several storerooms, then what may have been the entrance to the kitchen. We entered a large expanse of open lawn and came upon a strange addition to the rear of Ethamside Palace.

The main part of this bizarre extension appeared rather industrial—a two-storey concrete block like a windowless River Etham pumping station. A row of large rusty pipes came out of the ground and poked into the side of this monolithic building. Joining this concrete blockhouse to the palace was a one-storey building with red brick walls, a gabled glass roof, and several tall chimneys. Although this smaller part of the extension had ample windows, the rooms inside were dark.

"What do you make of this, professor?"

"I wager the smaller of the two buildings is a laboratory of some sort. I've seen a similar design before in the Scientific Quarter. But the larger one? I can't fathom its purpose."

Argos and Ben growled, straining on their leashes, anxious to run free. The putrid smell had returned with a vengeance.

"Release the dogs," the professor ordered. "Follow them."

The beagles ran across the lawn straight towards a door on the laboratory's side that made an exit into a small courtyard. They barked and paced along the bottom of the door, sniffing and scratching, their claws scraping at the door's wood.

Professor Carr checked the knob. "The door isn't locked. Cover my entry."

I positioned to one side and tripped the loading catch on my petronel. A cartridge slid into the firing chamber. "Ready."

The professor turned the knob and the door swung outwards. A cloud of noxious fumes burst forth, forcing us back. We gagged as we struggled for clean air to breathe, running backwards on our heels a good twenty yards before collapsing on the grass. The two beagles arrived beside us, yelping.

"By all that is holy, professor, what in God's name is that?"

"I don't know. But if a door has been opened that leads into the interior of the palace, the house must be full of that gas. No wonder the blaggards brought masks."

The billowing plume, tainted with the most outrageous stench, climbed into the moonlit night sky. A sizzling sound emanated from inside the laboratory, a faint persistent hiss.

"A pipe must be leaking. How long it's been like that is anyone's guess," Carr remarked. "The smell is not the kind of gas that lights our lamps. If it were, and it met with a candle or spark, there would have been an explosion. Those pipes go underground. Perhaps storage tanks have been buried. But containing what chemical?"

The cloud's intensity dissipated as the opened laboratory door released the trapped volume of nauseous vapours high into the atmosphere. Argos ventured back to the door and barked. I placed a kerchief over my nose and went to retrieve him. As I did, I spotted the body of a man inside, near the exit, one arm extended, his abdomen twisted, as if the man had taken a desperate lunge towards the door.

"Professor, come quick."

The deceased wore a white laboratory coat, ripped and stained with blood. His face was ashen and his arm scarred with deep cuts. Rigor mortis had frozen the agony of his death throe—his mouth held open, gaping; his eyes bulging. As we looked closer, the lower half of one leg was missing.

"I hear whispers from the grave," Professor Carr said as he peered inside. "This is the true Baronet, Dr. Arthur Billingsworth, confirming the other as his imposter. Billingsworth must have tried to escape the fumes and was overcome by suffocation. And here, inside…the source of his misadventure. I see what's been leaking."

Professor Carr stepped gingerly around the body, his boots crunching over the broken glass of shattered test tubes and beakers. Equipment on either side of the body had been knocked over and the origin of the hissing—a pipe that ran overhead—was cracked open and bent in a vee-shape as if pulled down from the ceiling. Only someone seven feet tall could have reached up to do this, and that someone…or something…had exceptional strength.

"Don't be foolhardy, professor."

"If the gas was meant to poison us," he coughed. "It would have done so when we first opened the door. The vapour appears benign in its own right. Disgusting, yes. But asphyxiation appears to be the only danger. If Billingsworth had smashed a window, he might have survived."

The hissing pipe drooped down near a window. Kerchief pressed to his face, the professor lifted the sash, yanked on the pipe until the bracket holding it to the ceiling gave way, and pushed the broken end that was spewing gas outside.

"He never had a chance. By the character of his injuries, something got to him first."

The opened door and window ventilated the space, giving us the chance to see in the moonlit shadows the nature of the laboratory built behind Ethamside Palace. Large lamps like inverted bowls hung from the ceiling over a row of surgical tables whose edges dripped with leather straps.

"What manner of laboratory is this?" I asked.

"One of malevolent intent," came the reply. "Experimentation of the most peculiar kind."

The laboratory was a shambles. Papers and journals had been tipped on the floor. Desks and tables turned over. On the lab's opposite side, a wide set of solid doors had been broken open. Claw marks ran in jagged diagonals across the paint.

A loud noise, like splintering wood, echoed through the high ceiling. It originated from the direction of the opened doors, the gateway from the lab into the main house.

A woman screamed, a blood curdling sound of shear dread.

The gas had confused the beagles, its effects masking the trail they'd been following. They circled our legs aimlessly, whimpering.

"Leave them," the professor ordered. "They've done their job. Quickly, this way—"

We ran through the chaos and debris. The doors opened into a library, perhaps one of the biggest I'd seen in private hands. It spanned the full width of the adjoining laboratory, bookshelves reaching the ceiling. Leather sofas and armchairs were arranged like the interior of a gentleman's club. Gas vapours hung in the air, trapped under the library's ceiling in a murky brown fog.

We raced across the library, through glass French doors that had been similarly clawed open, and arrived in a well-lit two-storey reception hall. The banister of its grand staircase had been broken halfway down. Thick wooden spindles littered the floor. Paintings had been dislodged, tables upset, and the vases on them smashed. The woman in the brown petticoat, wearing her gas mask, lay sprawled on the floor, waving the jagged end of a broken spindle in front of her, her legs pedaling backward but making up no ground.

Out of the shadows emerged the beast, our first real view of the silhouetted terror we'd chased in the gloom the night before. Five foot tall as it hunched on all fours, its head was snakelike, smooth and featureless. A loose flap of wrinkled skin extended under its chin. The colour of its leathery body ranged from a grey-green to an ocean blue, with a line of black speckles running down its back. On its sides, below its shoulders, a pair of small wings hung stiffly as the creature moved, its body and tail swinging from side to side as it crept forward. Thick patches of scarred, calloused skin, almost barnacle-like in appearance, joined the wings to the body. These wings lacked any of the creature's colourings, as if these appendages were foreign to the beast's true nature.

The 'dragon' hissed and slunk menacingly towards the woman, its mouth baring teeth as keen as a sawmill's blades, its talons like those of a bird of prey. The woman screamed again as it drew closer, its razor-like claws inches from her foot. She swatted its snout with the spindle. The creature's head leaned back then it resumed its predatory advance.

I raised my loaded petronel. "Professor, I fear I must shoot. But the creature will be lost."

"Do what you must. With haste!"

I fired, a volley of steam-driven rage. The petronel's cartridge blasted clear through the creature's chest and out the other side. Blood, flesh and shrapnel sprayed on the wall behind it. The 'dragon' reared up as it was struck, then fell to the floor with a heavy thud. A long pink tongue slithered out of its mouth as a last rush of air escaped its lungs.

"Julie!' someone yelled from the opposite side of the reception hall. The man in the doctor's frockcoat rushed over. His other accomplice followed close behind—the coachman, double-barreled pistol in hand, walking with a swagger, lugging a suitcase heavy with booty.

"Stand fast and surrender!" I commanded, ratcheting another shell into my petronel's chamber. I pointed the barrel at the coachman as he raised his pistol.

He sneered and cocked the trigger. I knew that look and I didn't hesitate.

My shell found its mark. Its impact on my opponent forced his pistol hand upwards as he fired, his bullets lost in the ceiling. The coachman dropped like a felled forest timber, flat on his back.

Life in the slums had taught me villains with pistols rarely stop to debate their fate. Shoot first and ask questions later has always been the motto of the street. I cocked the petronel again and addressed the other two, ready to do the same again. "Stay where you are. It's over."

The faux-doctor grabbed a dagger from inside his coat, lifted the woman to her feet, and put the knife to her throat. He backed away, the woman in front of him, his other arm gripped tightly around her waist. "I know we'll both hang. So do your worst. But you'll have to kill her first."

"No honour among thieves?" I replied.

"Julie here knows the score. Don't ya, darlin'?"

The man staggered back with his captive. As he reached for the sack of booty he'd dropped, his arm slid down the woman's waist. As it did, she bit the wrist that held the knife, loosening his grip. In one swift movement—as if she'd had to do this once or twice before—she snatched the weapon, twisted free, then plunged the dagger into his chest.

"Sure, I knows the score. I'll take my chances with a judge, thank you very much," she said.

Dr. Billingsworth's imposter slumped to the floor, blood gurgling up his throat and down his chin, a most astonished look on his face.

"An honour to have made your acquaintance, you filthy pimp," she added, as she wiped the bloody knife clean on the man's frockcoat and spat on his corpse. The deed done, she turned towards us. "What a business, eh? We would have got away with all this, if it weren't for that monster." She walked over to the lifeless beast. "Who's the real villain here, anyway? To create such a thing as *this*?"

"You know how this happened, don't you?" Professor Carr surmised.

"Doc Billingsworth's doing," she replied. "He was a regular of mine. Not bad in the sack neither, and he paid well. One night, he insisted I stay over. Said the place was empty and he wanted the company. He'd sent the staff away as he'd 'work' to do. Surgery? On defenseless animals? Stitchin' body parts from one to other, like they were some sort of patchwork quilt? A bat's wings on this big lizard? I mean, cor blimey, what kind of madness was that?"

She plucked one of the wings on the dead 'dragon', trying to stretch it out. It wouldn't flex, stiff as a board. "Didn't work, did it? Anyway, I'd had too much gin in me. Couldn't handle any more of his nonsense so I went to bed. What a fright I found in the morning. The stench from the gas. And him dead as a doorknob, half eaten. And this monster he cobbled together, lurking in the garden for his next meal. Lucky it didn't catch sight of me."

She poked the dead 'dragon' with the dagger. "Dead enough, thank goodness. Yeah, the doc told me everythin' he was up to. *He* was the real monster. Most of these lords are, when they get their pants off. So he got what was coming. And then—" She pointed to her two dead accomplices. "We took what we could, when we could. Struck while the iron was hot."

"You stole his identity papers, his clothes, and His Lordship's steam-Clarence, didn't you?"

"Too right, mister." She touched a finger to her temple. "Got brains, I do. Not like the other girls. The guards don't check papers on the way out. Only on the way in. Silly nits. And I can drive anything with a steam pipe inside it. Can do all sorts if I have to. You've seen that. The guards knew me, so pretending we was the doc and his tart wasn't hard when we came back. I said to Jimmy here, one visit was enough. The plunder that first night was a real cracker. Would have set us well on, without a second trip, let alone a third. But these two greedy louts weren't havin' it. Now look at 'em."

Professor Carr took the petronel from my hand. "Jeremiah, go outside and send up a flare. I think it's time."

"Right you are, sir."

"And I'd get someone from the Royal Zoo to come clean up the Darwin Room, if I were you," she said. "Before more of 'em take exception—like this one did—and scarper."

"The Darwin Room?" I inquired.

"That's what the doc called it. That big stone warehouse out back. Dark, stinky place. Unfit for man nor beast. That's where the rest of 'em are kept. Cooking in his evolutionary soup, or whatever it was. What nonsense he kept spoutin'. Even a poorly schooled slut like me knew he was bakin' a madman's cake, even if he didn't."

"Rest of them?"

"The other critters. God knows what you'll find in there. But the Devil does. From what he showed me—and I couldn't stomach more than a peek—it's enough to send a sinner back to church on Sunday."

She threw the dagger on the floor. "Here, then. I don't feel like fightin' no more. So what's to become of me? A hangman's noose? For what? Tryin' to earn a livin'? That's all it was. What about the slimy toffs that live in places like this, eh? Doin' evil like *this*? They're plunderers too. Just a different sort. They say it's all legal what they do, like we don't know any better. But to us, it's just pimpin' of another kind."

Professor Carr stroked his mustache and raised an eyebrow. "I'm tempted to let Madame Justice, blind as she always must be, take stock of your crimes, ma'am. But I'm equally tempted to say you're a victim of a much more heinous crime—a most shocking condemnation of the scientific community—one the Imperial State Police perhaps might bury in total obscurity, should enough political pressure weigh in. News of this travesty might fan the flames of anarchy. Flames that would be hard to put out."

"What you suggestin', m'lord?" she asked.

"You're a witness to an incredible act of scientific evil. Which makes you a valuable insurance policy against a potential cover-up of the truth. I can offer temporary freedom—a safe haven in hiding at my Institute—in exchange for your future testimony. You'll be *my* prisoner, not the beadle's. More comfortable, I promise. And better food. When the time is right, and your evidence is given, I'll petition the Grand Marshal for leniency. If he's as much a friend of mine as he says he is, then transportation to the colonies might be your due. A new life. Perhaps a better one. Certainly better than the alternative offered by the gallows."

"You'd do that for *me*? How peculiar."

"Peculiar," Professor Carr said, "is what I do."

SOUL RIPPER

PART I

I could not help but return her stare—a haunting, forlorn gaze of dead eyes and sallow cheeks. Young and otherwise quite pretty, she looked tired and distraught; her pale complexion hidden by a hint of blush stroked gently across her cheeks, brightening an otherwise sad countenance.

She'd entered the aero-tram at my station, Hebbingdon Square; a petit soul, green eyes, brown hair with dangling curls, wearing a green velvet jacket with matching lace-trimmed bonnet. She carried a fur muff to warm her hands against the December chill. I'd watched her run to catch the tram—her emerald jacket a spot of colour in a dull-dressed crowd—and then search the carriage as if specifically to find me, eventually taking a seat across from mine.

How can I be that special to draw such a woman into my presence? I consider myself quite ordinary, neither handsome nor ugly. Perhaps my suspicions were entirely conceited. Perhaps I was reading far too much into how our fates had crossed paths and her inclinations had nothing to do with me at all. But still, of all the many people I encounter in my daily travels, her face and its piercing stare bewitched me from the very start.

Our eyes met each time I raised my head. I tried to ignore her but to no avail. There was a sorrow in the way her eyebrows arched and a subtle rage in the way the creases tightened around her eyes. It was as if her mind was re-enacting a Greek tragedy between each stop on the Dentwich Line. I felt her presence throughout the whole journey, a companion who spoke no words but said so much. It was that sadness and angst that drew my gaze to her. But I knew not what purpose, if any, drew her gaze to mine.

Relief came when the aero-tram shuddered, grinding to a stop at Barnaby Circus. Its sudden lurch rocked the passengers, stirring them out of their faux sleep. With a hiss of steam, the doors released their captive grip on the carriage's occupants and they flung themselves upon the world like snorting horses at the start of a steeplechase.

I rose from my seat and stepped out onto the landing platform, a steamy iron plinth heaving with people, bumping and jostling for no particular advantage. Newspaper vendors harangued the passers-by as they left the station—mostly solicitors, bankers, and their puppy-like assistants, none of whom seemed particularly fazed by the newspaper sellers' barked announcements of the latest political scandal in the capital, or of some distant military defeat in some forgotten corner of the Empire.

On the street, a plethora of women with frazzled hair and soiled pinafores pleaded their case to exchange a copper for a single red rose or white boutonnière, their presence ignored in the rush, their voices lost in the swirl of a hurried crowd whose thoughts were consumed more by the golden coins of their remits than the fancy of romance. Only a single pie-seller on the street corner felt any comfort. Her tray was soon emptied as the newest throng passed.

As I exited the station, the statue of Air Cavalry General Horatio Barnaby was hard to avoid, perched on his steam-dart high atop a column in the centre of Barnaby Circus as if directing the traffic of an army of ants. As I fought my way through the crowd, the distinct emerald jacket of the woman on the aero-tram appeared from time to time as I glanced behind me. Despite many turns down the maze of streets that branched out from General Barnaby's statue, she remained in my footsteps, even stopping when I did, so as not to overtake me.

Was she following me?

My journey had a singular purpose: an appointment at Wainthorpe's Apothecarial Emporium in Windsholme Mews, a narrow cobbled alley little changed since 1666, its tightly squeezed buildings of black-stained oak beams and soot-washed plaster spared incineration during the Great Fire of that year. The structures leaned against each other like top-hatted old codgers at a racetrack, crushed at the shoulders as they strained to see which filly had pipped the post. The alley was wholly unfit for either horse or steam carriage, its jumbled paving stones as unruly under foot as the shoppe fronts were misshapen with age. Nevertheless, Windsholme Mews was a pedestrian paradise of quirky shoppes, each proudly handed down within the same family of merchants whose fortunes over many centuries had risen only high enough to maintain the rent. Regardless, their love of the city and their own place in the hierarchy of its trading heritage had transcended any thoughts of abandoning their craft. For it was along Windsholme Mews that one could find merchandise and *objets d'art* that one could not find anywhere else in Her Majesty's Britannia. In fact, it was said that if one couldn't find what one coveted most, among the cobbles and shoppes of Windsholme Mews, it couldn't be found anywhere in the whole world.

Wainthorpe's Emporium was no ordinary apothecary and hence it warranted my journey of some distance. I was on a mission to procure a remedy for a malady that had afflicted me since my childhood, roaming the streets of Pritchard's Green. My affliction was called St. Agatha's worm. Why it was called that name I haven't the foggiest idea but it was a common intestinal parasite acquired by anyone growing up amongst the poorest citizens of the capital. The presence of these despicable creatures in the bowels yielded annual bouts of uncomfortable cramps as they ended their lifecycle in a final flourish of unrestrained procreation intended to ensure the survival of their nefarious species. There was no known cure; no known way to exorcise the beasts once they installed themselves in the gut. One had to just grin and bear the consequences until one's inner sanctum gained the upper hand. However, to those of significantly higher means, temporary remedies were available. Since coming into the employ of Professor Atticus Carr, my social status had been elevated to a level of good fortune. I possessed a purse that could accommodate the procurement of medicines as well as a higher quality of pies and peas. As such, I considered my annual pilgrimage to Wainthorpe's more as a privilege of passage from the lower classes than an inconvenience.

I was surprised when I entered to see the shopkeeper tending the counter. I was accustomed to being greeted by old Mr. Wainthorpe, the apothecary who seemed to transcend time. He'd been the custodian since time immemorial, perhaps even the decade before. How sad it was to find that the establishment's founder had passed. The man serving me was young, his son, Alexander Wainthorpe, a recent graduate in the Pharmaceutical Arts at the Londinium School of Medicine. He'd taken up the position on the passage of his father. The young man, tall and athletic looking with silky brown hair, had a bouncy glow about him, a projection of enthusiasm and gaiety that was often the demeanor of someone who'd stepped into good fortune immediately upon exiting their studies without need of an apprenticeship. His manner was courteous and professional, beyond his years. His father would have been proud.

Alexander filled my prescription as I watched, carefully measuring the tinctures of ingredients on an impossibly precise set of scales; compounds with Latin names dispensed from large bottles with gilt-framed labels that crammed the apothecary's shelves. He knew of Professor Carr—who didn't?—and also knew of my association with him, facts no doubt passed on from father to son. His curiosity expanded into quite a conversation, my presence in the shoppe being his only customer at the time. He inquired of the professor's most recent case, the haunting of Harandon Hall in Cymrushire, a tale that had mesmerized the city once its peculiar details had dribbled into the tabloid press. Our dialogue was cut short by the entry of an elderly gentleman clearly suffering from gout. I bid my good-days and left the apothecary well satisfied, a small parcel with two bottles of powerfully concocted worm powder carefully tucked in my jacket's pocket.

I strolled back up the Mews towards the station, lingering in front of the Watchmakers' Pavilion, an establishment housing several practitioners from the Timekeeping Guild, its window filled not just with the finest of timepieces but also clock-driven automatons, measurement instruments and navigational aids. My fascination planted me on the spot for several minutes, mesmerized by the intricate display of the latest clockwork technology.

I felt a gentle tug on my coat and turned to see who had been so bold. To my utter amazement, it was the young woman I'd traveled with on the aero-tram, her sad face framed by her emerald green bonnet, both unmistakable markers of her identity.

"Kind sir," she said, mewing like a kitten. "Please. A moment of your time."

Intrigued by her mysterious pursuit, I pointed to the chronometers in the window. "You have caught me at exactly the time when time itself has my attention. So at this moment, my time is yours. How can I be of service?"

Her chin dipped, her eyes momentarily hidden by the flutter of soft lashes. I saw a tear form, then trickle down her cheek. "It is on behalf of my sister that I seek your help. It is the relief of her despair that will satiate the hunger of not just my heart, but those of many others who love her, if she is returned to us. You see, she has disappeared, and is presumed lost forever. But I know that is not true."

"This seems a matter for the Imperial Police. Should not those resources be summoned to your cause?"

"Yes, they have been. And yet there is no progress. In fact, after many months, the police have abandoned the case. They said there are many causes for a person's disappearance, with some reasons quite innocent, and since their inquiries had produced nothing of substance, I should employ the services of a private investigator to find her. They referred me to a Mr. Sherlock Holmes. But even he could not help. After explaining my case, he said his services would have to wait. More pressing matters were on his plate. After reviewing the circumstances, he advised me to contact Professor Atticus Carr. You are his assistant, Jeremiah Boone, are you not?"

"How did you recognize me?"

"I followed you from Professor Carr's Institute of Peculiarities. The professor wasn't in. The porter pointed you out as someone I should engage with and gave me your card. But you walk too quickly for me. And the matter at hand was too delicate to discuss in public on the aero-tram."

"Quite extraordinary, Miss—?"

"Unsworth. Hannah Unsworth. My missing sister is Claire Unsworth."

"Unsworth? As in the Unsworth Perpetual Loom?"

"The same. My father's invention. There will be a substantial reward for the discovery of my sister's whereabouts."

"But why Professor Carr? His talents are best applied to incidents of the peculiar. This matter seems to require more conventional means of investigation."

"Claire is my twin. We have felt each other's feelings since birth. I have always known what she was thinking and she has always known my inner thoughts as well. It is an eternal bond we've shared throughout our lives. Ever since her inexplicable disappearance she has come to me. Not in the physical sense or else our discussion today would be moot. But in the spiritual sense. Is this kind of manifestation not in the purvey of Professor Carr's talents?"

"Yes, indeed it is. But regrettably, his aethereal communications are most often with those whose existence has passed on to a life beyond our own."

The young lady stiffened. Her face hardened. "Claire is alive! I know it. I feel it. It is indisputable to me. Her spirit wanders but her body rests. I know how strange that might sound. It is indeed most peculiar. Have you ever heard of such a thing?"

"I have not. But the peculiar has undiscovered dimensions waiting for us to explore. Don't look so down-hearted. Can you accompany me today upon my return to the Institute?"

"Of course. Anything."

"Then let's meet someone who I'm convinced will know exactly the situation you speak of."

PART II

Professor Atticus Carr bent forward and held the magnifying glass close to his eye. Inside the large rectangular terrarium was a small bush with spindly branches and hardly any leaves. The bush was a specimen from the Sultanate of the Harisian Sands, a desert sage.

Our footsteps did not deter the professor from his task. "The Harisian sand spider," he said, alerted to our presence but not looking our way. "It doesn't weave a web. Instead, it lurks in a shallow channel dug beneath the sage's roots. The spider's body displays the same tone and texture as the sage's trunk, a means of perfect camouflage as it runs up to catch its prey. Nature's master of illusion, surviving by subterfuge in one of the world's most inhospitable climes. If one is to be a master of illusion, one must study those that already are."

"I hope we're not intruding," Miss Unsworth said.

Professor Carr lowered the magnifying glass and smiled at the young lady in the green jacket. "Of course not. It's about your sister, isn't it?"

Miss Unsworth's jaw dropped. "How did you know?"

"I'm reading your aura. Sadness. Despair. A loss. But not the loss of a male relation or acquaintance. It's a feminine vapor I see. And the loss of someone of maturity, not a child. Your mother perhaps? If your mother had passed, she would speak to me from beyond. But I hear no one. Besides, the maternal bond is quite pronounced in aura and what I see dancing in the aether around you is not that. To be sure, it is much deeper than mere friendship. This attachment stirs your blood with a kindred sorrow. So where does this leave us? This is not about your mother, and since I sense no aethereal presence with us at all, I'm making a bold assumption this matter has something to do with a living sister. Perhaps a lucky guess?"

"My God." Miss Unsworth swayed on unsteady feet. "Dear Lord, thank you. I've finally come to the right place." Her hand clutched the back of a chair. Her legs wobbled.

I helped Miss Unsworth into the seat. "I fear the young lady is exhausted in both body and spirit, professor."

I poured her a glass of water. Once refreshed, Miss Unsworth recounted to Professor Carr the extent of her fruitless attempts using official channels to ascertain her sister's whereabouts. Then her story took a decidedly strange turn, recounting incidents she'd previously not spoken to me about, events that had transpired in the weeks after the Imperial Police abandoned their assistance.

"One day—a clear bright day—I felt it would be good to take my mind off things by tending my parent's garden. It's normally a chore for our groundskeeper but I thought the activity and sunshine would brighten my spirits. I was pruning some roses—my sister's favorite variety, a deep crimson in colour—when I looked up and saw Claire standing on the other side of the bush. As you can imagine, my heart was instantly filled with joy. She's come home! I dropped the shears. My mind could only think of how to escape the thorny rosebush between us so I could reach over and give her a hug. In my fit of excitement, with my eyes darting around the garden bed to see a way around the roses, I diverted my gaze for just a split second and when I looked back in her direction, she was gone. I was despondent. But then, my heart lifted again. I heard her voice. Quite clearly. Quite distinctly. She called me by my pet name, Hannie."

Miss Unsworth retrieved a kerchief from her purse. "I couldn't see her but I could hear her. Hannie, she said. I don't have much time. I can feel *it* dragging me back. Help me. I'm trapped. Help me." Miss Unsworth sniffled. "Then, Claire's voice went silent."

She reached over the desk and clutched Professor Carr's hand. "She sounded so frightened. I called out to her. I ran around the garden like a crazed person. My parents heard me. My mind could not settle. They had to send for the doctor to give me some calming waters. I slept for nearly the entirety of the next day."

"Did this happen again?" he asked.

Miss Unsworth took a deep breath. "Twice more I saw and heard her, both times in the same manner and with the same disappointing result. Once in town, right in the middle of shopping with my mother in a very crowded department store. This time Claire was behind the counter, standing next to someone serving us. She spoke virtually the same words, pleading for help, something I couldn't offer. Several days later, the same thing occurred at an aero-tram station. You may think I'm crazy. My parents do and it frightens me. When I sleep, I dream of a dark room with stone walls and a strange machine with flashing lights. This vision is unbelievably realistic. I feel I'm there with her. I can feel the dampness around us and the smell of the musty air, like the stink of an old root cellar. I have a great-aunt who's in an asylum due to the dementia of her age and my dream reminds me so much of the place where she's housed, a grim place, like a prison cell, with no hope. One could hardly call it a home. Just cold machines, and even colder attendants. Could Leedham Hospital for the Insane be the kind of place where Claire has been taken?"

"It's possible. But the very fact she's your twin explains much to me," Professor Carr said, in an assuring tone. "And because your sister's spirit is not present with us right now indicates she has not passed. The deceased will always reach out to comfort those they have left behind. Her wandering in the aether has another cause. Based on your account, I feel your inclinations are correct. Your sister is very much alive."

"If she's not a ghost, then what is the spectre I see?"

"Her soul has left her body and for a brief time has been allowed to drift free. You said she felt something dragging her back? Dragging her back to *where*? I would say, back to her body, wherever that is. That can be the only conclusion to be reached."

"Then these are not the hallucinations of one suffering mania? I'm not crazy?"

"Not in the least. Your sister's body has been imprisoned in some manner, as yet unknown, and her spirit has become detached from it. Because you're her twin, it's likely you're the only person in the whole world she can communicate with when this happens."

Miss Unsworth's eyes grew wide. Her mouth opened but no sound came out.

"How is this possible if Claire Unsworth is still alive?" I asked on her behalf.

"This phenomenon is more common than you think, Jeremiah, but it is rarely spoken of. Why thus? As in so many cases of the peculiar, without overwhelming scientific proof, the scientific establishment, including doctors of medicine, disavow its possibility. Claire Unsworth has become a 'traveler'. And just like physical travelers whose shoes leave footprints in the soil, we must follow in the footsteps of someone who has traveled this way before. That is our next port of call. Are you both ready?"

PART III

The aero-cab lifted off from the Institute's roof. We left the banks of the River Etham, the pulsing vein of commerce that bisected the city, and turned on a heading to the north of the sprawling metropolis. After an hour, the aero-cab soared over a district called The Barrens, many miles beyond Londinium's central core. Here, rancid air swirled as if alive; a plumed beast smeared brown by puffing chimneys and billowing grit; the distant city's Imperial chancelleries and famed cathedrals fading into shadowy silhouettes through the lens of an industrial mist.

I'm an uncomfortable passenger even on the most placid forms of transport. Professor Carr on the other hand could sleep through a hurricane. His mind tunes to a frequency few others can, his psychic abilities unquestioned. Professor Carr slumps into a nearly catatonic state when he travels. Where he goes in his mind, he rarely reveals. Within minutes, the professor appeared as a cat on a chair often does, sleeping with eyes part open.

Miss Unsworth shared my discomfort with the journey and I sought conversation to distract my mind and my stomach from the unpredictable jostling of the aero-cab.

"If I have siblings," I said. "I know nothing of who they are or what travails consume their lives. I'm an orphan you see. At the age of twelve, I was acquired from the charity that took me in, to work as an errand boy at the Theatre Macabre, Professor Carr's entertainment establishment. But like you, Miss Unsworth—although not entirely for the same reason that brought you into the Institute—I often have feelings that someone in a crowd is someone I'm deeply attached to, through my blood. A brother or sister perhaps. An aunt, uncle or cousin. Even once, I felt strongly that my father was within a stone's throw of where I stood. Professor Carr believes I may be connecting with spirit and encourages me to train my mind to expand that possibility."

"Then you share the torment I feel. I saw that in your eyes when we were on the tram. Your face exudes a quiet confidence. But your eyes do not. Why is that?"

"Professor Carr elevated me from a potential station in life that would have put me even below the level of a street vendor. I comport myself the way my current position as his assistant requires me to do, professional in all regards, whether I'm with him or not. But I surmise, deep inside my soul, I'm still the street urchin who begged for scraps and foraged with rats. My greatest fear is that my good fortune could be taken away at a moment's notice, in much the same way as it arrived unannounced and plucked me off the streets. It's a wariness, a vigilance; a prudent guardedness that warns me that perhaps an unkind word, a deceitful action, a lapse of moral standing, might throw me back on the streets at any moment."

"I see. I can't possibly understand what that feels like," she replied, her voice apologetic.

I've heard that voice many times before, coming from those of born gentry. It's a sound that binds regret with resignation as if the plight of others is a distant predicament, as if those in poverty are marooned on a deserted island beyond reach.

I turned the conversation to find a happier subject. We settled on gardening, on roses in particular, as this was a subject I knew nothing about, having grown up with only rare instances when green grass touched the soles of my feet. It was a discussion where my curiosity was genuine and her responses came with great sweetness and fluidity, in sharp contrast with the journey. For what seemed like forever, our aero-cab chugged with its own breathless abandon through the muggy atmosphere, bobbing up and down in shafts of rising heat from the forges and ironworks below us, places where muscled men toiled inside raging infernos under girders thick with rust and oil.

My conversation with Miss Unsworth stopped suddenly as the aero-cab passed through a particularly noxious cloud. Gagging from a whiff of its sulfurous fumes, she clutched a perfumed handkerchief to her face, eschewing the mask that I offered, a breathing apparatus mandated in cabs by law but whose sometimes soiled and unhygienic condition often made them more dangerous to wear than to suffer without their use.

At the edge of The Barrens—as if to buffer Mankind's might from Mother Nature's comforting arms—lay ragged fields littered with shanties; an unincorporated scar on the landscape of civilization, a town more like a war-bombed encampment than a human habitat. We approached our destination, Gravemen's Hollow, where transients seeking a better life arrived from all corners of the realm to bear witness to the brutality of The Barren's factories and if they survived without injury, begrudgingly stayed on to procreate.

As the aero-cab descended, it bumped in a stiff wind, being the constant draught that sucked fresh air from the countryside into The Barrens' industrial furnaces. What claimed to be a green field, but was in fact a meadow of nettles, surrounded the public landing pad. The pad's cracked planks were stained by rot, an appearance that was not a good omen for a safe arrival. The cab's charapilot plunked the carriage down on delicately sprung stilts then maneuvered the vehicle's fluid-ballast so as not to put the aero-cab's full girth to bear on the deck and risk the landing pad's collapse. The jostling compartment brought Professor Carr out of his cataleptic state. The aero-cab, its weight still half aloft, wobbled like a plate of jelly, making egress a tricky climb down.

"Remember this, Jeremiah," the professor commented as I helped Miss Unsworth off the rotten decking to solid ground. "If the task is difficult, employ the best. Anything less invites failure. And failure can beget disaster. Choosing the right charapilot for a journey like this should not be left to chance. And pay well. Vote for experience, not thrift."

"What a hellish ride, professor." I said, scanning the horizon around us. Hovels with ragged moss-strewn thatch. Sheds with corrugated tin roofs. Rickety fences enclosing pigs and goats. "What could possibly have brought us out to this godforsaken place? If our aim was to seek counsel from a medium, surely there was someone more readily available in Londinium at a more suitable venue?"

"Good point. In most cases, as you know, I'm expeditious in my inquiries. But we have in this circumstance, a most peculiar mode of aethereal conveyance. Remember what I just said. If the task is difficult, employ the best. Anything less invites failure."

A cart and horse arrived to take us on the next leg of our journey. I helped Miss Unsworth into the back. We sat on simple plank seats that faced each other, the stench of dried manure under our feet. The farmer, our coachman, cracked a whip; the poor horse reared, straining its bridle; and the cart lurched forward on its way down a bumpy grass track towards what appeared to be the ruins of an old stone church.

"During séance, mediums leave their body," the professor noted, unfazed in his discourse by the banality of the local transport system. "In turn, their body is occupied by someone deceased, a spirit who uses the medium's voice to communicate with the living. Have you ever been to a séance, Miss Unsworth?"

"I must admit, I have not, professor. Although the tabloids provide quite graphic, and might I say, *imaginative* accounts of such events."

"Far from imagination, my dear. And soon, such wonders will be fully illustrated to you."

Her eyebrows raised and her mouth curled down as if tasting something sour.

"Fear not. I assure you, you will come to no harm."

Miss Unsworth frowned again, unconvinced. I felt the pain of her rejection.

Professor Carr noted her apprehension. "You might ask, what is the nature of the phenomenon we are about to investigate?" He gestured with his hands. "Well, just like this cart ride, it's a temporary transit, an aethereal portage—a gap between bodily life on the one hand, and spiritual death on the other. The yogis of Pajastan practice this skill, for it is a skill of the most accomplished minds. But where does the medium's soul go when this practice happens? Can it indeed control where it travels? Or is it merely at the whim of unknowable aethereal forces? All we do know is that when the séance ends, the spirit returns to reunite with its body and the medium's world becomes right again, as if nothing had happened."

The church and its overgrown graveyard loomed ahead. "As Jeremiah has so eloquently said," the professor continued, "why have we come to this *godforsaken* place, Miss Unsworth? One answer. We are here to seek counsel from the very best, lest we fail in our quest to reunite you with your sister."

"Then I shall suspend my skepticism and await further enlightenment on this subject."

Miss Unsworth retrieved her perfumed kerchief and pressed it to her nose.

***

Professor Carr had knocked on the heavy oak door of St. Dunstan's-in-the-Field several times without answer. We'd been waiting for a good ten minutes since his first knock.

Bored, Miss Unsworth wandered into the church grounds, strolling between the gravestones, her emerald green jacket drifting in and out between thickets of grey stone stumps.

"Perhaps we should find the rectory and inquire there?" I asked the professor.

"There is no rectory."

Confused, I could only say, "Then perhaps we are too early."

"Hardly, Jeremiah. Since there's no way to make an appointment, there's no possibility to be either early or late. She's here, inside."

"Who's here? The pastor of this church is a *she*?"

"Madame Jeanette, the current occupant. You may call her a pastor of sorts. But this building, such as it is, has not been a church for many centuries."

Carr swept his hand into the air as if to cast aside the cobwebs and ivy and conjure up the church's more ostentatious past. "Well before the Great Mechanization," he noted. "Gravemen's Hollow became a frequent stopping point for highwaymen that preyed on stagecoach traffic en route to the Wolds. The Church built St. Dunstan's with the hope that its pastors could rehabilitate these scoundrels' souls. It appears in this instance, the Devil won out. The church was abandoned in the 17th century and fell into ruin. The building has been reincarnated in many guises since—coaching inn, brothel, illegal gin distillery, and other quite notorious conversions of purpose."

"As always, you're well informed. Have you been here before?"

"Several times, each for a different reason, but leaving each time with a renewed wonder. This is the home of the special kind of medium we seek. And, as you will soon see, to her unusual charms. During our journey here, I meditated, contacting her through psychic means to establish an arrangement for our convenient arrival. We simply must wait our turn. She has other clients ahead of us. Her specialty works to no exact chronometer."

Miss Unsworth returned from her sojourn. "How strange. Most of these gravestones have just one name inscribed. A first name. Quite simple names. Tom, John, Uriah, Jacob."

"For many men, whose past they wanted to hide," the professor said, "that single name was the only one they were ever known by during their lives. Farmhands, peddlers, gravediggers, thieves. When the factories of The Barrens erupted from the Earth like brick volcanoes, men such as these turned away from the grind of daily subsistence and went to the furnaces to seek regular work. To them, work was work. To those interred here, hard work—honest or otherwise—held no morality and shed no shame. The leather purse that kept their pay coins warm, bore only a first name to declare their owner. These purses were often the only possession these men had left to identify them after death, the meager contents that jingled inside used to pay for a pauper's burial."

"This is a grim and foreboding place." Miss Unsworth shuddered, rubbing a shaking hand up and down her arm as her eyes darted around the graveyard. "I wish to leave. I wish I had never engaged you."

"Fear has its purpose, Miss Unsworth. It teaches us caution. It raises our inner strength. For at heart, we are primitives who will do anything to survive once confronted with our worst fears. Take solace in your fear. It is an attribute you will harness to your advantage in the hours ahead. You are stronger than you think. You will turn your fear into fortitude when the need arises."

"I dread that moment. But you have made it clear, dear sir, that I have no escape from this adventure. As you hold my fate in your hands, I urge you to provide for its safety."

The door into the dusty carcass of St. Dunstan's-in-the-Field opened with a loud creak.

A couple emerged, of middle age, both of them in rags with straggly, unkempt hair. The man held the woman by the shoulder; their faces pale, draped in sorrow, their eyes blank. They trudged out of the church, the woman weeping gently, her energy spent.

An old man, stiff wisps of grey hair protruding from the sides of an otherwise bald head, bade us entry. He was very short, almost childlike in stature, dressed from head to toe in black—a plain black jacket with no lapels, cut in the Oriental manner, closed by a single row of white pearlescent buttons; black pantaloons and black shoes; and strangely, wearing black gloves.

"Gregori," he said in a Russkan accent, placing a gloved hand to his chest. He pointed into the church. "This way, please."

A single window over the entry door let a beam of sunshine into the vestibule. It cast a spotlight on the baptismal font whose bowl was filled with rock crystals of yellow, blue and green. Jagged facets broke the light into the colours of the rainbow, spreading the spectrum onto the bare stone floor between the font and the sparse rows of old pews behind it. The interior of St. Dunstan's was dark and cold; the arches, where former stained glass windows once shone, now boarded up. Candles on tall stands flanked an altar, a rectangular table covered in a black cloth but devoid of altarpieces. Behind the altar, black velvet curtains hung across the width of the church to separate the congregation from an ante-chamber, the back room's presence indicated by the flicker of a candle creeping above the top of the curtains.

Miss Unsworth clutched her crucifix and pressed Jesus tightly to her lips. "Where have you brought me? This is a hall of Devil worship!"

To think we had persuaded such a demure creature as Miss Unsworth to attend such a place of ill-reputation seemed in hindsight a wholly unworthy and impolite act. However, Professor Carr was steadfast in his resolve to use whatever means necessary to morph the unknown into the known.

It was with this determination we allowed Miss Unsworth to step inside the ex-church's dismal walls, regardless of its history, and more importantly, wholly ignorant of the task that lay in her future, for in possession of either knowledge surely she would have fled.

I, on the other hand, with the benefit of many prior experiences as Professor Carr's assistant, approached the unknown with my uniquely distilled mixture of tepid courage and suppressed fear. "Hold onto your faith, Miss Unsworth," was my less than consoling reply.

"You will not find a more Christian woman than Madame Jeanette," the professor said, deflecting the church's obvious failings as a house of worship. "Yes, she forswears the gilded trappings of the Britannic Church, but she is not faithless. She ministers to those of poverty whose torments are often deepened by envy and greed. She wishes to cast off their spell of want, that earthly sin that traps their minds, and thus provide sanctuary for the simplicity of what is truly essential to their souls. This blackness around us is a blank canvas upon which an open-minded imagination can wield its colourful brush."

"That sounds more like an excuse than an apology," Miss Unsworth replied, her tone sharp. She drew a deep breath, her chin rose, her back stiffened. I felt her hand searching by my side and when it found my own—a quite surprising show of kinship—its grip had the strength Professor Carr had spoken of. "Lead on, professor. Let's get this over with," she said, her fingers entwined with mine.

We followed Gregori down the central aisle towards the altar. Once there, he turned, his hand indicating we should stop where we were. He disappeared behind the velvet curtains. A moment later, the curtains parted, skimming to the sides on rollers, the sound like marbles crossing a wooden floor.

What appeared before us, made both Miss Unsworth and I gasp.

A semi-circular table of the darkest oak invited as many as five people to sit on its curved side while what can only be described as a Tudor throne, a carved seat of considerable height, occupied the straight-edged opposite side of the table. If wood was the only material present, it would not have elicited such an immediate reaction. It was what was attached to the top of the table that took our breath away.

The visitors' seats had tall backs with plush, cushioned headrests. In front of each, bolted to the tabletop, was what could only be described as a copper manacle—a top and bottom band to bind both wrists. Clamped at the centre of each of these shackles, a copper rod extended outwards to a bright copper platen resting in front of the medium's throne. The ends of the rods were firmly clamped to the platen, joining the five sets of manacles to one central station, the whole apparatus resembling one half of a bicycle wheel's spokes, laying flat on the table. On top of the central platen were two vertical grips, about a foot tall, again made of copper; their purpose indicated by undulations in the metal where fingers could be curled around. Similar grips were used by charapilots to steer their aero-cabs.

The chamber was dimly lit, a single thick candle on a tall candlestick placed in one corner. Outlined in the gloom, below the candle stand, sat an array of objects on a small adjacent table—a brass holder with a smaller unlit candle, a jar of white powder, a large spoon, a brass Petri dish, and a rather oddly configured, very narrow, long glass dome. At the open end of the dome was a brass ring tipped with a rubber surround.

"Please be seated," Gregori announced, guiding Miss Unsworth to the seat directly opposite the throne.

She released her grip on my hand, her eyes fixed on the manacle, her mouth downturned as if in the presence of a dead fish.

"Place your hands in front of you on the table," Professor Carr instructed. "Close your eyes. Let your fear drain away."

Miss Unsworth did as instructed. Once her eyes were shut, Gregori closed the shackle over her delicate wrists in a single swift movement, so quick he overpowered her natural instinct to withdraw.

In turn, Professor Carr and I were shackled in a similar way. Gregori gently turned dials on the sides of the manacles until the copper met our skins, but not so tight as to hurt us. The inside surfaces of the manacle were velvety soft, worn smooth like old gold. Regardless, my brow grew clammy, my palms sweaty.

"Are you comfortable?" the professor asked.

Miss Unsworth replied, "As comfortable as a prisoner can be."

"As in all things peculiar, there is purpose," Carr assured her. "With these wristbands, a connection can be made through the copper rod to the medium, and thusly, an electro-luminescent link is created to the strong aethereal forces she will bring to bear. It's an unfortunate procedure, but this bondage ensures you do not break that important connection during the séance. That would prove wholly catastrophic. We wouldn't want to lose you."

"Lose me?" She tugged on the manacle, the motion of her hands constrained. "Where am I going?"

"Patience, all will be revealed."

Behind the throne, a door opened from its place at one end of a grey-paneled backdrop riddled with woodworm. A plump woman entered the ante-chamber, her body swaddled in a flowing silk caftan decorated with embroidered purple dragons on a black background. She wore a purple silk headpiece shaped like a turban. She took her seat opposite us. The dimness of the faint light from the single candle behind her hid her facial features.

Gregori went to the side table, lit the small candle in the holder and placed it on the table in front of her. In this candle's more direct light, the fulsome aspects of her face were revealed.

Miss Unsworth screamed.

She pulled back on the manacles in a fruitless attempt to rise from her seat, jolting upwards to no avail, her hands locked in copper. She settled back, still wriggling, turned her head away, buried her face into her shoulder, and sobbed.

"There, there, child. Have you never seen a leper before?" the medium asked, in the dialect of the tropics.

My own sense of natural revulsion kicked in. Madame Jeanette's face produced an instantaneous shock to the visual senses. I felt my cheeks contort into a wince. Viewing the macabre was an inevitable hazard of my occupation. In this moment, I tried to remain stoic and keep my focus but Professor Carr shot a glance my way that admonished the defeat of my courage by my fear.

To be sure, one could tell Madame Jeanette was negro; her skin as ebony as molded chocolate. But beyond that humanity, one could not help but notice the ravages of the dreaded disease, an affliction from a more distant land. Her face was covered in ugly lesions; her hands equally tainted, deformed, bent like coat pegs.

"Men of medicine say my condition will not convey so long as you do not touch me," Madame Jeanette said. "For that reason, a distance must be maintained. So I had these channels of copper built—the Wheel of Spirit, I call it, a linkage that will bind us together as one, as if I could hold your hands in mine."

Madame Jeanette waved at Gregori. Her assistant scooped a spoonful of powder from the glass jar and poured it into the brass Petri dish. He passed the dish over the candle in front of Madame Jeanette until the powder bubbled and turned brown like burning sugar, sending a plume of white smoke in the air. Madame Jeannette breathed in its vapors, her chest rising until it was full.

The diminutive man returned to the jar and put another scoop of powder in the Petri dish. He heated it as before, but this time held the open end of the glass dome over the burning powder. White smoke filled the tube-like glass chamber. He approached the back of Miss Unsworth's chair, grabbed her forehead with one hand, pulled her head back like a dentist ready to extract a tooth, and once convinced she was secured on the headrest, placed the rubber-sealed end of the glass dome over her nose.

Miss Unsworth wriggled and sputtered but was helpless to prevent smoke being drawn into her lungs as she struggled for breath. In a short time—a mere tick and tock of a pocket watch—her shoulders slumped, and the stiffness in her body melted away. Gregori removed the glass chamber from her face. Hannah Unsworth sat up, her eyes weepy, her lips pouting, her head wobbling ever so slightly.

"Enjoy the vapors, Jeremiah," the professor said. "They do no harm. The opium smoke is simply a relaxant, a means to an end, an avenue down which we will glide to our destination with Madame Jeanette's guidance as our torch."

Gregori placed the cylinder of smoke to my nose and I dutifully inhaled. My eyes looked down the length of glass pressed to my face, this object of séance being the last vestige of reality before my mind was swept away. Fully immersed in the realm of the unreal, I stepped out of a cloud, imagining I had shrunk. I walked along the glass tube's curved surface. A dark space appeared at its end; a blackness, expansive in its depth and bounds yet I felt no fear.

A bright white light grew from a pinprick in the void, its throbbing glow silhouetting three figures—a man whose profile sported a goatee; a petit outline my heart told me was that of a young woman; and the shape of a portly person, her wide body draped in flowing robes that billowed in an unseen wind.

"Welcome to the aerophane," Madame Jeanette said, her features completely devoid of leprosy. She was indeed beautiful, her former countenance restored in a trick of the aether; her plump cheeks unblemished, soft and happy; her outstretched palms supple and inviting.

The pinprick of light rose into the dark until it appeared as a single star in a night sky. Its glow illuminated our surroundings. The four of us—Professor Carr, Miss Unsworth, Madame Jeanette, and myself—stood in the centre of a circle about ten yards wide. The ground beneath our feet swirled with fog, ankle deep. To the outside of this circle, four beds of roses grew; rose bushes of various colours, each bed separated from its neighbour by a path. Beyond the roses, there was nothing, the same blackness of infinite dimension as the 'sky' above.

"We are guests here," Madame Jeanette continued. "Guests of Miss Unsworth. For it is her spirit that defines where we are."

"I don't understand," Hannah replied.

"Child, you are the one who has created this sanctuary. This aerophane is your mind's place of comfort, a place of unity with your sister. An aerophane is but a slip of aethereal fabric in the bigger cosmos. But for you, it's an important oasis, for it is here where you will begin your travels."

"There is nothing but blackness beyond those roses."

"No, that is what you perceive. Choose a path and follow it. Let your mind open the darkness to other possibilities."

Miss Unsworth took cautious steps through the mist at her feet. One of the paths lay beside a bed of roses of the same deep crimson she'd described the time her sister's wandering spirit appeared before her in the garden. With each of her steps, the darkness that lay beyond the path lifted as if opening the pages of an illustrated pop-up book. From the void, wooden steps with two arched handrails appeared until a small bridge like those that straddle country streams emerged full length.

"That is a pondletomp," Madame Jeanette said. "From the Aquitanian, *le pont du temps*, the bridge of time. Press your hands together, dear. Concentrate on a specific memory as you cross, and you will be taken back to it. If you cross the pondletomp with a blank mind, your travels will be in the present. But in no circumstances should you ponder the future. Walking there is too dangerous, a path reserved for only trained minds like my own, lest one's soul becomes lost between today and tomorrow and cannot find its way home."

Hannah hesitated.

"Cross the bridge, child," Madame Jeanette urged. "Don't worry. You will be able to return. See what waits for you on the other side."

Hannah walked between the gap in the flowerbeds, stepping up on the bridge that emerged at the end of the path. She hadn't gone far along it when she stumbled back, clutching her hand to her chest. "Claire? Dear sister, is that you?"

"For most of us," the medium said. "The pondletomp is a solitary gateway into our own minds. But for a twin like you, Miss Unsworth—one who shares memories and emotions with another—it will join you spiritually to your sister as if an aethereal umbilical cord stretches between you. Go across it. Walk with her in her footsteps. Think deeply of a time in the recent past, for it is within this trail of times-gone-by where explanations of her disappearance lay. Think back to the last day you saw her. Travel that memory with her."

Hannah crossed the bridge of time, her smile growing ever wider on her face with each step. Her eyes expanded into orbs of wonder at what she saw ahead of her, a vision invisible to us. Her gait quickened until she disappeared into the blackness on the other side of the bridge.

Once Miss Unsworth was out of sight, Madame Jeanette followed. The medium reached the middle of the pondletomp, stopped, and called back to us, "You must stay there. I can follow her because I'm her guide. We are connected by the Wheel of Spirit. I will keep watch, but from a stealthy distance. I cannot interrupt her thoughts. She must choose the direction she travels without influence or prejudice."

Instructions delivered, Madame Jeanette disappeared into the void, and as she did, the pondletomp folded back on itself, and vanished.

"Let me understand, professor," I said, as we stood alone in the centre of the circular garden of roses. Beyond the sanctum of flora floated an endless black void. "We are—well, *where* exactly are we? Can I take a bridge back into my own memory?"

Professor Carr chuckled. "Why don't you try and see what happens."

I was less than heartened by his response. Undeterred, I accepted his challenge and walked between the rose bushes. No bridge appeared as it had done for Miss Unsworth. Instead, my feet sank deeper down into the mist until my legs were buried to my knees in vapor, as if I'd entered quicksand.

"Help, professor! I'm stuck."

He laughed again. "And you want me to get stuck alongside you?"

"Don't be cruel, sir. Don't punish my curiosity."

"Very well. But you don't need my helping hand. Close your eyes, believe you are at the centre of the circle, and so it shall be."

I did as I was told. When I opened my eyes again, I was standing beside Professor Carr. Incredulous, I asked, "But how?"

"We are all travelers, with no bodies to constrain us. Thoughts are our means of motion. But this is Miss Unsworth's aerophane, her creation, and it has boundaries you cannot cross on your own. We cannot venture beyond this circle, as you have just found out. Madame

Jeanette on the other hand, has the power to follow and guide. She is a student of the Akashic records—knowledge contained not in books, but in the aetheric plane, the library of the mind. It took her a lifetime to master the skill of traveling away from her body. She's been teaching me that skill, but unfortunately due to the burdens of a busy schedule, on far too few occasions. Alas, my days are consumed by other matters of the peculiar, and I fear I may never acquire enough competence to guide a traveler on my own."

"How long must we stay here?"

"Not long. In fact, I sense the return of Miss Unsworth and Madame Jeanette as we speak."

"Surely not? They've not been gone for very long."

"Ah, that's where you're wrong, dear Jeremiah. The mysteries of time, indeed. Miss Unsworth could have been gone for hours or even days. Perhaps weeks and months. Or years. To her, time stretched around her like the coils of a spring, expanding and collapsing her memories to suit her desire to find answers. To us, elapsed time seems relatively short. To her, that same amount of time grew infinitely long. At some point in her wanderings, she will end her search, have the answers she needs, and travel back to the present, with Madame Jeanette's guiding hand preventing her from stepping into the dangerous realm that is her future. Regardless of the relativity of time, to Miss Unsworth, she will feel she's been on a journey of considerable length."

And so it was. The pondletomp emerged from the void and atop its arch, the forms of a young woman and her portly guide re-appeared.

Miss Unsworth descended with a quick gait, running towards us, short of breath. "We must hurry, professor. Claire is in great peril. His experiments, I fear, will lead to the permanent separation of her soul from her body. He's a dangerous fool, with malevolent lusts. And my sister is not the only one he holds."

"My work is done," Madame Jeanette said. "And haste is required."

With those words from our guide, the oasis of roses dissolved into the mist. The vapors rose up my legs until they obscured everything, the swirl around me like thick cigar smoke. For a brief moment, I felt weightless, floating as if in water, unsure of what was up and what was down. A moment later, I could sense I was turning. My eyes caught sight of a white light. It expanded, and as it did, the fog cleared. As I floated, I could see quite clearly below me, down into the very room we'd left behind in St. Dunstan's church. I was above myself—looking at my physical self from outside my body, detached, the weirdest feeling I'd ever felt.

As I looked down upon myself, and the bodies of the professor and Miss Unsworth, we sat motionless in our seats, in a state of trance. The room around us glowed with a blue luminescent energy. Madame Jeannette's fists held tight to her device's copper grips. Bolts of light ran from her hands, down the rods to our manacled wrists. The Wheel of Spirit had joined us as one. Suddenly, Madame Jeanette released her grip and the ribbons of blue energy disappeared with a loud sizzle. A suction, like that of a giant industrial vacuum, caused me to plummet from above, down toward myself, where it sucked me back into my body.

I woke in my seat to the touch of a cool wet cloth being dabbed on my forehead. I gazed into Gregori's wizened face. "Welcome back. Thank you for coming to see us, Mr. Boone," he said. "But you must go now. Madame Jeanette's next appointment is here."

PART IV

A beastly rain fell; a deluge that drained soot from the sky. The wind gusted, threatening to turn my umbrella inside-out. I stood across the street, hidden in an alleyway, a draught at my feet and a rivulet running across my boots. The canals are sure to flood tonight, I thought, as the relentless rain beat down.

With dark clouds looming overhead, day had succumbed to darkness. I checked my pocket chronometer. The time was half-past six in the evening. Closing time. A man extinguished one gas lamp after another inside the shoppe until the merchandise in its front window lost all definition. The man emerged, put up his umbrella, turned to lock the shoppe for the night, and scurried down the street toward the aero-tram station.

I followed, my pace matching his. The shadow of Professor Carr emerged from the alleyway opposite mine. We knew where the man worked—the shoppe easily identified from the sign above the door in Miss Unsworth's description, a result of wandering back in time with her sister Claire. But Claire's memory had a crucial lapse. She had lost consciousness in that shoppe at the point of her abduction and awoke as a captive, in the same dank room that her sister Hannah had dreamed about, its exact location annoyingly unknown even to Claire.

Claire's spirit had offered Hannah few solid clues, but the ones we did have proved useful in our pursuit. Professor Carr was concerned that where her abductor lived—a flat in a densely populated, fashionable district; a record we easily obtained once his place of business was known—may not be the location where his victims were being held. Following him from his shoppe was the only solution. Whether he returned home to his flat after his day's work, or to some other place that housed his victims, the help of the Imperial Police was as close as the nearest public alarm box. Professor Carr did not wish to engage the police until absolutely necessary. More often than not, the methods of the police force were clumsy. A premature or ham-fisted enquiry could scare the perpetrator into silence or turn him away from the route to his hidden lair.

Our suspect followed the maze of streets leading to the nearest aero-tram station. The iron-roofed atrium over the tramway's forecourt banged with the drumbeats of pounding rain. What a relief to be inside its shelter. As always, Barnaby Cross bustled with life, busy with people taking outbound connections to all points of the city. We feared losing the man in the crowd. Thankfully, he stopped to buy an evening paper, allowing us to catch up. We were still unclear of his intended destination as Barnaby Cross serviced many tram-lines.

Whistles blew on a nearby platform to signal a tram's imminent arrival—the Northeast Line to Woolford Mill, a borough of clothing shoppes and artist colonies, a place with an agreeable ambiance where the city's university students, and those newly graduated, could find reasonably priced rents, decent grub and satisfying ale. The man bundled the paper under his arm and took flight to catch that tram.

We boarded a carriage behind the one he alighted, so as not to draw attention. Professor Carr's face was well known, and to this man, mine was known as well. We kept a careful watch through the rattling windows that separated our carriage from his.

Tension grew with every stop. Where would he step out?

Far down the line, the aero-tram finally arrived at its terminus, Woolford Mill. We lingered on board until he was safely twenty paces away from the tram, then disembarked and resumed our pursuit.

Outside Woolford Mill station, a sea of identically-colored umbrellas mingled like lilies floating on a pond. So many people, so many men similarly dressed—dark suits and dark raincoats, walking down a dark street. My heart skipped a beat. Had we lost him?

"Go that way," Professor Carr ordered. "I'll go the other."

"How will you find me?"

"Call out with your mind. I'll find you."

"I wish I could do the same."

"Don't worry about me. Now go!"

I turned left and hastened through the crowd. Professor Carr turned right. With the men's coat lapels drawn up to their ears, and their umbrellas tight to their shoulders, it was nearly impossible to know who was who. I wandered for several blocks not knowing if the man we'd followed from the shoppe had made his escape in the other direction.

Each time I thought I had my suspect in sight, I had to discount those who stopped at an alehouse or inn. We suspected this man operated alone, isolated from society. We theorized that since he held captive not only Claire Unsworth but several other young women too—a revelation Hannah had learned from her sister—he was keeping them prisoner in some sort of perverse private collection of beautiful things, locked away for his own amusement like a case of dried butterflies on pins. That they were not yet dead was a blessing. But what were his plans if he tired of viewing them alive? What then?

The rain stopped. Our suspicions that he shunned social contact were correct. Eight blocks down from the station, the crowd thinned to a trickle. As the umbrellas came down, one man stood out from the rest. He walked with a disciplined determination and in some haste, nearly knocking over a pie seller as she re-opened her cart to the night trade—a man with a destination firmly in mind; a man on a mission, his strides clocking with the regularity of a metronome.

He turned down an alley between two clothing shoppes. I approached with caution. As I peered around the corner, he fumbled with a set of keys in front of a doorway. A single gas lamp shone overhead, illuminating his face. Yes, this was the same man that had left Wainthorpe's Apothecary in Windsholme Mews, boarded a tram at Barnaby Cross, and had now arrived at a warehouse of some ilk in Woolford Mill. The man, known to me, and I to him—young Alexander Wainthorpe, the apothecary's son—had much to answer for; a young man whose inheritance had blessed him with a worthy position and ample funds. What was the meaning of these abductions? What macabre experiments in aethereal conveyance had he concocted?

Wainthorpe entered the building. As I proceeded down the alley, a figure ran up the alley from the other side of the lamplight.

"Jeremiah," Professor Carr said. "We have him. Summon the police! Hurry, man."

A public alarm box stood next to the alehouse I'd passed a moment ago, a block away. I ran back, nearly slipping several times in the wet. I pulled the alarm and a flare shot high into the sky to signal the nearest patrol ship. In this vastly populous city, these flares were a most effective ways of summoning the police. It took a few anxious minutes to bring a patrol ship down to my location on the street but thank goodness one was nearby.

When I'd left Professor Carr, he'd been standing outside the warehouse's door. But upon arrival with two constables, we found the alley deserted. "In there," I said, pushing the door. It swung open on unlocked hinges. "Hurry, my good men."

Light from the alley's gas lamp shone through a large window, breaking up the shadows of an otherwise unlit building. Crates of various sizes were scattered about its cobbled floor, several of them opened, straw tumbling out.

"Oi, oi! What have we here," one of the constables said, as he flashed a hand-torch around the boxes. "Contraband?"

I pushed his torchlight toward the floor. "Cut the light, you fool. You'll give us away."

The constable grumbled but did as I asked.

"We're looking for a way down. Perhaps into a cellar," I whispered. I heard a noise at the far end of the warehouse, the scuffling of feet. "There! Over there!"

The constables and I raced toward an iron railing surrounding a set of steps that descended into the bowels of the old building. Arriving at the bottom, gas lamps lit the way through a passage that dripped water from its arched ceiling.

Ships, Claire Unsworth had told her sister Hannah. She'd seen ships in the wanderings outside her body. Londinium was a port of some significance, but that clue had little relevance to pinpointing her exact place of imprisonment in a city teeming with canals and wharves. Until now. We must be near a canal, I thought. What better way to deliver goods to a warehouse? And dripping water. Was this a sign that one of the many canals connected to the River Etham had reached flood stage and was spilling its waters over the warehouse's loading dock?

"Quickly! Before this cellar floods," I yelled.

The door at the end of the passage was locked. On the other side, I heard Professor Carr's muffled voice. He grunted and groaned as if in a struggle.

"Stand aside, sir," a constable said.

The pair of policemen, tall, broad-shouldered, and fit, took a flying leap together and slammed into the door. It smashed open, and fell flat to the floor, the wood around its hinges weakened by the damp.

"Stand back!" Alexander Wainthorpe cried.

We had burst into a very large room, its considerable height drifting into darkness despite the gas lamps that flickered around its perimeter. Wainthorpe stood at the far side, holding a large knife to Professor Carr's throat. The keen blade flashed with malice. Blood dripped from a wound on the professor's head. His hands had been wrapped in copper wire, a material stored on several large wooden rolls around the chamber. Once a storehouse of some kind, the large room had been converted to a laboratory of bizarre construct.

Behind Alexander Wainthorpe, an electrical panel hummed. Colored bulbs flashed and the needles of a bank of meters twitched. In front of the bastard and his hogtied victim stood flat tables, like those in a hospital's operating theatre, but made of copper. The bodies of four very beautiful young women lay prone and motionless on their surfaces. Around each girl's head was a copper cage. Blue sparks danced in between the gaps in the cages' mesh.

"On your knees," Wainthorpe barked at Professor Carr. He stiff-armed the professor to the floor.

"It's over, son," a constable said. "You've been found out. And there's no escape now. Don't do anything rash."

"It's over when I say it's over," he screamed in reply.

Wainthorpe took a step back, his eyes locked on us, the knife in his hand pointed down at the professor, ready to lunge. Without letting his gaze wander from ours, he reached back to the electrical panel and grabbed the handle of a stout switch, a fork-shaped circuit breaker, the kind that if flipped from 'up' to 'down' would douse the power in an entire building.

"If I pull this lever, the current to my aurotropic cages will be cut. And when that happens, there will be no means by which the souls of my specimens will be able to return to their bodies. They will be lost in the aether forever."

"These girls are not specimens," I said, my legs itching to pounce on the scoundrel, should he let down his guard. "They are young women of flesh and blood, who deserve better than this."

"They are pioneers, and will be honored as such when the philistines at the university finally attest to the breakthrough I've invented. Research they steadfastly denied to fund, but I undertook with my own resources."

"Denied with good reason," I countered. "You cannot use someone's soul as if it were gelatin in a test tube. That's prohibited by law. Our work at the Institute is careful to avoid such evil experimentation."

"Don't argue with him, Jeremiah," Professor Carr said, spitting out blood.

Wainthorpe pushed him forward and as he did, the professor braced his bound hands on the edge of a vacant copper table, a gurney waiting for its fifth victim.

"What is your plan, Wainthorpe?" Carr asked, coughing. "Are we to stay frozen in this standoff until we die of hunger?"

"You," Wainthorpe shouted at the constables. "Lay down your truncheons and walk over there." Wainthorpe gestured with his knife towards a small room with a door of iron bars, one of the cells where he'd no doubt held his captives. "And you too," he said to me. "Lock yourselves inside. Do it, or I'll skewer this man's neck."

The police did as instructed and so did I. The cell had a chain with a padlock, previously opened. I entered the cell with the constables, closed the door, slung the chain around the bars, and turned the key to seal the lock.

"Throw it on the floor," Wainthorpe ordered.

The key bounced across the flagstones, out of our reach.

Professor Carr, his bound hands firmly atop the copper table, rested his head on his forearms as if in prayer. Alexander Wainthorpe released his grip on the electrical switch. His knife hand shook. He hovered over Professor Carr like a vulture. I feared for my mentor's life, unable to come to his aid.

Suddenly, the gas lights in the laboratory dimmed. They brightened briefly but the lamps dulled again until all their flames went out. The room fell into semi-darkness, illuminated solely by the flashing bulbs of Wainthorpe's electrical equipment and the blue sparks dancing through the copper mesh over the heads of his four motionless victims.

"What's happening?" Wainthorpe exclaimed. "How did you do this?" He shook the knife within inches of Professor Carr's neck, twisting his hand, gritting his teeth, spitting out the words, "How did you do this?"

A bolt of electricity jumped from the wires that bound the professor's hands, onto the copper surface of the table. The flash squirmed down the table like an electric eel. When it reached the bottom, an explosion of white sparks burst out from the edges of the copper gurney, so bright it blinded me.

The flash was momentary, like an intense firework. Gloomy semi-darkness returned. I squinted. My eyesight re-adjusted. The sparks had caused Wainthorpe to cower backwards. In doing so, he'd stumbled over a chair and dropped to his knees. The knife had fallen to the floor beside him. Professor Carr stood up, kicked the knife away, and placed himself between Wainthorpe and the switch that could cut electrical power to the apparatus.

Angered, Wainthorpe rose and lunged forward, knocking the bound professor back against the electrical panel. The deranged apothecary's son reached again for the switch, a lever that if pulled would doom four innocents. Again, the professor tried to stop him, but the young man's hand held him back by the throat. Veins throbbing on his forehead, eyes wild, Wainthorpe, with his other hand, grabbed the lever and pulled it down.

It stuck, halfway between the 'on' and 'off' position.

"What's wrong with this?" he muttered.

An electrical charge emerged from the switch, wrapping its bright tentacles around his arm. The charge buzzed like a swarm of angry bees, its size increasing. The charge followed Wainthorpe's arm up to his shoulder, crossed it, and then ran up his neck. Finally, bright bands of electricity encircled his head. Wainthorpe, rooted to the spot, could not let go.

"Aargh!" he cried out in pain, teeth clenched, body shaking. Smoke rose from his head as his hair burned off.

A charge of that kind could electrocute a horse. Just as I thought Alexander Wainthorpe's moment had arrived, a white spectral form stripped away from his body, like wallpaper being peeled off a wall. The form gathered shape, mirroring his height and girth. What can only be described as Wainthorpe's spectral essence, floated away from his body like a small passing cloud swept up by the wind.

At one end of the laboratory, a dark shape crystallized out of the gloom, at first inky black, then glowing with an aura of purple. The shape took human form—a portly woman in flowing robes. Her arm reached out and snared Wainthorpe's spirit as it floated by, as if snatching a cat by the scruff of its neck. The spectre squirmed but was unable to break free.

"Ah, you received my message," Professor Carr said.

"How could I not?" the spirit of Madame Jeanette replied. "Did you shoot it out of a cannon?"

"Copper is a great conductor," he replied.

"Try not to be so melodramatic next time," she said.

"What can I say? A flare is a flare. Whether in the sky or in the aether."

"Come, Mr. Wainthorpe," Madame Jeanette said to the spectre trapped in her grasp. "Let's travel a bit, shall we? How about looking into your future? I'm sure Her Majesty's Constabulary has some interesting things in store for you."

With those words, the phantom that was Madame Jeanette's spirit collapsed into itself, sucking with it Alexander Wainthorpe's spectral double. As soon as they vanished, the electricity surrounding the insane young man's mortal flesh disappeared and his body slumped lifeless to the floor.

With Madame Jeanette's departure, the gas lamps came back on. Professor Carr limped across the room and picked up the padlock's key to free us from incarceration.

"With haste, fine gentlemen," he said to the constables after being untied. "I don't know how long we have. To you, our evil friend's wanderings will appear brief. The first order of business is to ensure the physical side of Alexander Wainthorpe doesn't escape when his spirit returns."

"No worries, sir," a constable replied, unbuckling handcuffs from his belt. The other constable left the laboratory to rally reinforcements.

"Jeremiah, help me with the girls. I think I know how to reverse the polarity of these ghastly traps and return their spirits home."

We tended to the instruments—ingenious in their diabolical simplicity—and over the next hour, one by one, Claire Unsworth and the other three of her companions-in-horror emerged from trance, somewhat groggy, but with a gratitude that was quite overwhelming. I could only imagine the delight on sweet Hannah's face when she and her sister were reunited.

Shortly after Madame Jeanette returned—having finished guiding her reluctant new client around the cosmos—a full squad of Imperial Policemen arrived to secure the premises, cart off the perpetrator of these extraordinary crimes, and assist with the repatriation of Wainthorpe's captives. Disgruntled, his head blackened by soot, the newly reconstituted Alexander Wainthorpe was led away in chains to face justice.

We were about to depart, battered and bruised but otherwise satisfied, when one of the constables who'd witnessed the earlier affray said in a sheepish tone, "Excuse me, Professor Carr. I'm not quite sure how to put this…but *um*—"

"Spit it out, my dear fellow."

"What are we going to say about…all of…*um*…all of *this*…when we write our report in the morning?"

Professor Carr rubbed his sore neck and smoothed his sweaty goatee. He looked around the laboratory—its copper tables, electrical panels and mesh head-cages unlike anything known to modern science—and said, "All of *this*? Quite easy, constable."

"Easy, sir?"

"I recommend keeping it simple," the professor replied, smiling. "Perhaps begin with…something very peculiar happened in Woolford Mill yesterday…"

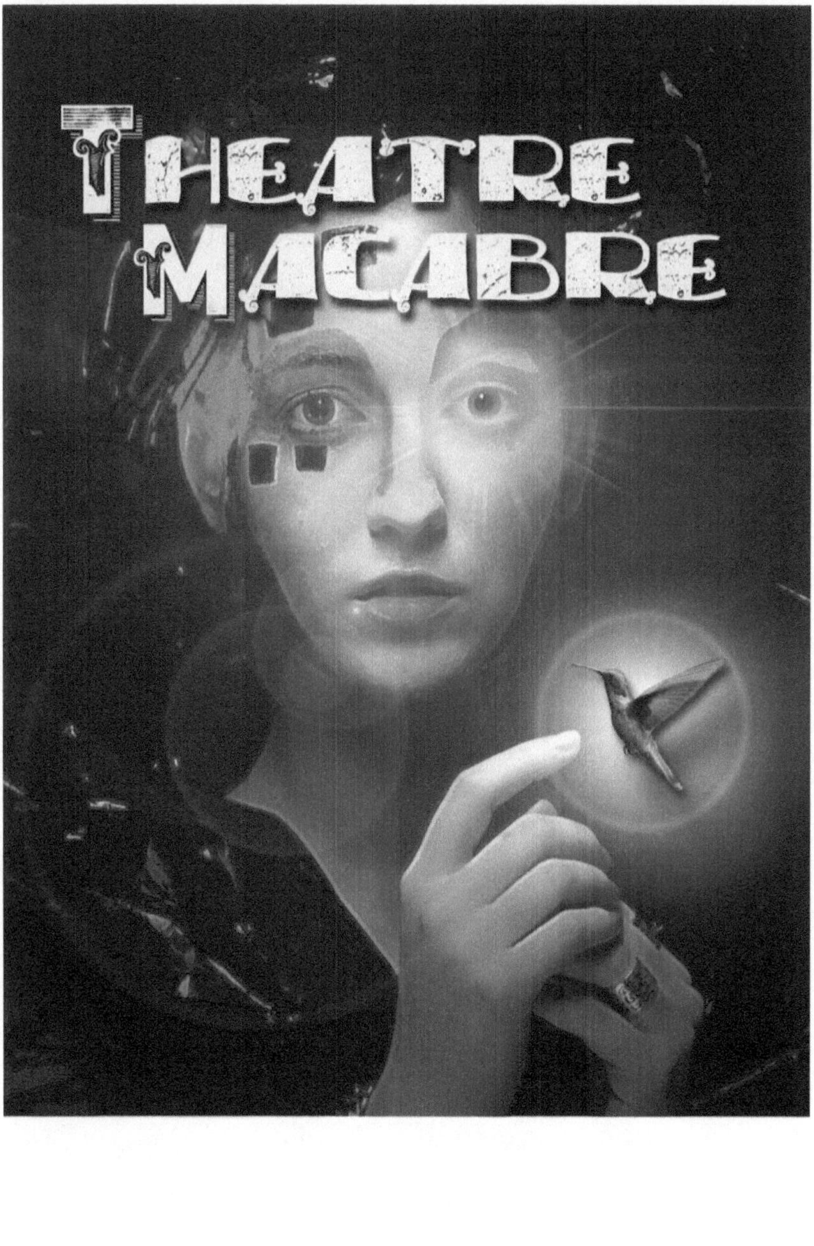
THEATRE
MACABRE

THEATRE MACABRE

PART I

How did I know her?

Inspector Mars of the Imperial Corps asked me this question as we waited for an assassin to strike. My answer then was brief, matter of fact, simply a detail the security services needed to pursue a course of grave concern.

That question probed deep inside my heart. This account, if it be honest, must therefore begin, not with an exposition of intrigue, but with an understanding of love. For tragedy is born when love and death intertwine.

When one is young, one doesn't stop to pause, to think, to contemplate consequences. Such is the nature of youthful abandon. Impassioned young men wander the world, explore, and seek love with every glorious step.

Fate, an ever so cruel mistress, brought Emma and Rosemary into my life, together in the same place, at the same time. Infatuation, my great enemy, drew me to one, thus diverting me from the other. It cast a cloak of ignorance over me, of the unnoticed flirtations of someone who would have suited me much better.

Foolishly, I thought love brewed from bedeviled passion as easily as one distills a powerful ale; the ingredients—captivation and primitive sensuality—harvested from the earth of one's soul and placed in a great pot of emotional fermentation until an intoxicating liquor emerges from the blend. One of life's great paradoxes is that as one ages, infatuation loses its potency as if the brew has the strength of a strong gin when one is younger but the tepid effect of watered-down wine as one grows old. Sadly, in my case, I knew of true love only when it had been lost, and as such, arrived at that conclusion too late to rescue it.

Londinium is both blessed and cursed. It is many things, but if anything, Londinium is not a forgiving place. Far too often it embraces darkness like a long lost brother. Londinium is by no means a city one can take for granted, not for a single stroke on a chronometer's dial.

For the fortunate few, the city's gold glitters, its champagne pops, and its heady air is scented with lavender perfume, fancy pastry and soft leather. But for many others—hundreds of thousands, if not a million souls—life simply lurches from birth to death in a dire loop of hopeless circumstance, daily survival a steady grind of ceaseless toil, seasoned with generous measures of desperate ingenuity and thieving guile.

I, Jeremiah Boone, live among the silent majority, a middling ground that occupies the space between two starkly contrasting worlds; a place, thank God, of relative comfort and relative ease; a spectator to what providence brings to some but abjectly denies to others.

The city can be a genteel lady, green and pristine, with cultured walks under old oaks, a place of lazy ponds glistening in the morning frost. But underneath its finery, it's an intemperate old curmudgeon; a money-hoarding churl who smells of iron-quenched water and rusty rails, its moldy clothes reeking of percolated steam. Regardless, it is beyond doubt the city I love. And at its very core, throbbing with life, as if holding in its hands the beating heart of the metropolis, sits The Theatre Macabre.

To say the Theatre Macabre is not an establishment of considerable import, not just in Londinium but in the entire world of the performing arts, would be a crime of impropriety. And speaking of crime, the theatre has, on more than one occasion, been the site of murder and mayhem.

By the time I was twenty-three, several years before I became Professor Carr's apprentice at the Institute, I became the Theatre's clerk of acquisitions. I'd developed quite a celebrated weekly run, flying the aero-van east at dawn to pick up the latest advertising bills at the printers; then south to the Ironmonger's Circus for hardware and wood; then onward to the Garment District to pick up cloth, thread, and lace for the costumières. Across from Putnam's Haberdashery sat McMarton's Pies, purveyor of fine Celtish delicacies that were the favourite of the Theatre's staff. A list in my pocket contained their orders and my arrival back at the Theatre, just in time for the luncheon hour, was met with great enthusiasm. McMarton's pasties with minced lamb were sublime.

Emma Langsford, a tailor's daughter, tended the shelves at the professor's favourite book shoppe, The Peculiarium, directly adjacent to McMarton's Pies. When Professor Carr learned of my route, The Peculiarium was added to my itinerary, as the book shoppe's rare collections were ever-changing and the professor had little idle time on his calendar to casually peruse its latest finds.

Emma Langsford was quite shy, although her timidity came with a great intelligence. As I learned on repeated visits, her intellect had given birth to ambitions of being a playwright. Emma was a great observer of human character; her position the perfect muse to take stock of the varied custom that stepped through The Peculiarium's doors. She was a slight, frail young thing, just turned nineteen. At twenty-three, no longer boyish in looks, I was the kind of man with strong shoulders and earnest prospects young girls fancied. Her skin was almost pure white, her profession allowing little exposure to the sun. Her face was slender, her lips a natural pink. She eschewed cosmetics but her captivating smile was all that was needed. Her almond-coloured eyes, mousy brown hair, and plain, almost matronly dress reminded me of the young women who called on establishments unannounced, books of scripture in hand, to solicit attendance at some local prayer meeting. In truth, Emma Langsford held no pretenses of being anything other than herself; her natural womanhood, of wholesome virtue, and thoughtful perspective, fully on display as soon as I walked into the book shoppe.

On many occasions, when Emma introduced me to a newly acquired publication of some antiquity, we struck up a conversation as if the professor's wants were my own. However, her informed commentary overpowered me. Ashamed at my poor schooling, I feigned an educated interest and offered responses more akin to fraud than opinion. I knew she could see into my failings. But she was kind, ever so gentle with her guidance, most instructive. The professor was always well pleased with what I brought back from The Peculiarium. In truth, it was not my judgment at the root of the purchases, but hers.

Rosemary Fenhaligon on the other hand was a cheeky lass, audacious, almost recklessly so. She tended the counter at McMarton's Pies. A child of the market stall, and brassy with her pitch, she could sell hot coals to an undertaker, wrapped in a fish skin. Bold and buxom, her blond hair flouncy and wild, Rosemary and I had an instant connection, an electricity that sparked every time I walked through the pie shoppe's door. We were born from the same origins, had worked hard from nothing to better ourselves, and wanted nothing more than to enjoy our meager success. When I returned to the Theatre Macabre, I would sometimes find in my basket an unordered clootie dumpling or a jam-filled buttery, her way of blowing me a kiss, although the flutter of her eyelashes was enough to enrapture me. In return, I would bring Rosemary a ticket for admission to the

Theatre, even though it was Emma who would have benefited more from that gift.

My duties on show nights prevented me from sitting with Rosemary, who came alone, but rarely left that way. Regardless, our rituals proceeded unchallenged by other suitors as far as I knew, until finally on one of my weekends off, I met up with her for a pint and a tot of gin at her local alehouse. From that point on, I was hopelessly smitten and further weekends brought the carnal pleasure a young man coveted. None are more beautiful than a maid scented by a desire equal to your own and impassioned thus to respond to your touch.

Yet I still held feelings for Emma Langsford. Her shyness never allowed her to reveal what she truly wanted of me, but I saw in her eyes an unmistakable longing. In hindsight, my sense of reason had been taken hostage by infatuation. Rosemary grew more brazen with her requests, knowing they would be met. With Emma, it was as if one pole of a magnet were too weak to pick up a pin, while with Rosemary, the other so strong it bent metal.

Twelve months came and went before the two of them finally encountered each other, in the most bizarre of circumstances given how physically close their occupations had kept them. One night, when I was finally given leave to attend a performance rather than stage one, I escorted Rosemary Fenhaligon to the Theatre Macabre. I spent every copper I had on her—a meal beforehand, flowers for her hair, and so many tipples it was a wonder she could make it up the Theatre's front steps. The latter was a terrible mistake. I should have known a beast roused in her when liquor met her lips. I'd met that creature before but had foolishly discounted its devilish traits as the joyous merriment of youth.

That night, at the Theatre Macabre, comedy and tragedy met one another head on.

The audience in the Theatre buzzed with their usual mix of astonishment, apprehension and fright. But whatever mood our fellow theatergoers felt, Rosemary expressed the opposite. She heckled the magic as bogus, using words of such coarseness the women around her gasped. When the tension of the performance increased and the audience adopted a cemetery quietness—in the midst of some death defying high-wire drama, or while a tiger-tamer had but a stick of wood between herself and jaws that would crush her—Rosemary blurted out some drunken nonsense that elicited angry looks. Before the finale—Professor Carr's *performance célèbre*—I removed her from her seat. I could not face the embarrassment she might cause me during his act. I wished to leave, to take the aero-tram back to her flat, and call it a night. But Rosemary said the night had only just begun. She insisted we stay. I compromised and took her to the Theatre's bar, where drinks cost double the price of a few blocks away.

A great roar of cheering and applause announced the end of Professor Carr's performance. Once again, he'd not failed to please. A noisy crowd emerged from the auditorium's doors, full of wonder, recounting the night's magical highlights. Patrons drifted into the bar until the tide turned into a flood and I found myself fighting for every inch to get Rosemary another drink. The bar became stuffy and airless. Rosemary grew pale, the drink taking its toll.

"Let me take you outside," I said.

On show days, the least wealthy patrons at the Theatre Macabre arrive by foot or by public rail-plane to Radwith Station, a quarter mile distant. The more well-to-do are dropped by steam-driven Broughams under the portico of the Theatre's *Entrée Grande* or land by balloon cab on the roof of the South Annex. Those whose position in society warrants the utmost in privacy and security—the Imperial aristocracy; foreign nobility and high diplomats; personages of wealth in industry—are conveyed by their private aero-coaches to a special landing pavilion behind the auditorium, a place the staff of the Theatre affectionately named the Berth of Gold. After being greeted by elegantly attired footmen with welcoming trays of canapés, patrons of high rank and their guests are ushered into their private boxes by an assigned concierge.

I'd promised to show Rosemary the Berth of Gold where the famous and wealthy depart the Theatre, my stage pass allowing me access. The Pavilion of the Empire, as it is officially known, is enclosed entirely with glass, its roof held up by bronze pillars. The effect is to bring the stars down from the heavens on calm evenings while sheltering the patrons during inclement weather. Its function was to let the glitterati revel in one last orgy of luxury as they waited for their private aero-coaches to take them home.

With her speech slurred and a newly found champagne glass in hand, Rosemary kissed me and made an empty promise to behave herself. To my chagrin, we found the Pavilion heaving with men and women of much higher social status but in much the same inebriated condition as her. Not long after entering, she latched onto a group— total strangers—and caroused with them as if she'd known them her whole life. The gentry, once ploughed with rich food and drink, often behaved with the most astonishing boorishness as if decorum was something one simply put on and took off as easily as a hat. She was in her element.

That's when I saw her, gliding into the Pavilion as if on silken wings—Emma Langsford, her slim form swallowed inside the ruffles of an elegant black satin blouse, its puffy sleeves and matching bustle growing her small frame. A necklace of rich red garnets hung around her porcelain neck. It was the first time I'd ever seen her in makeup. How beautiful she looked. She was on the arm of a man more than thrice her age, streaks of silver-grey in his slicked black hair and goatee. He wore a black tuxedo with white shirt, ivory brocade waistcoat, and white bow tie. A sash of blue satin draped across his chest, pinned tight by a bejeweled star-shaped brooch with enameled insignia, indicating he was a diplomat of some sort.

Our eyes met, Emma as startled to see me as I was to see her. She pulled on the man's arm as if to separate from him, but he saw someone in the crowd he knew and quickly dragged her away. As he whisked her off, her mouth opened slightly, as if to say her goodbyes before we'd even had the chance to say hello. Her eyes filled with that same longing, almost apologetic in their regret.

An aero-coach arrived, emblazoned with a crest I couldn't make out. The tuxedoed gentleman brought Emma to the coach and was about to help her on board when its door flew open. A man in soldier's leathers, a bandit's scarf hiding his face, sprung from inside, pistol raised. He aimed directly at Emma, fired a single shot, and leapt back inside the coach. The aero-coach took off in a burst of engine flame, its murderous highwayman inside, accelerating steeply into the night sky with the determination of an angered steed.

Emma fell to the deck of the landing pad, clutching her chest. Her escort, the diplomat, retreated from her body in more apparent concern for his own safety than for hers. I broke through the crowd—the boozed-up congregation frozen in shock—and rushed to Emma's side, placing my hand under her head to raise it off the cold stone. The paleness of her fingers, pressed hard to her chest, quickly turned red. Blood oozed between them.

"Jeremiah," she gasped as she recognized my face. "Oh Jeremiah—"

"Help is coming," I replied, not knowing if it was, not knowing what else to say.

A moment later, she slipped away in my arms; her eyes a glassy relic of what she once was, a young woman with unfulfilled ambitions and rare gentleness.

Chaos reigned around me. The Imperial State Police swarmed the Pavilion. I knew nothing much of what transpired next, my mind a blank. The only thing I remember was holding Emma in my arms and rocking her lifeless body. *Who would do something like this? And why?* I asked myself, oblivious to the pandemonium.

How Rosemary Fenhaligon got home that night was as mysterious as the reason for Emma's murder. I called on McMarton's Pies the following day and they told me she hadn't returned to work. Fearing for her safety, I made inquiries back at the Theatre Macabre. A concierge said he saw her leaving in the company of a wealthy patron. Rumours, he informed me, had been circulating among the elite of the Pavilion that she'd been his mistress for quite some time. A month later, the concierge learned she'd left Britannia with her rich lover for Aquitaine.

Emma's murderer was never caught. The Imperial State Police deemed her assailant to have been a member of the Union of Anarchists who, with others, had hijacked the aero-coach. The newspapers reported her death as incidental to the assassination attempt on the diplomat, the ambassador from the Grand Duchy of Alzenburg. I knew that assertion to be wholly false, a politically convenient excuse for the authorities to blame the anarchists. No effort had been made by the assassin to target anyone but Emma. The subsequent inquiry was a similar sham. I was not called to testify, my position in society apparently unworthy of bearing witness to the atrocity. Most of those who did supply testimony had been cockeyed with drink, their recollections worthless.

These vagaries of life, combined with one's unyielding responsibilities, and the dulling of emotion as one matures, have produced in me the most obstinate cynicism, a curse I fight to this day. The years have drifted by. I have left my twenties behind and entered my thirties. Still young by any standards, I temper the power of infatuation over my heart. Many women have sought my attentions, more than those I choose to woo in return. In Emma's soul I might have found my true match, had she been able to seduce me through intellect alone. I own the deepest regret for that blindness.

With each change in the calendar, the cynical spell of reality attempts to douse the unbridled flames of passion beyond hope of rekindling them. It took a devious plot to show me that true love is indeed eternal and perhaps has been with me all this time.

PART II

The flotz stretched the tips of his giant wings until they touched either side of his cage, a full measure of twenty-five feet wide. The massive bird's hawk-like head bobbed up and down, a sign of curiosity, his handler Guillermo told me. Tufted feathers of orange, red and green, emblazoned in a crown above bold yellow eyes, contrasted with the pure angelic white feathers of the rest of his broad body.

Guillermo plucked a river trout from a basket and pushed the fish's tail through the bars of the cage. The bird inched forward on razor sharp talons the size of meat hooks and bent his curved black beak towards the bars of the cage. The flotz tilted his head and blinked several times, as if asking permission to take it. The handler wiggled the fish in reply. The bird gently pried the meal from Guillermo's hand with his beak—not with a grasping jerk, but a grateful, delicate touch.

"What a polite beast," I said.

"More loyal than the most loyal of hounds," Guillermo said. "But only if raised from birth. The wild crested flotz is a bird of prey feared even by jaguars. But once tamed, as placid as a kitten."

The flotz lay the trout on the cage's floor and nibbled at the fish, pausing to take careful looks between each bite as if some sly little creature of the jungle might snatch it from under his talon.

"The legends of the Tarawaks," Guillermo continued, "say the first man and woman flew down from Heaven on the back of Itiki, a crested flotz just like this one. Itiki taught mankind how to fish and hunt, and most importantly, to live in harmony with the other animals of the forest. Wisdom, the people of Amazonia say, was Itiki's divine gift to mankind and a flotz feather is a page from nature's Book of Knowledge."

Performers from all four corners of the globe, whether permanent members of our troupe or transient entertainers, ensure that a full menagerie of rare mammals, birds and reptiles, and even the odd trained spider, are omnipresent on site at all times. On Sundays, the Theatre Macabre opens its vast array of halls, exhibition spaces, aviaries and animal cages free to the public so children can marvel at the wonders of the natural world, a collection of exotic species from faraway places, housed under the soot-laden rooftops of inner Londinium.

Beside the large cage housing the crested flotz of Amazonia, stood a smaller aviary about eight feet tall and ten feet wide. Inside, a trumpet bush with yellow flowers sat in a large pot, surrounded by other exotic plants from Amazonia—delicate white orchids, bright orange honeysuckles, pinkish-red fuchsias and lobelias. A dozen hummingbirds buzzed around the cage, competing for the flowers' life-giving nectar, their tiny bodies a blur of motion as they hovered, hungry bills darting in and out of the petals.

Princess Ayleena of Amazonia, tonight's star performer, walked into her private aviary in the North Annex dressed in a short loincloth slit at the sides, strapless sequined brassiere, shoe-less feet adorned with jeweled anklets. Dark alluring eyes, long ebony hair; her midriff bare, her body a deep native bronze with curves that brought a flutter to my cynical heart. On her head, a crown of jungle vines was graced with a spray of multi-coloured feathers radiating several feet in the air, plumage that swayed like a peacock's fan as she moved.

The flotz let out a shrill cry and flapped his wings.

"Hungry, my sweet Kati?" the princess asked.

Ayleena plucked a fish from the basket then entered the cage, a structure barely big enough to fit the flotz by itself. She nestled under the bird's outstretched wings, his shoulders a foot above her head. The flotz took the fish from her hand as gently as before, then nuzzled her like a cat stroking the side of a chair, confirming his gratitude with a throaty purr.

"Tarawak myths say the first flotz stole that sound from the black panther," Guillermo said, as we stood in awe of Ayleena's power over the giant bird. "To acquire the big cat's stealth and cunning."

"I never fail to be amazed by the love that it shows her," I replied. "Their affection casts a spell over the audience greater than the illusions she performs. That love is the true magic everyone sees on stage."

"They are not illusions, señor," he replied. "The magic of Amazonia is powerful. Jungle spirits guide her hand. Itiki watches over her and protects her. Such is her birthright."

"I can't argue with that. Her show is extraordinary."

Ayleena fed another fish to Kati, his beak a lethal scythe that could sever her hand if he so wanted.

Guillermo checked his pocket chronometer. "Princess, it's time," he advised.

Princess Ayleena's performance, the finale of *The Extravaganza Exotica*, lasted more than an hour. It followed Sheik Ali Masood and his snake charmers from Pajastan; Georgina Spiznov and her dancing white tigers of Siberska; and the escapology of The Great Garaboldi. Professor Carr was not performing. He'd taken a commission to entertain the King of Aquitaine at the Royal Chateau outside Spari and had put me in charge of the Theatre Macabre in his absence, a daunting honor but a heavy responsibility. I took comfort that the professor's staff had considerable managerial talent in every facet of production and audience care, a situation that made my temporary position of authority nearly superfluous to the efficient running of the Theatre. Regardless, I felt an obligation to attend to every little detail and thus had been run ragged from building to building inspecting each performer's preparations, Princess Ayleena's being the last.

She inspected the flotz's leather saddle to ensure its straps were holding firm and nodded to Guillermo. He opened the door of the hummingbirds' aviary and the squadron of tiny birds streamed out. The hummingbirds at first scattered randomly in the air but soon gathered in a swirling formation akin to an aerial ballet. Ayleena led Kati out of the cage. One would think that a glimpse of unfettered freedom would cause any bird to take flight, as the hummingbirds had done, and with a winged beast as large as this one, I'd challenge anyone to stop the flotz doing just as he wished. But it was not to be. Kati was as placid as a faithful horse being led from the barn for its daily cantor, more curious at its sudden liberty than anxious to escape.

With Kati resting by her side, Princess Ayleena held a hand in the air and snapped her fingers several times. She pursed her lips and a warbling sound—part coo, part cluck—brought the hummingbirds to her, circling her plumed headdress until the flock alighted on her crown of vines. The iridescent blue-green of their tiny bodies formed a tightly packed band along the twigs. On stage, the audience would not notice them until Ayleena warbled a command and they would take flight, scattering outward in an explosion of color, buzzing over the astonished crowd, before returning to her waiting arm. The hummingbirds adored her the same way the flotz did, and the magic she held over them produced the most extraordinary array of tricks. The tiny birds retrieved orchid blooms, danced through a spectacular maze of glass tubes, and in the most incredible display, hovered in front of a line of dangling chimes, each beak ringing its part in a tune Princess Ayleena conducted to create a concert of wondrous delight.

Tonight's bill was the last night of *The Extravaganza Exotica*. At the end of her act, Princess Ayleena would climb into Kati's saddle and fly him around the auditorium, landing on a variety of perches. In her final feat—a spectacle of heart-stopping abandon—the bond between her and Kati was tested to its limit. Her daring never ceased to bring knots to my stomach. From the highest perch, she would dismount from Kati, letting the flotz fly away and land alone on the stage. Then, eighty feet above the audience, the princess would leap off the perch, plunging headlong, untethered, towards the gasping crowd. Kati would spring from the stage and catch her in his talons when she was barely ten feet from the audience, returning her unharmed to the perch.

The giant bird's lumbering gait tottered side to side like a metronome as it followed Princess Ayleena down the arched gallery that connected the North Annex to the back of the main stage. As they disappeared from view, one final duty remained before I could take my own place backstage, and that was to ensure the smooth arrival of our most prestigious customers at the Berth of Gold.

The Theatre Macabre is not a single structure as the name may imply but a cluster of buildings, a small town in its own right, nestled off the Radwith Road, one of the main arteries in Londinium, an avenue which if followed to its terminus six miles hence would arrive at the gates of the Imperial Court. The principal edifice, by far the largest, contains the theatrical auditorium with a seating capacity of three thousand. On the outside, its red-bricked dome proclaims its heritage as a former zeppelin factory, once bankrupted by a notorious swindler, one of many scoundrels that have disgraced the Empire by their greed. The building's transformation to the current Theatre— funded by Professor Carr's substantial inheritance from his father's copper mines and brass foundries—was as much a work of magic as the pageants of illusions he hosts.

The auditorium is connected by arched galleries to two annexes containing innumerable ante-chambers, dressing rooms and props stores. This trio of buildings plants its foundation in the shape of the letter 'U' and within these embracing arms, a cobbled plaza invites the public to entertainment provided by street performers of every ilk. Spinning off the two annexes are clusters of ateliers and costume workshops; training rings and equipment sheds; and a miscellany of other smaller structures whose contents are often unexplored for years.

As a young stagehand, I was often called to fetch an article or prop from a particular store, or retrieve something forgotten by an artiste in their dressing room. I know every hidden passage, every underground tunnel, every shortcut through the maze of buildings, big and small, some of them I believe unknown to anyone but myself, unless one possessed the architectural plans.

It was down one such passage I ventured, en route to the Berth of Gold. A narrow alley, formed by the brick walls of two separate storehouses, runs to a spot where a set of iron stairs climbs up the side of the building and into the girders of the roof. Catwalks crisscross the inner space between the ceiling of the auditorium and the building's exterior dome, and these walkways I have found are the fastest routes from any point in the Theatre Macabre to another. The catwalks bypass the many backstage dressing rooms around the building's perimeter whose corridors before a performance are always filled with activity. Light in this sanctum is scarce, just a few bare bulbs of the new Tesla variety, strung on wires through the beams. The transit through the catwalks, although efficient, is dark and tricky, suitable only for those who know the route intimately, as the hand rails in some places are rusty and lack strength.

The Berth of Gold, or the Pavilion of the Empire as it is rightly named, rests at the northeast corner of the Theatre complex, positioned to be quite separate from the transport links used by the general public. From the northeast corner of the roof, a door exits the Theatre's dome to the outside where another iron staircase runs down the side of the building. The stairs end at the base of the aeronautic tower whose telegraphy signals direct the private aero-coaches to land. From there, the Pavilion and its landing pad are easily reached down a ramp.

I climbed and reached a point halfway across the girders in the roof, a junction of two catwalks. A light appeared ahead of me where no such bulb existed. No new Tesla extensions had been installed. I was sure of this and most puzzled. This light was a singular glow and of a colour quite distinct from the other bulbs, more red than yellow. At the junction, the left turn led to the door outside, the right turn to a point where projection lamps hung on gantries accessible through panels in the ceiling. The unusual glow reappeared in my peripheral vision. It had moved from its original position and now hovered over the catwalk accessing the lighting gallery. The intensity of its glow increased, waned, and grew bright again, a signal not unlike the rotation of a lighthouse's lamp. Concerned this anomaly might be some failure of the Theatre's electrification system, a fault that might give rise to a fire of calamitous consequences, prudence dictated I investigate its cause.

I ran briskly across the catwalk but despite covering much distance, the light always stayed the same size, wandering away from me as I ran towards it. I passed the lighting gallery and could hear the preparations of the Theatre's engineers in the auditorium below. The glowing orb then descended down a set of stairs until it reached the service door. The door was ajar, and to my amazement, the light squeezed through. I followed, the exit bringing me to a side corridor leading to the Royal Mezzanine, a broad, plush-carpeted foyer where patrons of nobility and high rank gathered ahead of performances before concierges escorted them to their private boxes.

I caught sight again of the glowing orb as it entered the Mezzanine's main gallery. Panting and ignoring the stunned looks of the waiting concierges, I resumed my chase until I finally caught up with the mysterious object which had now stopped and was hovering outside the door leading into a private box. A crest on a plaque identified the owner of the private box as the Grand Duchy of Alzenburg. The door suddenly swung inward and the orb zipped inside.

There's no escape from this point, I thought, *save over the balcony's rail to the seats below.*

I entered the box and gasped. Buzzing in the air, several feet from the edge of the balcony, was a hummingbird, its wings beating in a blur. A ring of red light, like a halo, surrounded the tiny bird. We stared at each other as one might do when discovering a deer in a forest, both man and beast exchanging glances of suspicion.

Had one of Princess Ayleena's hummingbirds wandered away from her control?

The hummingbird darted off, flying across the Theatre's open air before stopping inside the Imperial Loge, the most central and most opulently decorated of all the private boxes. Flanked by tall, gold leaf decorated columns and hung with royal purple velvet curtains, the Imperial Loge was reserved for the exclusive use of the Imperial Family. Inside the box, I spotted a woman sitting in the chair used by Queen Ellinora when she attended the Theatre. From this distance, I couldn't make out the woman's features, except that her face was rather pale and the dress she wore was dark and had a satin sheen.

A sense of alarm returned. I bolted from the box and ran down the corridor, nearly knocking over one of the concierges. "Quickly," I said back to him. "The security of the Imperial Loge has been compromised. Hurry, man. We must see who dares such a thing."

The concierge and I rushed along the corridor and bounded through the opened door into the Imperial Loge. There was no one inside. *What trickery is this?* I thought, peering over the railing to see if someone had climbed down. *A lady in a dress could surely not have done so.* Confounded, I sent the concierge down the other end of the corridor to see if a lady of my description had taken flight.

The Imperial Loge extended outward several feet further than any other private box and had tall partitions on either side for maximum privacy and security. It wasn't possible to climb from there into an adjoining box. Upwards might be the only escape route, but again, I saw no evidence of a rope or other climbing device.

The concierge returned. "The corridor is empty."

As I approached the balcony's railing to scan the interior of the auditorium, I spied the hummingbird again, its glowing halo quite easy to spot in the semi-dark Theatre. The bird hovered inside the box I'd just left, the one belonging to the Grand Duchy of Alzenburg.

What game was it playing? Catch me if you can?

The hummingbird flitted back and forth, as if signaling to get my attention, but once my eyes locked onto it, the bird flew away, buzzing down to the main stage where it disappeared behind the curtains.

My pre-show inspection at the Berth of Gold had been thoroughly sidetracked by this most peculiar and alarming incident. I felt my skin going clammy, the sweat of the chase like a cold cloth on my face.

Focus, Jeremiah, I thought.

I descended more stairs to the Premier Balcony, one level below. It contained further loges, less private than on the Royal Mezzanine but still quite luxurious. At one end of its corridor, a service door led into a flyspace to the right of the stage, another shortcut I knew that would take me to the Berth of Gold. Here, the Theatre Macabre's system of ropes, counterweights, and pulleys allowed stagehands to move sets, screens, and trapezes on and off the stage during performances.

The flyspace was a platform like one might find in a church's belfry. Ropes, chains and ballast bags hung from the ceiling; control levers and winches crowded its ill-lit space. As I arrived, a sudden movement in the shadows caught my eye, a figure silhouetted in the faint light—the silhouette of a woman, her bustled dress moving behind the ropes.

"Come here where I can see you," I ordered in a brusque voice.

No answer came.

I crept around the ropes, hoping to catch sight of the woman's face. For a brief moment I did—at least I thought I did—but the shadows around her darkened, until they absorbed her countenance into the blankness of the unlit wall. I advanced, pulling aside a set of chains with some urgency. But what I thought I'd seen—someone lurking in the shadows, a definite physical presence—had disappeared.

I rested a moment, perplexed. A hummingbird that flitted from box to box? An intruder, a woman, urging me to set chase but then, when cornered, yielding only to shadows? *Was I going mad?*

Confused, I turned back to resume my duties.

A pistol thrust out of the darkness. The end of its barrel pressed firmly into my forehead. This time, its cold steel was no illusion.

"Move and I'll blow your head into the next borough."

PART III

She walked backwards and bade me follow, her pistol pointed at my chest, its trigger ready to do its worst. Stage lights streamed into the flyspace from behind an opened curtain and lit up her face. Her hair was a silky black, her eyes a penetrating blue. She was tall, nearly six feet, and by the smooth shape of her young face, no older than thirty. She wore a red velvet military jacket, close fitting with a braided front, epaulets and gold buttons; black pants with a red stripe; black knee length leather boots.

"We haven't cleared this area yet," she said. "Which makes you under arrest."

"Under arrest? For what? Don't you know who I am? I'm Jeremiah Boone. I—"

"I don't care *who* you are. I care *why* you're here."

"This is preposterous! I'm in charge of this theatre."

"Professor Atticus Carr is in charge of this theatre."

"He's away. And in—"

"And in my absence," a familiar voice said as he climbed the stairs into the flyspace, "Jeremiah Boone Esquire has been put in charge of the Theatre Macabre."

"Professor Carr? But, but…," I stammered. "You're supposed to be in Aquitaine."

"That's exactly what we wanted the world to think. And by your reaction, I would say we've succeeded." The professor placed a gloved hand on the barrel pointed at my chest and gently pushed it down. "Mr. Boone was not aware of our plans."

"Good," the woman said. "But now that he knows?"

"You can trust him," he said.

"What's going on, professor? Who is this?"

"Inspector Antoinette Mars," the woman replied. "Of the Imperial Corps."

"The Imperial Corps?" I exclaimed. "Here? In the Theatre?"

The Imperial Corps were the elite of the Queen's security services, responsible for investigating 'enemies of the state' and uncovering acts of sedition and espionage. But its most famous regiment—or infamous, depending on which side of the pistol barrel one had the misfortune to face—was its League of Imperial Assassins, Her Majesty's overseas spy service.

"We have unexpected guests tonight," Professor Carr explained. "Her Imperial Highness, Princess Clementine, the Queen's daughter, and her husband, Prince Alexander. The Corps believes an assassination attempt will be made."

Inspector Mars holstered her pistol. "Now that you know why I'm here, you're either part of my security team or a security threat. Which one is it?"

"The former, most assuredly," I said, stunned by this revelation. "We must increase security immediately."

"Theatre security?" Inspector Mars said with a chuckle. "This is not about pickpockets. Don't worry. Everything has been taken care of."

"Assassination?" I asked. "But how? If no one even knows they'll be in attendance?"

"We suspect there's a spy inside the Palace," she replied. "The Imperial Corps has foiled several other attempts recently. These are dangerous times for the Imperial Family. The country is on the verge of anarchy. And foreign powers are funding the dissidents."

"I've been chasing an intruder," I announced. "A woman I believe. I couldn't catch her face but she's wearing a black dress with ruffled sleeves and a large bustle. I saw her enter the Imperial Loge. Is she one of your agents?"

"Black dress? Agents are working incognito this evening but no one of that description."

"So how will I know who's an agent and who's not?"

"You won't. And you shouldn't. We don't need an amateur revealing their identities to the plotters."

"But what you do need is *access*," I replied. "And I know ways in and out of these buildings only the architect would know."

A loud crash filled the air. The sound came from behind the stage. A piercing shriek followed, a cry no human could have uttered, a screech like a chorus of a dozen eagles. We bounded down the stairs to stage level. Behind the main curtain, Kati the flotz, his giant wings flapping, strained at his bridle, lifting Princess Ayleena off the ground as she struggled to contain him. A backdrop had fallen to the floor and the bird's wild strength threatened to topple more.

"*Pantokai! Pantokai!*" Ayleena cried. "*Pantokai, Kati!*"

"Guillermo, what's happening?" I asked.

"She's trying to calm him, señor," he replied. "I've never seen him so agitated."

"Evil spirits are coming," the princess said. "The hummingbird has warned us."

"Hummingbird?" I said. "The one that glows? You've seen it too?"

"Yes."

"What's going on here?" Antoinette Mars asked. "A hummingbird? Evil spirits? What nonsense is this?"

"Quiet," Professor Carr responded. He walked away, out into the center of the deserted stage, a finger to his temple. "Jeremiah," he called back. "She knows you."

"Who professor?" I said, coming to his side.

"The young woman in the black dress. I hear a name. Emma."

I had but glimpsed her from afar, in the Imperial Loge, and then again fading into the shadows of the flyspace. A pale, nearly ivory face. A black satin dress. "Professor, is it possible? Emma Langsford?"

Inspector Mars strode up to us. "*Who* did you say?"

"Emma Langsford," I replied. "I knew her. Many years ago. She was killed in this very theatre. Murdered. On the landing platform at the Pavilion."

"I know that," the inspector said. "I want to know how *you* know *her*."

"I loved her. I didn't know it then. But I know it now. She is here. In the Theatre Macabre." Vivid memories came flooding back. "I saw her sitting in the Imperial Loge."

"You didn't answer my question," Inspector Mars growled. "*How* do you know her?"

I recounted our frequent meetings at The Peculiarium, the antiquarian book shoppe where Emma worked, and the friendship we developed over many visits on behalf of the professor's collection.

"The important question," Professor Carr said, his voice hushed as he gazed around the empty Theatre, "is what stirs her spirit? Tonight of all nights?"

Inspector Antoinette Mars strutted across the stage, her eyes fixed on the Imperial Loge. "Why indeed? A ghost cannot be an assassin."

"Her spirit lives within the hummingbird," Princess Ayleena interjected. Her presence had slipped onto the stage behind us on the silent heels of her bare feet.

"The hummingbird?" I asked. "It's not one of yours?"

"To the Tarawaks, the hummingbird is our symbol for eternity. Each one bears the soul of someone who has departed but reborn for a specific purpose. I know the souls of all my hummingbirds. This bird is not one in my care. Sacred, little gods of the Air—they remind us to cherish truth and embrace balance in our lives. They bring us dreams and messages. This hummingbird carries the spirit of a young lady and brings a special message for the one she loves."

With every word the princess spoke, I felt the flush of memory cascading over me, the burden of regret. Tears ran down my cheek and my legs went weak. I closed my eyes. I could see the look of longing on Emma's face as she died. With her last breath, she seemed to want to tell me something, more than just a farewell, but a secret of some kind.

"Enough with the mystic mumbo jumbo," Inspector Mars sneered. "So what's the message, bird lady?"

"Follow me."

"That's it? That's all? *Follow me?*"

"The simplest answers are always enough for those who walk with wisdom."

"Now it's time for me to ask you a question, inspector," I said. "How do *you* know Emma Langsford?"

"The simple answer?" Mars replied. The thud of her black boots echoed around the empty auditorium as she paced. "She was one of my spies."

PART IV

"This is the very spot I held her in my arms as she died," I said, standing with Professor Carr and Inspector Antoinette Mars on the landing platform at the Berth of Gold. The sky above us had filled with airships. The aristocracy of Londinium were arriving for the performance. "It has never been explained to me, or to the public, why the assassin shot her, and only her. Why he never aimed for anyone but her, even though the Ambassador of the Grand Duchy of Alzenburg was her escort that night."

"What do you know about Alzenburg?" Mars asked, as the first aero-coach landed in front of us.

"That it lies between Durchland and Korolya. And that, out of necessity, its allegiance is to neither. It protects its neutrality with vigour. Which is very sensible, given it is such a small nation, squeezed between two of the most powerful ones in Europa."

"And it's claim to the throne of Britannia?"

"It has a claim?"

"A distant one," the inspector replied. "But an important one. One of blood, not marriage. Queen Ellinora has but one child, a girl, Clementine. Tonight, she and her husband are coming here to celebrate. Tomorrow, the Palace will announce Princess Clementine is expecting. Should she give birth to a boy, he will inherit the throne when he comes of age. My sources within the anarchist movement had been alerted to this pending news. How did they know? From the spy within the Royal Household. That is our only conclusion."

"Evil spirits," Professor Carr said. "Just as Princess Ayleena does now, I felt them too, several weeks ago. Their evil has been focused on the Theatre Macabre like a prism placed in the hot sun. I alerted the Grand Marshal of my fears and the Imperial Corps enlisted my help.

But this is an evil that stalks the streets. It's not made of aether, but of flesh and blood."

"If Clementine is killed, bearing that child heir," Inspector Mars continued. "The direct bloodline of the House of the New Tudors ends. There are those within Imperial circles who believe the Grand Duke of Alzenburg, a distant cousin to Queen Ellinora, would be next in line to the throne of Britannia. That claim has more to do with politics than heredity. In politics, opportunity rules supreme. A period of anarchy would likely follow any assassination. Then, upon the death of Queen Ellinora—a monarch with no heir—factions within the nobility would battle each other to the death to stake their claims to her throne. These factions would promise the world. And no promise is more hypnotic to the populace than bringing order to chaos. So you see, those that support the Grand Duke as the rightful heir have every reason to support the anarchists as well, perhaps even control them. It is a path to power in Britannia."

"And Emma?"

"Emma Langsford had been recruited by the Imperial Corps because of the influential clientele who patronized The Peculiarium. She became an invaluable source of information for us. The ambassador was one of those who frequented the book shoppe. We suspected his involvement in providing funds for the anarchists. We told her to encourage his advances. She was rewarded with an evening at the Theatre Macabre. But her identity as an Imperial spy was uncovered, as the fatal events of that night testified. The ambassador was never the target of the anarchists. She was."

"And Her Imperial Majesty's government covered that up," I remarked.

Aero-coaches bobbed in the light evening breeze as they lined up in formation to discharge their passengers.

"Truth," I mused. "Her spirit has come back to restore the truth. If only I'd brought her to the Theatre instead of Rosemary that night, perhaps Emma would still be alive."

Inspector Mars laughed. "Truth? You seek truth? You can start by casting aside that deceitful memory."

"How dare you! Emma was perhaps naïve in the ways of espionage, but regardless, you put the state's purpose ahead of her protection and thrust her in the middle of a clandestine war she couldn't possibly have comprehended in the full."

"Emma knew the dangers she faced when she accepted the Queen's shilling. But you and the truth are indeed strange bedfellows. How was Emma betrayed? Ask yourself, what became of your paramour that night, Rosemary Fenhaligon?"

"Rosemary? What has she got to do with any of this? She was just some churlish lush who cast civility into the gutter. She absconded with my honour to Aquitaine, rich lover in tow, never to be seen on these shores again."

Inspector Mars clapped. "Oh, Mr. Boone. Bravo! You should scribe for the tabloids. Those newspapers are not worth the farthing they cost, meant to whisk coin from the pockets of the foolish. Titillation is their purview and you have much to offer in that regard."

"About Rosemary? You know different? Speak then, if fidelity is even possible to find in a spymaster's arsenal."

"McMarton's Pies might be a clue to Fenhaligon's calling, her certificate of birth another," Mars replied. "Rosemary Fenhaligon was a Celtish separatist, terrorists in league with the anarchists. She was both their spy and their whore. With her rich lover in Aquitaine, you say? Excellent. Please forward her address. She's disappeared into the netherworld. Perhaps still roams our shores. Or perhaps she's plying her trade in the souks of the Harisian Sands. Who knows? You don't, obviously. Whatever the bearing of her compass, she was the one who betrayed Emma Langsford to the anarchists. They and the separatists had eyes on the patrons of The Peculiarium, for clandestine reasons of their own."

"Rosemary? I...I—" Words escaped me. My chin nearly touched my chest. "It's so—"

"Tell your story to the tabloids, Mr. Boone. See if they give a farthing for the truth."

Professor Carr put a hand on my shoulder. "Don't torture yourself, Jeremiah. Emma Langsford's vocation might have led to the same fate regardless. As the inspector said, the life of a spy is a dangerous one. And fate is the cruelest lover of all."

"If I were you," Inspector Mars chided, "I'd focus on what's important right now, not some mushy tripe that addles your brain."

"She's right, Jeremiah," Carr agreed. "Cast painful memories aside and put the appropriate priority on tonight, on thwarting this plot."

"This whole affair is a total muddle to me. But reluctantly, I must accept reason," I replied, wiping tears from my face. "So let me think for a moment like an anarchist."

I paused, reflecting. "I have it! If I wanted to assassinate an Imperial Princess, I know *exactly* when I would strike."

"There, I knew you could do it," Mars chirped. "Your wits have cleared. Go on."

"It would be at a time in tonight's performance when no one in the Theatre Macabre could possibly have eyes on me. A time when no one in the theatre will see where the bullet has come from, making my escape possible."

Inspector Mars grabbed my arm. "And what time would that be?"

"The moment Princess Ayleena jumps from her perch and plummets towards the crowd."

***

One by one, aero-coaches delivered the elite of the Empire to the Theatre Macabre. Aristocratic men in their valet-brushed tuxedos, lapels festooned with medals. Ladies swaddled in satin and silk finery, jewels sparkling like little stars, their coiffed hair swept into sculptures of a salon-keeper's art. Regardless of wealth or rank, a legion of Imperial State Police inspected every clutch, frisked every gentleman's frock coat. No one—whether arriving by private aero-coach, by public aero-tram, or on foot; whether of substantial means, or barely able to purchase a ticket—would escape the scrutiny of Inspector Antoinette Mars' cordon of security. Pickpockets would never make it past the first flagstone in the forecourt.

As master of ceremonies, Professor Carr left the Berth of Gold to prepare for *The Extravaganza Exotica*. Even without the unannounced attendance of Princess Clementine and her consort, Prince Alexander, this final performance had brought much anticipation with it.

For me, anticipation of a more personal kind sent a chilling tingle up my spine. As I caught sight of the crest of the Grand Duchy of Alzenburg on the side of the next aero-coach in line to land, the hairs on the back of my neck bristled. If ever there was a daemon I wished to vanquish, it was the pain of that night many years ago.

As the ambassador stepped out of the coach, I faced that daemon head on.

The diplomat had aged, a mere slip of the silver-haired, debonair gentleman who'd escorted Emma Langsford to her fate. Time had aged all of us, but it was with a tinge of smugness that I leered at a man that time had not treated gracefully—nearly bald, his skin wrinkled as a turkey's, his shoulders droopy, back bent, a body that wobbled on feeble legs. A footman retrieved his walking stick from the coach. The cane was sturdy and tall; made of thick black ebony; topped with a silver handle in the shape of a boar's head, the emblem that featured on the crest of the Grand Duchy. The ambassador planted his gloved hand on the top of the cane and stepped forward, gaining for that brief moment a measure of the imperious posture he'd lost with age.

A constable from the Imperial Police reached for the cane. The ambassador shouted, "Good God, man, can't you see I'm lame!" He whacked the constable on the shins. "Hands off."

"Let me, Your Excellency," I said, placing my hand under the diplomat's elbow to hold him up. "These searches are a routine precaution." With a firm hand to steady him, I wrested the walking stick from the ambassador's grasp. The policeman frisked his tuxedo jacket, completed the search, and nodded, all clear.

"There," I said, handing the ambassador his cane, as if a moping child had lost his toy. "All done."

"An outrage," the old man muttered. Unaccompanied, he struck a lonely figure, a shadow of the man he once was.

"You handled that diplomatically," Inspector Mars said as the ambassador waddled off. "I will have eyes on him throughout the evening. Many eyes."

"Can he really be the orchestrator of such a sinister plot?"

"Don't let the old coot's feebleness fool you. Power can be wielded in infinitely more ways than muscle and brawn. But if the ambassador expects to sit back and watch a diabolical spectacle unfold, he will be in for a surprise. My agents will remove him from the Grand Duchy's box before Princess Ayleena performs, assuring the box will be empty of any assassin during her finale."

The landing platform cleared. The one remaining airship to arrive would be the Imperial Barque, transporting Princess Clementine and Prince Alexander from Rockingham Palace to the Theatre Macabre. The Imperial Police hustled the few lingering members of the Britannic nobility out of the Pavilion until it was devoid of anyone not in uniform.

Inspector Mars, deep in thought, turned to me and said, "Mr. Boone. It's too easy."

"I'm sorry, *what?*"

"This was too easy. The anarchists and their traitorous supporters are well aware of Imperial security procedures. We've searched the Theatre high and low. Now we've searched every man, woman and child whose set foot inside. Their plan is a test of our wits. You can be sure of that. I've been mulling over something you said earlier. That you know ways in and out of these buildings only the architect would know."

"That's correct."

"Suppose the anarchists had access to those plans."

"Hmm." I thought a moment, running through a mental list of every public entrance, every stage entrance, the delivery gates, the service doors, the catwalks through the roof. "Yes. I see what you mean. There are still a few ways to gain entry once every official door has been bolted tight and put under guard. Difficult ways. But not impossible."

"That's what I suspected. We must hurry to shut down those opportunities."

"How many agents do you have?"

"How many agents do you need? They're yours. Tell me where and it will be done."

"And what if our assassin is already inside?"

"He needs a weapon and a location to use it. Let's assume, despite everything we've done to prevent it, he has the former. So, weapon in hand, if you were an assassin, and the Grand Duchy's box was not available, where else would you go that would be within a gun's sight of the Imperial Loge?"

"I can think of several places."

"Good. Take me there."

PART V

The arrival of Their Imperial Highnesses caused the opening curtain of *The Extravaganza Exotica* to rise an hour later than scheduled. The delay was soon forgotten as the circus of wondrous acts, with its marvelous sets and exotic creatures, held the audience captive, whisking them away to a palace in Pajastan and to the windswept steppes of wild Siberska. The magic of The Great Garaboldi brought tension and suspense followed by relief and awe as the *escape artiste* wormed his way out of a barrel whose flaming rope threatened to send him plunging to his death when its last filaments were consumed by fire.

I made my way from backstage to the Royal Mezzanine just in time to hear the The Great Garaboldi's empty barrel crashing in splinters on the stage. That sound signaled agents of the Imperial Corps, dressed as concierges, to descend on the private box of the Grand Duchy of Alzenburg. Two men dragged the ambassador through the loge's door, his protests drowned by the noise of the audience's applause.

The diplomat was a feisty old sod, wriggling free of one, then twisting around to strike the other. "Unhand me, you louts," he cried, pushing them away until he stood apart, encircled by the Imperial Corps.

"This way, Your Excellency," Inspector Mars ordered. "It's for your own safety."

"Balderdash! What is the meaning of this?" he barked as he stumbled down the Mezzanine's broad carpeted steps towards her. "This is outrageous. Under what protocol have you the right to treat a sovereign ambassador in this manner?"

"I don't need any protocol when the security of the Imperial Family is at stake. You will be taken to your aero-coach. Your evening is over. Take solace. Think of it this way. You'll be back in the embassy, snifter of warm brandy in hand, before the air corridors over Londinium become jammed with traffic. I'm doing you a favour."

The ambassador huffed, wrestled again with the agents, then marched, unaided, in the direction Inspector Mars pointed, to the exit. With the incident under control, the business of the Theatre resumed. Concierges, who had been held back while the agents of the Imperial Corps did their work, hustled down the corridors in either direction. Trays of drinks and platters of food were delivered, these services in high demand during performances.

The double doors to the Grand Duchy's box had been left wide open. One could see through them to the performance below. Princess Ayleena took the stage. I wandered in, the pageantry that was the Theatre Macabre in its full glory on display in front of me.

"You can watch from here if you wish, Mr. Boone," Inspector Mars said. "I will post guards outside. From this point on, no one will be able to enter this box but you. My agents have taken positions around the building in the locations you instructed. Every corridor is being patrolled. Their Imperial Highnesses are secure. I ask only that you remain ever vigilant and on call should the need arise."

"I will rest easy only when the night has ended and the Theatre is empty."

"I share that sentiment."

Inspector Mars closed the doors to the loge, leaving me alone in the vacated box. I chose one of the six armchairs—the one at the front, so I could peer over the balcony's railing—and slumped wearily into its plush velvet cushion.

Princess Ayleena's performance enthralled me. Her beauty and grace were unmatched, the magic of the hummingbirds mesmerizing. Despite this, my eyes could not stay rested for long. They wandered the Theatre Macabre, interrogating every face in view, probing every shadow in every corner for an unseen hand on a trigger. My heart raced. My throat tightened. My mouth drained dry.

Time had marched halfway through Princess Ayleena's finale when the sense that something was not right overwhelmed me. A voice came into my head, not that of Inspector Mars, but repeating the phrase she'd used, the phrase that earlier had troubled her. *This was too easy.*

"What is it?" I said out loud, alone in the box. "What is nagging at my mind?"

This was too easy, the voice replied. *Think, Jeremiah. Dear Jeremiah.*

I wheeled around. Standing with her back to the closed doors was Emma Langsford. An aethereal mist swirled around her. She floated upwards until the bottom of her black satin dress was several feet above the floor, her young face as clear and bright as a warm summer's day. She whispered with gossamer breath, *Think, my love,* her voice as soft and gentle as morning dew.

I stepped towards her and in my clumsy haste, toppled a chair. I felt a hand push me away but saw no hand on my chest. The spectre of Emma Langsford drew me closer but as I rose again the invisible hand returned, tipping me sideways. Off balance, I reached down and grabbed the arm of the fallen chair to steady myself. As soon as I did, the aethereal force knocked me back again.

Think, Jeremiah. Dear Jeremiah.

The vapours around her grew thicker, consuming my Emma in a billowing cloud that expanded until her face faded into a mist of its own.

"No! Don't leave me!"

A deep enveloping aether was all that remained in the loge. But the force of a hand returned. It pushed. I resisted, holding onto the chair. "What is the meaning of this, Emma?" I pleaded. "All I want, is to embrace you one last time. Yet you force me away. Push me down so I need a crutch. Like some cripple. Why?"

A glow emerged at the centre of the swirling cloud of aether. A small red orb.

"Push me? So I need a crutch?" I said, stunned. "Of course. His crutch!"

I scattered the chairs to search the floor. I entered the swirling aether to inspect the corners of the loge. "It's gone!"

The mist condensed until the only spectral presence left was the glowing orb. Inside its red halo, a hummingbird buzzed and bobbed.

The double doors flung open. No hands had turned their handles.

Follow me, I heard in Emma's voice—the message Princess Ayleena said the hummingbird had been given specifically for me.

Follow me, the bird repeated, bouncing in the air as if to signal me, before zipping out of the loge, and out of sight.

I burst into the foyer of the Royal Mezzanine. The guards, stunned by the violence of the out-swinging doors, had summoned Inspector Mars. I ran to her. "His walking stick," I asked. "Where is it?"

"What?"

"He fought his arrest. *Unaided.* He marched out of here. *Unaided.* Did he leave the walking stick behind in the box? No. He did not. It's not there!"

"The *weapon?*"

"It was heavy. I held it. The shaft was too heavy to be hollow. It's the assassin's weapon!"

"But *who?*"

"A concierge. That must be the answer. When the commotion of his arrest distracted us, he must have slipped into the box and retrieved the cane. That's why the ambassador came alone. So no one could interfere with their plan."

"You! Down that corridor!" Mars yelled at her agents. "You! Down that way! Get ready to evacuate Their Highnesses."

My head swung from side to side, searching the Theatre. The hummingbird. Where had it gone? Which way now?

Follow me.

Emma's voice came from behind. From the Grand Duchy's private box. I raced back. The hummingbird hovered in the open air of the auditorium ten feet from the edge of the balcony rail.

"Follow you? I can't follow you there."

"Who are you talking to?" Inspector Mars asked.

"The hummingbird. There. In front of us."

"I don't see anything."

"You don't?"

Follow me.

The hummingbird darted across the open space, high above the audience. I could not follow. It was impossible. The orb stopped, clear across the other side, smaller now in the distance but still visible, at least to me. It bounced up and down, its signal. *Here I am*, it seemed to say. *Now watch what I do.* The hummingbird flew straight up into the ceiling and disappeared into the beaming stage lights.

"The lighting gallery!" I pulled Mars by her jacket. "No time to explain. Keep up with me if you can."

I ran out of the box, turned right and sprinted down the corridor to the service door at the end, the Theatre Macabre's double roof being one of the possible entry points for an enterprising assassin I'd told her about earlier.

As I reached the door's handle, it wouldn't open. "He's locked it."

"Stand back!"

Inspector Mars whipped out her pistol and fired. The door knob flew apart. I flung the door open and bounded up the stairs towards the catwalk over the Theatre's ceiling. The Tesla lights had been doused, not by accident I thought, plunging the girders above the auditorium into complete darkness, save the scraps of light leaking through the access panels of the lighting gallery below. I ran along the catwalk and tripped over an obstacle. It felt like I'd run into a sack of potatoes. It was a body. I heard footsteps behind me, the clunking of heavy leather boots.

"My agent!" Inspector Mars cried out.

A muffled shot rang out from somewhere on the opposite side of the catwalks, its sound escaping into the Theatre's domed roof. A bullet clanged off the railing near me. Inspector Mars returned fire, but it was hopeless to aim true in this darkness.

The access panels into the lighting gallery lay twenty feet in front and ten feet below me. A panel had been moved aside for someone to climb down. Behind a light stand, I saw a man's shadow, cradling a long thin object in his hands.

"Down there," I whispered back. "Our assassin."

"It looks like he's assembling some sort of gun."

I spotted a shadow passing across the light stand. "The flotz," I said. "Ayleena is riding him. The performance must be continuing and she's nearing the end. The gunshots have not been heard."

I crept forward on hands and knees, feeling for the gap in the catwalk that marked the short stairway down to the gallery. Another shot rang out. Another bullet whizzed over my head.

"More than one anarchist is hiding up here," I whispered.

"Midnight optics," Mars said behind me. "A new tool for assassins."

"He can see us, but we can't see him?"

"Precisely."

"Then if we can't proceed, we have no choice, inspector. Someone must rise into the line of fire and leap over this railing. It's the quickest way down. Then someone—someone with a gun—must fire everything she has, in whatever direction she thinks she should, and hope like hell she hits something that makes the man with the midnight optics duck."

With no hesitation, she replied, "On three. One…Two…"

A halo of red light, the hummingbird, flashed by my face as I stood up, whizzing across the girders into the darkness. As I jumped over the railing, the hummingbird's bright glow lit up Inspector Mars' target.

"Three!" Inspector Mars fired several rounds.

I descended towards the ceiling panels. The panels were made of thin pine boards, light enough to be moved easily but not strong enough to hold a man falling from a ten-foot drop. A loud crack of splintering wood accompanied me as I fell through. I landed where I thought I would—on a narrow walkway where the lights were fastened to adjustable stands. My arm caught the brass housing of a lamp on the way down. A sharp pain seared my elbow. Instinctively, I cried out.

The assassin turned toward my voice. His gun had been completed, its barrel and sight had been cleverly hidden inside the ambassador's walking stick, its ebony exterior discarded on the floor beside him. The barrel's end was sheathed in what appeared to be a wool wrap, perhaps to silence the retort, the reason his accomplice's gun also lacked sound. The rifle's trigger mechanism was the boar's head handle, attached beneath the barrel. Being as slim as it was, and without a magazine, I surmised the weapon held but a single shot. What the design lacked in firing power, its sight made up for in accuracy. Using a pistol from this distance would be a wild, random act, and quite noisy. He and his accomplice planned to escape and this weapon of stealth was their choice.

Would this assassin be a martyr to the anarchist cause, or was he employed as a craven mercenary?

I was about to find out. One bullet meant he must choose one target, and one target only.

He chose Princess Clementine, shouldering his weapon then aiming it toward the Imperial Loge.

My arm throbbed and hung limp by my side. Regardless, I rushed the would-be assassin, colliding head first like a charging bull just as he pulled the trigger. Had I jolted him enough to miss?

Its single shot now spent, the assassin swung the rifle at my face like a metal club. Reflexes brought my hand up. I felt the hot steel of the gun's shaft smash into my knuckles. The sound of cracking bones preceded the most excruciating pain. I fell on my back, one arm broken at the elbow, my other hand crippled and bloody. The glint of a blade flashed in the dark as the anarchist drew a knife from a scabbard strapped to his leg. A shot rang out from above my head, its round hitting the assassin in the shoulder. He fell to his knees and crawled towards me, knife still clenched in his fist. A second shot rang out, but the bullet from Inspector Mars pinged off the brass housing of a stage light.

I squirmed, my legs trying to push me backwards. My feet could not find any grip on the smooth metal platform. The assassin's hand pulled back, knife high in the air, ready for a final, fatal thrust downward to my chest. Suddenly, the lighting gallery shook on its brackets as if an earthquake had struck. A piercing shriek stung my ears and I felt the wind from the fluttering of wings. The assassin screamed—a desperate cry I'll never forget and I never want to hear again—as his knife hand was severed at the wrist by the guillotine-sharp beak of the flotz.

Kati dragged the disarmed assassin out of the gallery, his shirt firmly clamped in the bird's beak. The man dangled in the open air, his feet kicking without effect. Princess Ayleena yelped a command in Tarawak. The flotz dipped his wing and turned their flight down towards the stage. Princess Ayleena issued another order and Kati dropped the assassin from a height meant to stun but not kill the man, then landed on top of him, talons drawn. The flotz pinned the bleeding man to the stage like a plucked fish.

Triumphant, the massive bird stretched his giant wings out, reared his head back, and produced another piercing shriek so shrill it must have shattered some of our patrons' eyeglasses.

It wasn't the finale that had been planned. But a thunderous applause followed just the same.

Exhausted and in pain, I lay on my back on the lighting gallery's walkway, my eyes staring up at a splintered hole carved in the panel of soft wood above me. A glowing orb with a red halo buzzed out of the darkness and into the opening. It bounced in the air as if to signal me. I smiled and blew it a kiss, tears welling up in my eyes. It bounced one last time, then zipped away.

I never saw the hummingbird again.

But I will feel the love of Emma Langsford until the day I die.

ABOUT CHARLES A CORNELL

When Charles isn't trying to survive the chaos of everyday life, he's dreaming up all kinds of bat-shit crazy fiction. He specializes in science fiction, science fantasy, dieselpunk & steampunk. He's known to write award-winning mystery thrillers too!

Charles has a BSc. degree in Metallurgy & an MBA. He worked in materials engineering, quality management, logistics & purchasing for a big name Fortune 500 company.

Charles A Cornell was born in England, raised in Canada and now lives in Florida.

His first published novel, *Tiger Paw*, won the 2012 Royal Palm Literary Award for Best Thriller from the Florida Writers Association.

His dieselpunk work, *DragonFly* is a retro-futuristic collision of science fiction and fantasy with a generous dash of alternative history. *DragonFly* was a 2014 Royal Palm Literary Award Finalist in Science Fiction, has received numerous Amazon Five-Star reviews, two prestigious Reader's Favorite Five Star Reviews, and won the 2018 Reader's Favorite Silver Medal in the Young Adult - Action category.

Charles's short stories and novellas have appeared in the anthologies, *The Prometheus Saga*, *Return To Earth* and *In Shadows Written*. His *Prometheus Saga* science fiction story *Crystal Night* won the FWA Royal Palm Literary Award for Best Novella in 2016.

CharlesACornell.com
SteampunkNovels.com
DragonFly-Novels.com

WORKS BY CHARLES A CORNELL

Steampunk:

The Most Peculiar Tales

Dieselpunk:

DragonFly
Spies in Manhattan
Die Fabrik / The Factory

Science Fiction Novellas:

Crystal Night
Children Of The Stars
The Orchid Man

Scott Forrester FBI Thrillers

Tiger Paw

Short Story Anthologies

The Prometheus Saga
Return To Earth
In Shadows Written

Satirical Non-Fiction & Fiction

A Survivor's Guide To Working At A Big Corporation
Harvey Drinkwater & The Cult Of Savings

MORE ABOUT DRAGONFLY

DragonFly explores the incredibly turbulent times during the 1940s and the 'what ifs' that might have been. *DragonFly* follows the journey of Veronica Somerset as she battles the odds to become Britain's first female fighter pilot. Packed with full color illustrations and black and white 'retrographs', *DragonFly* conjures up a whole new world of fantastic technology, dangerous fighting machines and wizards battling across the boundary between good and evil in a World War re-imagined like never before.

The characterization is top-notch! The heroine's character development intensifies with every turn of the page. The inclusion of the photography is icing on the cake in this extraordinary narrative. Insightful, creative and unique – be ready to be shocked and awed by **DragonFly**!
> — Cheryl E. Rodriguez for Readers' Favorite

DragonFly by Charles A Cornell is an extraordinary novel. The story is extremely entertaining, but it also made me think. It is indeed a truly adventurous tale: I could not put it down and read it in two days! The pace of the story, the superb illustrations, and the style of the author all make this novel a must-read!
> — Marie-Hélène Fasquel for Readers' Favorite

"DragonFly is brilliant! The Golden Age of Science Fiction is alive and well!"
> —Carol Kean, book reviewer for Perihelion Science Fiction
> Magazine & Amazon 'Vine Voice'

"A gripping and fast paced new adventure series..."
—Five Star Amazon Review

"I want to commend the author for writing a compelling and strong female lead... It's characters like Ronnie and the courage of authors like Cornell (to write such characters) that will help change the face of the sci-fi/fantasy/dystopian genre."
—Five Star Amazon Review

*"It has something for everyone. History wrapped in mystery draped in Sci-Fi makes **Dragonfly** a fast-paced winner!"*
—Five Star Amazon Review

"The thrilling climax... outdoes any big action flick for sheer sweep and menace. Cornell hits a home run!"
—Ken Pelham, award winning author of the mysteries, *Brigand's Key* and *Place of Fear*

*"There is a lot to like about **Dragonfly**... surprises... intrigue... in a world that doesn't particularly follow the history that we know."*
—Bard Constantine, author of *The Troubleshooter* novels.

"It was fantastic ... Charles has done a wonderful job blending alternate history with the mystical. His characters are well developed. I was disappointed when it ended."
—John Charles Miller, award winning short story writer & author of alternative history novels

DragonFly-Novels.com

www.ingramcontent.com/pod-product-compliance
Lightning Source LLC
Chambersburg PA
CBHW030247200626
46816CB00002BA/538